THE WHITE SOLITAIRE

Also by Elizabeth Mavor
Fiction
Summer in the Greenhouse
The Temple of Flora
The Redoubt
The Green Equinox

Non-Fiction
The Virgin Mistress
The Ladies of Llangollen – A Study in Romantic Friendship
The Grand Tour of William Beckford
A Year with the Ladies of Llangollen

THE WHITE SOLITAIRE

Elizabeth Mavor

HUTCHINSON
LONDON MELBOURNE AUCKLAND JOHANNESBURG

© Elizabeth Mavor 1988

All rights reserved

First published in Great Britain by Hutchinson, an imprint of Century Hutchinson Ltd, Brookmount House, 62–65 Chandos Place, London WC2N 4NW

Century Hutchinson Australia Pty Ltd
PO Box 496, 16–22 Church Street, Hawthorn, Victoria 3122, Australia

Century Hutchinson New Zealand Limited
PO Box 40-086, Glenfield, Auckland 10, New Zealand

Century Hutchinson South Africa (Pty) Ltd
PO Box 337, Berglvei, 2012 South Africa

British Library Cataloguing in Publication Data

Mavor, Elizabeth, *1927–*
   The white solitaire.
I. Title
823'914 [F]

ISBN 0-09-17356 5-3

Printed and bound in Great Britain by Anchor Brendon Ltd, Tiptree, Essex

For Peregrine and Toby Hodson

'. . . to think of Death, is to dye; and to be always thinking of it, is to be all one's Life-long a dying; 'tis Time enough to think of it when it comes.'

Captain Singleton

Historical Note

The following extract from *A General History of the Robberies and Murders of the Most Notorious Pirates*, by Captain Charles Johnson, is the only known biography of Mary Read apart from the brief account of her rigged trial in the Colonial Office papers.

Probably written by Daniel Defoe, Johnson's *Pirates* was first published in 1724 and swiftly became a bestseller in a world enthralled by tales of adventure and the lure of far-off places. Though there is no hint from where the author derived his information, subsequent historians have corroborated his stories from other sources, and have found him accurate even to the smallest detail.

E.M. February 1988

CHAPTER VIII: Of Mary Read and Anne Bonny, the female Pirates

NOW we are to begin a history full of surprising turns and adventures; I mean, that of Mary Read and Anne Bonny, *alias* Bonn, which were the true names of these two Pirates. The odd incidents of their rambling lives are such that some may be tempted to think the whole story no better than a novel or romance; but since it is supported by many thousand witnesses, I mean the people of Jamaica, who were present at their trials and heard the story of their lives upon the first discovery of their sex, the truth of it can be no more contested, than that there were such men in the world as Roberts and Black-beard, who were Pirates.

Mary Read was born in England; her mother was married young to a man who used the sea, who going a voyage soon after their marriage, left her with child, which child proved to be a boy. As to the husband, whether he was cast away, or died in the voyage, Mary Read could not tell; but, however, he never returned more. Nevertheless, the mother, who was young and airy, met with an accident which has often happened to women who are young and do not take a great deal of care; which was, she soon proved with child again, without a husband to father it; but how, or by whom, none but herself could tell, for she carried a pretty good reputation among her neighbours. Finding her burthen grow, in order to conceal her shame she takes a formal leave of her husband's relations, giving out that she went to live with some friends of her own in the country. Accordingly she went away, and carried with her her young son, at this time not a year old. Soon after her departure her son died, but Providence, in return, was pleased to give her a girl in his room, of which she was safely delivered in her retreat, and this was our Mary Read.

Here the mother lived three or four years, till what money she had was almost gone. Then she thought of returning to London, and considering that her husband's mother was in some circumstances, she did not doubt but to prevail upon her to provide for the child, if she could but pass it upon her for the same. But the changing a girl into a boy seemed a difficult piece of work, and how to deceive an experienced old woman, in such a point, was altogether as impossible. However, she ventured to dress it up as a boy, brought it to Town, and presented it to her mother-in-law as her husband's son. The old woman would have taken it, to have bred it up, but the mother pretended it would break her heart to part with it. So it was agreed betwixt them that the child should live with the mother, and the supposed grandmother should allow a crown a week for its maintenance.

Thus the mother gained her point. She bred up her daughter as a boy, and when she grew up to some sense, she thought proper to let her into the secret of her birth, to induce her to conceal her sex. It happened that the grandmother died, by which means the subsistence that came from that quarter ceased, and they were more and more reduced in their circumstances. Wherefore, she was obliged to put her daughter out to wait on a French lady as a foot-boy, being now thirteen years of age. Here she did not live long, for growing bold and strong, and having also a roving mind, she entered herself on board a man-of-war, where she served some time: then quitted it, went over into Flanders, and carried arms in a regiment of foot, as a cadet.[1] And though upon all actions she behaved herself with a great deal of bravery, yet she could not get a commission, they being generally bought and sold. Therefore, she quitted the service, and took on in a regiment of horse. She behaved so well in several engagements, that she got the esteem of all her officers. But her comrade, who was a Fleming, happening to be a handsome young fellow she falls in love with him, and from that time grew a little more negligent in her duty, so that, it seems, Mars and Venus could not be served at the same time. Her arms and accoutrements, which were always kept in the best order, were quite neglected. 'Tis true, when her comrade was ordered out upon a party, she used to go without being commanded, and frequently run

---

[1] A cadet was a volunteer who served, with or without pay, with the chance of obtaining a commission if proving of military ability.

herself into danger, where she had no business, only to be near him. The rest of the troopers, little suspecting the secret cause which moved her to this behaviour, fancied her to be mad, and her comrade himself could not account for this strange alteration in her. But love is ingenious, and as they lay in the same tent and were constantly together, she found a way of letting him discover her sex, without appearing that it was done with design.

He was much surprised at what he found out, and not a little pleased, taking it for granted that he should have a mistress solely to himself, which is an unusual thing in a camp, since there is scarce one of those campaign ladies that is even true to a troop or company; so that he thought of nothing but gratifying his passions with very little ceremony. But he found himself strangely mistaken, for she proved very reserved and modest, and resisted all his temptations and at the same time was so obliging and insinuating in her carriage that she quite changed his purpose; so far from thinking of making her his mistress, he now courted her for a wife.

This was the utmost wish of her heart. In short, they exchanged promises, and when the campaign was over, and the regiment marched into winter quarters, they bought woman's apparel for her, with such money as they could make up betwixt them, and were publicly married.

The story of two troopers marrying each other made a great noise, so that several officers were drawn by curiosity to assist at the ceremony, and they agreed among themselves that every one of them should make a small present to the bride, towards house-keeping, in consideration of her having been their fellow-soldier.

Thus being set up they seemed to have a desire of quitting the service, and settling in the world. The adventure of their love and marriage had gained them so much favour that they easily obtained their discharge, and they immediately set up an eating-house or ordinary which was the sign of the *Three Horseshoes*, near the castle of Breda, where they soon ran into a good trade, a great many officers eating with them constantly.

But this happiness lasted not long, for the husband soon

died, and the Peace of Ryswick being concluded, there was no resort of officers to Breda, as usual. So that the widow, having little or no trade, was forced to give up house-keeping, and her substance being by degrees quite spent, she again assumes her man's apparel, and going into Holland, there takes on in a regiment of foot, quartered in one of the frontier towns. Here she did not remain long. There was no likelihood of preferment in time of peace, therefore she took a resolution of seeking her fortune another way; and withdrawing from the regiment, ships herself on board of a vessel bound for the West Indies.

It happened this ship was taken by English Pirates, and [as] Mary Read was the only English person on board, they kept her amongst them, and having plundered the ship, let it go again. After following this trade for some time, the King's Proclamation came out and was published in all parts of the West Indies, for pardoning such Pirates who should voluntarily surrender themselves by a certain day therein mentioned. The crew of Mary Read took the benefit of this Proclamation, and having surrendered, lived quietly on shore. But money beginning to grow short, and hearing that Captain Woodes Rogers, Governor of the Island of Providence, was fitting out some privateers to cruise against the Spaniards, she, with several others, embarked for that island, in order to go upon the privateering account, being resolved to make her fortune one way or other.

These privateers were no sooner sailed out but the crews of some of them, who had been pardoned, rose against their commanders and turned themselves to their old trade. In this number was Mary Read. It is true, she often declared that the life of a Pirate was what she always abhorred, and went into it only upon compulsion, both this time and before, intending to quit it whenever a fair opportunity should offer itself; yet some of the evidence[1] against her upon her trial, who were forced men and had sailed with her, deposed upon oath that in times of action no person amongst them was more resolute, or ready to board or undertake anything that was hazardous, than she and Anne Bonny. And particularly

---

[1] That is, witnesses.

at the time they were attacked and taken, when they were at close quarters none kept the deck except Mary Read and Anne Bonny and one more; upon which, she, Mary Read, called to those under deck to come up and fight like men; and finding they did not stir, fired her arms down the hold amongst them, killing one and wounding others.

This was part of the evidence against her which she denied; which, whether true or no, thus much is certain, that she did not want bravery; nor, indeed, was she less remarkable for her modesty according to her notions of virtue. Her sex was not so much as suspected by any person on board till Anne Bonny, who was not altogether so reserved in point of chastity, took a particular liking to her. In short, Anne Bonny took her for a handsome young fellow and for some reasons best known to herself, first discovered her sex to Mary Read. Mary Read, knowing what she would be at, and being very sensible of her incapacity that way, was forced to come to a right understanding with her; and so to the great disappointment of Anne Bonny, she let her know she was a woman also. But this intimacy so disturbed Captain Rackam, who was the lover and gallant of Anne Bonny, that he grew furiously jealous, so that he told Anne Bonny he would cut her new lover's throat; therefore, to quiet him, she let him into the secret also.

Captain Rackam, as he was enjoined, kept the thing a secret from all the ship's company; yet, notwithstanding all her cunning and reserve, love found her out in this disguise, and hindered her from forgetting her sex. In the cruise they took a great number of ships belonging to Jamaica, and other parts of the West Indies, bound to and from England; and whenever they met any good artist[1] or other person that might be of any great use to their company, if he was not willing to enter it was their custom to keep him by force. Among these was a young fellow of a most engaging behaviour, or, at least, he was so in the eyes of Mary Read, who became so smitten with his person and address that she could neither rest night or day. But as there is nothing more ingenious than love, it was no hard matter for her, who had

---

[1] That is, a skilled craftsman.

before been practised to these wiles, to find a way to let him discover her sex. She first insinuated herself into his liking by talking against the life of a Pirate, which he was altogether averse to; so they became messmates and strict companions. When she found he had a friendship for her as a man, she suffered the discovery to be made, by carelessly showing her breasts, which were very white.

The young fellow, who was made of flesh and blood, had his curiosity and desire so raised by this sight that he never ceased importuning her till she confessed what she was. Now begins the scene of love. As he had a liking and esteem for her under her supposed character, it was now turned into fondness and desire. Her passion was no less violent than his, and perhaps she expressed it by one of the most generous actions that ever love inspired. It happened this young fellow had a quarrel with one of the Pirates, and their ship then lying at an anchor near one of the islands, they had appointed to go ashore and fight, according to the custom of the Pirates. Mary Read was to the last degree uneasy and anxious for the fate of her lover; she would not have had him refuse the challenge, because she could not bear the thoughts of his being branded with cowardice; on the other side, she dreaded the event, and apprehended the fellow might be too hard for him. When love once enters into the breast of one who has any sparks of generosity, it stirs the heart up to the most noble actions. In this dilemma she showed that she feared more for his life than she did for her own; for she took a resolution of quarrelling with this fellow herself, and having challenged him ashore, she appointed the time two hours sooner than that when he was to meet her lover, where she fought him at sword and pistol and killed him upon the spot.

It is true, she had fought before, when she had been insulted by some of those fellows, but now it was altogether in her lover's cause; she stood, as it were, betwixt him and death, as if she could not live without him. If he had no regard for her before, this action would have bound her to him forever; but there was no occasions for ties or obligations, his inclination towards her was sufficient. In fine, they applied their troth to each other, which Mary Read said she looked upon to be as good a marriage in conscience, as if it had been done by a minister in church; and to this was owing her great belly, which she pleaded to save her life.

She declared she had never committed adultery or fornication with any man, she commended the justice of the Court before which she was tried for distinguishing the nature of their crimes, her husband, as she called him, with several others being acquitted. And being asked who he was, she would not tell, but, said he was an honest man, and had no inclination to such practices, and that they had both resolved to leave the Pirates the first opportunity, and apply themselves to some honest livelihood.

It is no doubt but many had compassion for her, yet the Court could not avoid finding her Guilty, for among other things, one of the evidences against her deposed that being taken by Rackam and detained some time on board, he fell accidentally into discourse with Mary Read, whom he, taking for a young man, asked her what pleasure she could have in being concerned in such enterprises, where her life was continually in danger by fire or sword; and not only so, but she must be sure of dying an ignominious death, if she should be taken alive. She answered, that as to hanging, she thought it no great hardship, for were it not for that, every cowardly fellow would turn Pirate, and so infest the seas that men of courage must starve; that if it was put to the choice of the Pirates, they would not have the punishment less than death, the fear of which kept some dastardly rogues honest; that many of those who are now cheating the widows and orphans, and oppressing their poor neighbours who have no money to obtain justice, would then rob at sea, and the ocean would be crowded with rogues like the land, and no merchant would venture out; so that the trade in a little time would not be worth following.

Being found quick with child, as has been observed, her execution was respited and it is possible she would have found favour, but she was seized with a violent fever soon after her trial, of which she died in prison.

1

There is the glass, and who can exhaust that glass which, for whoever chooses to gaze into it, expresses such a fine double awareness. The awareness of what we look like, and the secret knowledge of who we are.

In the light from a candle held close to the mirror the iris of the eye expanded like a living jewel, driving the pupil to an inexpressive point before its chasing colour which, in the fourth quadrant of the left eye, was truly extraordinary, a deep, restlessly changing violet.

Within its gold asterisk, the narrowed pupil, only window into the Lockean mind which calmly contemplated its own reflection, took in the violet, and for a moment grew large pondering it. Wise people had considered this quadrant full of portent for its owner. One had spoken of its influence in the inheriting of land and much cattle, another had foreseen the acquisition of specie in abundance, yet another, a fine marriage.

Outside in the black air the bell of the cathedral struck. Its chimes flew out over Breda's fortress, its ramparts lined with princely elms and, snugly smoking below, the chimneys of 2,200 comfortable citizens and four inns; the *Cardinal Prince*, the *Orange*, the *Three Blackamoors* in Bergs Street, and the *Valiant Trooper* in the market place, in the Star Room of which Read now stood.

The great bell struck again, echoing far out over the fens towards Frieseland which, on a fine day, could be clearly seen from its magnificent tower.

This tower, like the fortress, stood sentinel over a strange and volatile region dependent in the first instance upon the moon for its working, its very existence being centred upon the tides. It was a region, so its inhabitants were fond of quoting, where Fire was consuming the Earth (as peat) and where Air (as windmills) was consuming the Water. Wags called it the Bog of Europe, the Buttock of the World, a Cantle of Green Cheese spread over with Black Butter, where spiders were as big as shrimps. Unsurprisingly it produced its own curiosities. Once a mermaid had been cast up by a tempest, and with some cozening had been persuaded to eat bread and milk and, more usefully, to spin. She was unable to speak, and was given to tearing off her clothes and running passionately towards water whenever she could, but in the end they succeeded in teaching her to make the sign of the cross, so that when she eventually died she was allowed to be buried in the churchyard.

In point of fact the whole country was a curiosity, approaching at times the fabulous, being one continued meadow cut through with a thousand hand-dug canals full of salmon, pike, carp, perch and gudgeon, and providing flights for migrant birds from the north. It was flat country, from which arose steeples and houses looking as though they floated on water. Twenty-six miles to the north-west of Breda was Rotterdam. Here ships of 200 tons sailed up to the very doors of the merchants' houses, so that in the wonderful confusion of chimneys intermixed with topmasts, the traveller could hardly be sure whether he was looking at a fleet or a forest. It was in the square at Rotterdam that children waited for the great clock to strike, so that when the statue of Dr. Erasmus heard it he would turn over the bronze page of the book he was reading.

High water at Rotterdam, during the full or new moon, was at three, morning and evening, and Breda could be reached on Wednesdays and Saturdays by sailing-boat. It was a rough and ready way of travelling, but cheap. Similarly a sailing-boat set out every fourth day from Breda to Amsterdam, tying up at the Cingel by the Jan Roon Porstooren. Amsterdam, Tyre of the north, surrounded by misty fens and built on fir piles. People told strangers how it had taken a forest of 6,000 trees, each rammed so close a coin could not be thrust between them, to support but one of its many towers and steeples. Dr. Erasmus, visiting it, had described finding himself in a fabulous city whose inhabitants lived in the tops of trees, a city smelling pleasantly of spice from the nutmegs and cloves that the East India Company incontinently tipped into the canals from time to time, to keep up prices.

The eye took in the still image of the face thinking, and the mind which it served idly pondered the immensities that the tiny lens had absorbed, or which perhaps (depending on your philosophy) some inner eye had invented, for the mind in question was of a quizzical cast and intrigued by such curiosities. Restless expanses of grey northern sea came to mind, night skies swarming with multitudes of stars, great plains . . .

The candle wavered, and for a moment the eye moved into some secret inward contemplation, then returned once more to search the face that gazed back from the glass. It may have been the candlelight that rendered the face (framed by the dark red hair that people call 'Titian') strangely ambiguous, unwilling to lend itself to accurate definition. It was an ageless face, a little like the portrait by Minet of Mary of Guise. *Naturus* – about to be made – came to mind, surveying the dreaming heavy-lidded eyes, the straight narrow-bridged nose, and the long, shyly compressed mouth that could equally have belonged to a pensive youth or a sybil.

The eyes withdrew from contemplating the face, and rested on the lean hands that looked as though they would be capable of making things; cutting, carving, pleating, splicing, braiding, though one knuckle on the right hand was painfully notched by an ugly granulated scar that ran over the back of the hand and up the underside of the arm to the armpit. On observing the scar the eyes left the hands, and the inner eye saw again mist rising from a broad flat plain early on a September morning. It was a plain like an arena, which indeed it was, for drawn up and confronting one another had been two great armies in the magnificent array that was later woven into the tapestries from Gobelin, and sung of in the popular songs for many years after. Near to, in the very foreground of remembrance, the yellow leaves were softly falling in the wood of Sars. The wood of Sars – and the dreaming eye with its curious violet quadrant filled slowly with tears.

But the thaw had set in, and the ice-fields on which whole villages of firelit booths had been erected to entertain the jocular parties hissing over the ice in sledges carved like lions, tigers, dolphins, peacocks, were melting at last. The Maes would soon be open, and the ships sailing out of Rotterdam. A few weeks more, and the Zuyder Sea would be free of ice and the ships beginning to leave the Amstel. The long period of enforced waiting was at last drawing to a close.

Read got up, and setting the candle on the floor, bent and lifted back the heavy lid of the Indian chest, rummaging down through the neatly folded contents that were like aromatic strata of a previous existence, drawing up at last a pair of green shag breeches. Three years of disuse had creased them into stiff folds. Read smelt them, half expecting a whiff of horse sweat or the choking dust of pipe clay, then slowly drew them on, neatly lacing up the placket. They felt rough and damp, but fitted well, and, thrusting hands into the deep cold pockets, Read took a tentative turn round the room, then sat down stiffly, stood up again, and laughed in amused disbelief...

2

Laughed in amused disbelief, though this in a way was singular, for much of Read's life until now had followed unexpected courses. Whether due to the influence of the violet quadrant or not, Read was unsure, but in any case before the quadrant there had been a kind of prologue. This had taken the form of a significant dream experienced by Read's mother shortly before she had been brought to bed.

In the dream Mrs. Read, experiencing a certain sense of constriction, had cautiously opened her legs, whereupon out had popped a large scarlet balloon. This, growing ever larger, commenced enthusiastically bouncing over hedges and ditches, graduating from thence to trees and finally to windmills and steeples, until a more vigorous jetée carried it up into the blue of the sky where, for a second, it burned, a hectic spot, then vanished altogether.

The midwife agreed that this was certainly an omen, but of what precisely neither she nor Mrs. Read felt competent to determine, though they made attempts. Perhaps the expected child would take cloth and become a canon of the Church, though might not the red colour of the balloon suggest an unhappy connection with Rome? Then perhaps the Law? Or the Army? The birth which followed proved further unusual in that the child was contained in a caul. This now lay safely wrapped between sheets of blue paper in the Indian chest, though there had been times when Read had been hard put not to auction it. When Read's infant eyes had opened, cleared and set, there was next revealed the violet quadrant, followed in its turn, not all that long after by a third feature of prognostic interest.

'Thou,' Mr. Wafer was commenting, 'art, I fear, like to be a little mischief...' He had just taken Read's small hand and laid it tenderly uppermost in his own, gently uncurling the soft white fingers, and laying bare the dirt-streaked palm. 'Yes, as I thought,' as the colossal black-backed gulls wheeled over the Broad Quay, 'thou art promised unusual celebrity! And indeed thou art altogether endowed with too much of the magic sort for thine own good...' For in Read's infant hand he had seen the tiny pucker on the Mount of Saturn caused by an unusual confluence of hairlines. The Star, sign of some mysterious fatality that pursues the person all through their career, singling out that man or woman for distinction, but a distinction to be dreaded, since it indicates that the possessor of this mark will be the plaything of fate, destined to be cast for strange roles in life, most of them associated with tragedy.

But in the exhilarating thump, whistle and shout of the tar-laden air of Bristol's Broad Quay, Read paid little attention to this grave pronouncement of Mr. Wafer's, preferring to hear the story again of how Mr. Wafer had found Monmouth, the incendiary, lying in a ditch covered with fern, and wearing peasant's clothes. When they searched him, his pockets, Mr. Wafer had told Read, were full of green peas on which he had been subsisting, and all jumbled up with the peas, his Garter George in diamonds, and he was weeping...

Perhaps it was just as well Read disregarded Mr. Wafer's forecasts, it making very little sense after all to be preserved from drowning by a caul, or to be in the running for mighty possessions by reason of a violet quadrant, or indeed threatened with hanging or worse by the ownership of the Star, since none of this could be of much consequence to Read. For Read was not what he appeared to be. Beneath the covering of his patched shirt and breeches, his impatiently crumpled stockings, Read was in fact – a girl.

The confusion that Read, eight now, must surely be expected to have felt, was in fact not ever-present. He could remember only hazily what it had once been like to be Mary. This was before he and Poll Read, his mother, had set out at the bidding of old Mrs. Read from Blossom's Inn, Cheapside, in the dark of an early September morning with the town bells merrily clanging to celebrate the Peace of Ryswick.

Even less could he remember the jolting laborious journey westward in the post-waggon which ended two days later at Holbrook's warehouse at Broad Mead, Bristol. This, not all that far from the lane off King Street where old Mrs. Read had her lodging-house.

'Bristolia, lofty, spacious, faithful, fair,' her citizens extolled their city.

'Sweet, famous, old, kind, dear beyond compare . . .' Though Doctor Johnson's friend, Mr. Savage, whom the city first chose to ignore and afterwards to imprison, was to write rather differently from behind his bars, calling it a low-browed, squinting sort of place, dark, ignoble and self-seeking, utterly given to the making of pelf.

Before Mrs. Polly Read and her child had set forth that autumn morning, the fateful transformation had already been made. Unprotesting, Mary had been breeched and hosed and shod to present the very picture of a cheerful little homunculus strutting bravely into the reign of the first Anne.

The penalty at the time for this kind of deception was enormous, and Poll Read should have known better than burden her four-year-old daughter so. Women had been whipped, pilloried, imprisoned, subjected to impertinent personal searchings by midwives, burnt alive, for assuming the clothing of the first sex, though, curiously, not for acting its part. But although

Poll had no doubt heard of such occurrences, she surrendered everything to the one consideration which occupied her in the summer of 1697, which was to preserve herself and her daughter from starvation.

To be fair, and even taking into account that men who had known her unkindly dubbed her a fire-ship or tart, Polly had been the victim of betrayal, not once but twice.

On the first occasion, for a not very great consideration, she had agreed to change her name and marry a young wastrel in order to fetch him out of the Common side of the Fleet Prison. Ned Read and she had gone together to the *Hand and Pen* in Fleet Street where, for a further consideration, the notorious Dr. Colton (known by some as the Bishop of Hell) had married them. After this they had repaired to the Blue Room of a nearby establishment and gone to bed, for Ned Read had a generous way with him, and Poll had grown expansive after feasting on four mutton chops and sharing the bowl of punch Ned called for by way of celebration. Three months later, he unaccountably disappeared. Some of his Deptford friends said that he'd taken ship and gone once more on the Great Account (or privateering) in the Southern Seas, while others gave out that he was still lurking incog. in his old drinking haunts on the other side of the river. Whatever the truth, Poll was left with very little to go on and a rapidly quickening belly into the bargain. Her expansive nature and an improving sense of survival carried her more or less unscathed through the months of her time, and out again the other side, to the day six months later when, mother now of a sickly boy, she received an unexpected communication from Ned's mother.

The letter from old Mrs. Read had been long on the way, and through many hands, though this had been of no consequence, for it was still miraculously folded round a draft bill for twenty-five guineas on old Mrs. Read's account with a Bristol merchant. The burden of the letter (Poll's next consideration) was that, before returning to sea again, her poor boy had acquainted his mother with the fact of his marriage and his suspicion (gathered somehow on the side) that there had been a son of the union. Since Ned was all that poor Mrs. Read had left in the world, she had a certain interest in his offspring. Having purchased a small interest in a sugar plantation, she had taken herself to the West Indies for a space of two years, after which she designed returning to her home town, when she would be pleased to view her grandson. Until that time the further sum of a crown a week was to be made available to mother and son against old Mrs. Read's return.

In the event, two years became nearly three, in the course of which Poll lost her infant son with the scours, and not long after, during a further bout of expansiveness, was let down again. The outcome this time was unfortunately not a son but a daughter. Poll was vague as to who had fathered the child, though of one thing she was positive, he had been a gentleman. There were times indeed when, expansive yet again, she was able to narrow the field down to two, one a gentleman from Scotland, the other a young gentleman from Virginia.

Suffice to say that by the time Mrs. Read had returned from foreign parts, young Mrs. Read had gone smartly about and settled on a scheme for avoiding disappointment to the old lady and discomfort for herself. This by the simple expedient of changing the child's sex. Her daughter fortunately inclined to such a part. Either the Scottish or the Virginian gentleman had bequeathed his child a fine pair of shoulders, long legs, and a sanguine and vigorous disposition that could well pass for that of a boy, to which was fortunately joined high courage and a keen interest in things mechanical. The only discordant note Poll could perceive was a certain habit of reflection, a tiresome tendency to question (perhaps inherited from the Scotsman), and what was perhaps too soft a heart. But for the time, being a practical woman, she thrust these incongruities to the back of her mind.

See then old Mrs. Read in her snug lodging-house off King Street, so handy for the *Llandoger Tavern*, favourite meeting place for various seafaring gentlemen, including some suspected to be not long off the piratical or privateering account. The unkind, not daring to say it to her face, called her a female crimp behind her back – one who enticed seamen to spend too much on drink, and then, once they were in her clutches, sold them off to ship's captains in need of crewmen. But the lodging-house included among its number Mr. Wafer, who had voyaged round the world with Captain Dampier.

'He's a well-grown rogue,' commented old Mrs. Read in the course of that first meeting, squeezing the calves of her supposed grandson as though he'd been a tender morsel of poultry, 'but he don't favour my Ned!' She then pinched his cheeks till his eyes watered, eyes which were not, however, on his grandma, but on the extraordinary spectacle afforded by Mr. Wafer quietly tapping out his pipe in the chimney corner. For Mr. Wafer, perfectly ordinary in all other respects, was tattooed like a maypole from head to foot in a bright pattern of yellow, red and blue stripes. This had the curious effect, as with certain jungle animals, of rendering Mr. Wafer all but invisible in certain lights, so that in old Mrs. Read's obliquely-shadowed parlour he appeared, without effort, mysteriously to come and go.

'What dost thou think of me then, little master?' asked Mr. Wafer, seeing the boy's great eyes fixed upon him. For a minute it seemed there might be a possibility of Read bursting into tears with terror, but then the essentially gentle deportment of Mr. Wafer sitting there peacefully drawing on his long clay reassured him, and he collected himself to answer slowly:

'Very bright and lovely, sir!'

'Then thou and I are to be great friends!' responded Mr. Wafer gravely. 'The Indians gave them me, little sir, in recognition for a small service I did them...'

Old Mrs. Read all this time was being vigorously restrained by Poll from attempting to unbreech her grandson in order to judge how well made he was. She desisted finally, and the two women moved to the window to discuss terms, old Mrs. Read, as her clients well knew, being a great one for terms. Rooms, it seemed, could be found for mother and son at the *Pineapple* two streets away, where there was the certainty of regular employment for Mrs. Poll, for although Mrs. Read had pressed for the boy to lodge with her, young Mrs. Poll had insisted that do without her dearest boy she could and would not. So it was finally agreed that Read should be with his mother in the week, and visit his grandmother for all of Sunday. The payment of a crown a week was to continue, and when Read reached six he was to be put to learn to read and write at Colston's in St. Augustine's Back, and if he showed promise, to attend the Latin class there. Though not explicit, it was very well understood that old Mrs. Read intended something of advantage, should Read prove worthy. Mention was passingly made of a small property that, had not poor Ned... but never mind poor Ned... a property being purchased at that very time with the fruits of fortunate investment in the sugar trade, this made possible in its turn by the careful management of a small legacy left old Mrs. Read by her mother, and with which the lodgings off King Street had been purchased.

'Li-li, lilibulero!' Mr. Wafer was growling, having laid aside his pipe to set Read astride his leg in its thick grey worsted stocking, which, for Read, had magically become one of the chargers of the Prince Eugene, a charger that was even now curving its neck and bouncing its dappled posteriors, eager to be off to the extraordinary sound booming from Mr. Wafer's parted lips. These, in the most natural manner in the world, having become the mouth of a war trumpet.

'Have a care, if you please!' cried Mrs. Read from the window, 'for my grandson's intellectuals!' But to the deuce with intellectuals, Mr. Wafer and Read were already at the charge, oblivious of all going on around them, the gabble of the ladies, the stink of cod blowing in through the half-open September window, the acid scrape of the sleds that shimmied (bursting the hearts of the poor beasts that pulled them) over the Bristol cobbles. For it was well known that wheel traffic would upset the sewers below, not to mention the wine caves, in whose deep cool the Bristol Milk, glory of the town, must mature undisturbed.

Certain it was that from that day forward Mr. Wafer and Read became one and, whenever possible, undivided, Mr. Wafer being in turn Read's nursemaid, father, mentor, with the old seafaring town of Bristol their country. Bristol, its streets and narrow wynds shadowed by the high wooden houses, whose topmost storeys jutted out towards one another, so that the poor seamstress and the poorer hack could lean out over the narrow abyss and kiss across it, or shake hands, like the whip, wig, parasol, rope, stay, clock and spectacle makers, the spinsters, sea captains, dancing-masters and etc. with which the place abounded.

Down Christmas Steps to the quay below, Read holding Mr. Wafer's hand and counting as they go, Mr. Wafer in his white Sunday periwig, short loose frock-coat, blue-grey with brass buttons, a coloured handkerchief about his neck. Then down dark wynds smelling of cat and night-soil, hot bread, wet linen, tarred rope, tanning leather, and out into the hot sunlit day of the Rope Walk surrounded by its tall, still elms. Then to a convenient bench, Mr. Wafer inserting thumb and forefinger into an inner pocket stuffed with raisins to lure Read into reading out his letters one at a time from Mr. Wafer's small chapbook, after which they like as not toddle off to the Hot Wells. The water they drew here was clear, and warm as milk, according to Mr. Wafer, abounding in air bubbles, and excellent, it was said, for complaints as various as hot acrimonious blood, consumption, hectic fever, heats, the *fluor albus*, purulent ulcers, the stone, the gravel, the King's Evil – all apparently afflicting the curiously cheerful-looking visitors to the Wells.

Some days Mr. Wafer took Read digging for Bristol diamonds in the strata of St. Vincent's rocks. He'd demonstrate how, when you struck the chocolate-coloured marble with a hammer, it cracked, emitting a strong sulphurous stench. But they always returned to their great loves, the shipping quays; Tontine, Broad Quay, Mud Dock, the Grove, the Back. And sometimes, for a halfpenny, they took the ferry over from the Gibb to Wapping Dock where the great sea-going ships were careened and refitted.

'What's the tide?' Read demanded of his grandma.

'The tide's the tide, let it abide,' she replied shortly, having been surprised at her accounts. 'I slave only in thy interest,' she added by way of explanation. But Mr. Wafer never spoke so. 'Up wind, up sea,' he'd instruct Read. 'Down wind, down sea.' So that with the wind blowing in from the Bristol Roads and soughing up through the wynds into Read's sleep as it rattled the casements, Read dreamed, for Mr. Wafer, who filled Read's Sundays with expeditions, commanded even his sleep. And as the wind soughed,

Read dreamed of the sea changing from its natural greenness to a white or palish colour, indication, in his ship of sleep, that he was approaching land. Sometimes it was the Galapagos, where six fathoms down green turtles could be seen browsing on banks of sea-grass like the sheep at home; sometimes it was Hispaniola, where Read could hear them blowing conch shells to summon the little fat pigs from their day's rooting in the woods; sometimes Gorgonia, where the nimble black monkeys came down at low water to dig out the periwinkles from the roots of the mangrove trees . . . Then Read would taste the King Avocado, whose leaves, Mr. Wafer had told him, were large and of an oval shape, the fruit big as a large lemon, turning yellowish when ripe, so that the rind slipped off from the delicious substance inside. Green, and as Mr. Wafer said, a little yellowish, and as soft as butter . . .

One night Read dreamed he was walking along the shore of a quiet island in the Bay of Honduras, when at the tideline he found a large lump of ambergris, so large that when they carried it off to Jamaica, it was found to weigh a hundred pounds. It was of a dusky colour towards black, and about the hardness of mellow cheese, and of a very fragrant smell, and there was a great multitude of bees caught in it.

'Now you will soon be asking me the manner of making a canoe,' Mr. Wafer was saying, for it was Sunday once more, and the church bells were ringing, and Read had just returned from St. Michael's with his grandma. He was sitting with Mr. Wafer in Mr. Wafer's snug with the hippopotamus teeth, and the dried alligator, and the shrunken head, and the seaweed mysteriously blooming in a corked bottle of sea-water, and Mr. Wafer's Indian chest with the lid lifted, breathing out such aromatics that Read's eyes watered. Among other things the chest contained a brace of pistols, Mr. Wafer's cutlass, which Read was not allowed to touch for it was razor-sharp (how many people's heads has it struck off? Read wondered, but dared not ask), also Mr. Wafer's sextant and folding brass telescope.

'After cutting down a large, long tree and squaring the uppermost side, and then turning it upon the flat side, we shape the opposite side for a bottom,' Mr. Wafer was saying as he knocked out his dottle into his striped hand. 'Then we turn her, dig the inside, boring also three holes in the bottom, one before, one in the middle, and one abaft, thereby to gauge the thickness of the bottom; for otherwise we might cut the bottom thinner than is convenient...' To all of which Read listened attentively. 'Now we leave the bottom commonly about three inches thick, and the sides two inches thick below and one and a half at the top.' And Mr. Wafer gesticulated with the stem of his pipe. 'Then one or both of the ends we now sharpen to a point...'

Read sighed with pleasure at the competent simplicity of Mr. Wafer's description, and with a corresponding competence stored each stage of this operation away in the as yet uncluttered attics of his mind...

'Ned! Ned! What's the lad crazing at now!' And old Mrs. Read was at their door and greatly on the hum, being taken up with airing the Purple Bedroom for a new gentleman coming in. Read must go down to the *Pineapple* this instant for a plate of griskins and a pint of Mountain. Read, six now, was increasingly being asked to do his duty by his womenfolk, old Mrs. Read, and Poll his mother. Indeed the days with old Mrs. Read were becoming a groaning under an Egyptian bondage, for in the lodging-house there had been much coming and going of late; sea-chests being trundled up, close and prolonged consultations between Mrs. Read and certain of the captains on private matters of common interest.

'You've served me thus (badly) too many times for breath of late!' cried his grandma when he got back with the griskins and the pint of Mountain; but for all that it was never so heavy with her, because she took Read as she found him. It was his mother, after all, who knew the secret, who had the power by word or look to wrench him from his sheet-anchor, so that sometimes after she'd been at him he no longer knew who or what he was.

'What will come of it I know not,' Poll would muse, seeing Read growing tall and strong and able now to read his letters, splice a rope, and sharpen knives and mend her brooms. 'Sure our hopes must be in the next world where fools like I may hope for some happiness, though despised in this . . .' For Poll had been hearing strange things of Mrs. Read's, that it was for instance, if not a nest of common pirates, then a nest of women crimps, a house of no good repute, which was lowering, for above all else Mrs. Polly longed for respectability.

'Sure you'll not totally forget you're a She,' she went on, 'for a She you was born . . .' And then his mother began filling Read's appalled ears with intimacies he didn't want to hear, intimacies concerning hitherto unguessed softnesses, covert explorations of thumb and forefinger, clammy squeezings . . . which Read neither now nor ever wanted any part of. When his mother spoke of such things, dabbing her eyes with her skirt hem, he felt himself becoming cold and sullen, flat and defeated as unproved dough, until desperation forced hot tears from his eyes in a passion of longing for the clean, stringent instruction of Mr. Wafer testing him on his A's and B's from the small leather chapbook, or, better still, demonstrating the nice slant of a chisel, or the dry, careful tap of a hammer. Failing this, he could better tolerate the tiresome litigiousness of old Mrs. Read herself, her constant complaints, her criticism.

'Be sure and remember never to make water before your schoolfellows,' his mother was saying, for Read had now begun at Colston's grammar school in the Latin class. 'Certain it is,' went on his mother, 'that the shock of such a discovery would unhinge me as I now am!' And she sipped her can of smack and began to snivel and to justify herself all over again for turning Read into a He in the first place, which had been solely for Read's own sake.

But Read had long ago perfected an acceptable method of making water standing up. And from the first morning in the old dark classroom, with sunlight filtering through the founder's arms in the window, staining the young faces heraldic gules, azure, murrey as they prayed ('We pour forth our most humble and hearty supplications, that He, remembering the calamities of mankind, and the pilgrimage of this our life, in which we wear out days few and evil . . .'), he had begun as he meant to go on. He had made his first point by smacking an abusive redhead hard on the mouth, after which he and the redhead became firm friends for the remainder of the day, fighting for a back bench together as far away as possible from the dreadful Mr. Pope and his *qui, quae, quod* so that they could carve their names in peace upon the hard black wood of the desk.

'And pray, for my sake, be a good and diligent scholar, and do as you are bid,' cried his mother, well on into her third can, 'for should Mr. Pope have occasion to let down your breeches to whip thy posterior, why then I'd be ruined again . . . and I don't know for what!'

'Eight parts, two numbers, six cases these,' they chanted in the grammar class. 'Three genders, five declensions, three degrees . . .'

Read had so far managed to evade any such eventuality by taking Mr. Pope's random though vicious blows on less political portions of his anatomy; permitting his ears to be twisted, his nose pulled, his hair tugged and his knuckles cracked, by which means Mr. Pope seemed ever hopeful of instilling the *hic, haec, hoc* and the *ipse, ipsa, ipsud*.

'Nineteen pronouns, four kinds of verbs, and they
Three persons, though two numbers do convey . . .'

He had even managed to avert near catastrophe by diplomacy. When Matthew Ffish and Tom Hunnicot were one day measuring the lengths of their yards behind the stables, in furious competition, stretching and pulling at those unhappy organs and inviting Read to make a third, Read took a sideways step and set up as arbiter and finally resolved the quarrel. In the course of judging his friends' nakedness, however, he felt a treacherous movement like a fine knife sliding into his belly, which at the time he didn't know for what it was, but instinctively hated himself for it, and was ashamed of that humming secret part of himself that had made him feel so.

When all was said and done, Read acquitted himself well that first year at Colston's. By the end of it he could hurl stones as far as anyone of his age, and often with greater accuracy: could run and climb and jump and swing hand-over-hand equal to any of them, though for reasons of his own he did not play the truant. His only weakness was a tender heart.

They had got the sow badger in the tongs, and had set two lean dogs on her, and although they had taken the precaution of breaking her jaw she gamely took on the dogs a second, a third round. When the tongs slipped on her hams that were covered with foam and blood, knocking the frantic beast's eye out, Read choked and ran. Afterwards he had to wrestle hard and yet harder with his treacherous heart which, like the sly shift of desire he had experienced some time before, felt at once part of him and at the same time insufferably alien. It was about now that he developed the rare but furious fits of anger that both frightened and impressed his fellow pupils, so that into his second year he began to be regarded with respect and accounted one of Colston's leaders. The first real trial for Read's heart, however, came in the April of 1701, the year when he was almost nine and the new Queen came to the throne.

'Queen Anne, Queen Anne, she sat in the Sun,
As white as a lily – as brown as a bun!'

they chanted in Colston's yard. What remained in his memory from Coronation Day, however, was not so much the tumultuous bells and the dancing and scattering of hot pennies to the volatile Bristol mob, as the carrying on a hurdle of a wax effigy of the Pope, in red silk canonicals and triple crown, to the blaze on Broadway. The cortège in the April night was preceded by tumblers and jugglers leaping by torchlight, like creatures afflicted with St. Vitus's dance. Screaming like maniacs, they tore to the huge pyre that had been built in readiness. Jabbing and kicking and wading through the wrestling crowd, Read and Ffish were forced apart, and Read would have been trampled underfoot had not a great rum-smelling seaman hoisted him up on his shoulder in time for him to catch sight of the flames licking out at the scarlet robes, and to see by their hectic illumination the rouged wax face soften hideously, gape and then melt, running down in flaming streaks over the scarlet breast. At this the crowd hesitated for a moment as if shocked, then it opened its great throat and roared. Hard put whether to huzzah or sob at the sight, Read remained silent, so silent that, disappointed, the rum-smelling seaman let him slide back into the churning well of the crowd again from where, sickened, he struggled to the periphery and, by dark short-cuts, home.

It was three days after, with a full white moon rising in the night sky, that old Mrs. Read sent word to the *Pineapple* that the Captain had been struck down. Read was to come.

To Read's unpractised eye Mr. Wafer's appearance looked frighteningly similar to the melting effigy. Here was the same waxy yellowness, the fiery spots high on the gaunt cheekbones, the same toothless gape from which issued a terrifying sobbing like wind blowing beneath an ill-fitting door. As the breath sobbed, Mr. Wafer's breast worked painfully, and watching, it seemed to Read that the underlying bone structure of the face, from which the eyes stared out like dusty stones, was giving way.

Cautiously Read approached, steered firmly in the small of the back by Mrs. Read.

'Speak to him, Ned! Hold his hand!' Read did so, seeing that the striped pattern on the back of it had withered, like a flower caught by the frost, the colours gone dim. He could just feel the delicate thridding of the old man's pulse beneath his fingers.

'Speak to him!' insisted Mrs. Read, holding the dip-light closer.

'Mr. Wafer . . .' Read hesitated, then choked and pressed his lips against the old man's hand. It was cold and dry as a snakeskin. 'Mr. Wafer, sir!'

Mr. Wafer turned very slightly, his lips slowly trying to mouth round words already slipping away.

'Thou art too young to make a sailor yet,' he whispered at last. Then added – 'My little lass!' Then Mr. Wafer's eyes suddenly opened very wide, he gave a great sighing yawn, and for whole minutes it seemed he fought to draw breath as Mrs. Read and Read struggled to raise him.

'What did the Captain say?' pressed Mrs. Read.

Read lowered his eyes so as not to see his friend's agony, wildly pressing the slackening dry hand between his own.

'You can leave hold of it!' he heard his grandmother say a few moments later. 'The Captain's gone!' And she laid Mr. Wafer back on the pillows and waddled to the window and flung open the rattling casement . . .

And now began a terrible time for Read. Hours passing like days, and the days like weeks. When possible he lay in bed, trying to dream in the old way.

'Up wind, up sea!' he'd cry to himself. 'Down wind, down sea!' And sought to sail again to where the sea lost its natural greenness and turned to white or palish colour, indicating he was not far from land. But he could not.

'Stretching over to the Guinea coast,' he repeated brokenly as he retraced their old ways down to Rope Walk, the Grove, Mud Dock. 'A hankering to the windward bow,' he tried louder, 'a slatch of fine weather!' Searching, as it were, for Mr. Wafer on the Tontine, even taking the halfpenny fare from the Gibb over to Wapping, but he could not find him, could not by now even recall what Mr. Wafer looked like.

Lost, he wandered out to the St. Vincent rocks where, so long ago, it seemed, they had dug for diamonds. Then from St. Vincent's rocks to the Hotwell House, thrumming now in the May sun with the start of the season. 'We leave the bottom commonly about three inches thick . . .' But as he shuffled by, eyes on the ground, his mind refused to remember any more.

At that moment he heard a sharp 'Snap!' and raised his head to meet two blue eyes disturbingly quick in the quiet dead face. They were surveying him appraisingly from the lowered window of a sedan chair.

'Such pretty melancholy! I conceive a fancy for him!'

The face was ivory-smooth with a high-bridged nose,

the pronounced cheekbones smoothed over with carmine.

'Ask him why so melancholy!' This to an odd Crinkle-Crankle of a person, all ribboned gauntlets and vast periwig, out of which peered a yellow face like a shrew's, with a crimson patch at the corner of its vermilion mouth.

The panel of the chair was painted with a scene that captured Read's attention. It was of a moonlit forest, with a secret moonlit pool in which women were bathing – naked.

'Ask him if he recognises the story depicted on the panel. Tell him it is of Diana and her acolytes. Has he heard tell of Diana?' The long, very long, thin fingers resting on the chair sill began softly beating a tune, so that the chair-women, mistaking it for a direction, stooped to take up the poles.

'No, wait!' The hand was raised. The bracelet that encircled the wrist tinkled with its gold charms, one of which appeared to be a small microscope.

'Tell him poor Scipio is dead, and that I am in need of another footboy. . .' The fingers stopped drumming and the lips moved. '"Scipio Africanus,"' they recited. '"Negro Servant to ye right Honourable Lady Laverstock."'

> 'I was born a Pagan and a Slave,' (the lips intoned)
> 'Now sweetly sleep a Christian in my grave.
> What tho' my hue was dark my Saviour's Sight
> Shall change this darkness into radiant Light.
> Such grace to me my Lord on earth has given
> To recommend me to my Lord in heaven.
> Whose glorious second coming here I wait
> With Saints and Angels Him to celebrate.'

'Poor Scipio . . .' repeated the voice dreamily. Then, 'Ask him if he has a mother living.' Crinkle-Crankle approached. He exuded an odd smell that Read had not smelt before. 'Tell him that my agent is in Temple Street, tell him . . .'

'If indeed you have a mother living, boy,' said Crinkle-Crankle in an odd high voice, 'tell her Madame seeks permission for you to join her family in the office of footboy. Madame leads a retired life devoted entirely to the study of Philosophy, Mathematics, Physics, Poetry . . .'

'I'll not have my Ned's son a pander!' cried old Mrs. Read. She was newly returned from the Bristol visit of the Queen. Two hundred virgins clothed in white coming to meet her, she told them, all dressed as Amazons with bows and arrows by their side, and attendant shepherds with their crooks and tar-boxes, singing and playing on pipes of reeds. Mighty fine!

'I'll apprentice him!' cried old Mrs. Read. 'I'll not have him moping and eating his head off, and what if he do have to forgo his *qui, quae, quot*, he can add, and knows his letters . . .'

This was surely sufficient for Mr. Lynch with his blue nose, and thin as a lath, who lived in Wine Street and dealt with, among other things, the intricacies of old Mrs. Read's West Indian business. Possibly also with the business of her lodgers and captains, which was to do with the coming and going of ships. Possibly Mrs. Read was in the crimping business, possibly not. At all events, ships were fitted out and bound for the Gambia to trade loadings of brass buttons, glass, calico and clay pipes for slaves. Then the slaves, stowed neatly head to tail, were taken over to Montego Bay to be exchanged in their turn for tobacco, rice, indigo, logwood, rum, mahogany and sugar. Mr. Lynch totted up takings, multiplied, divided, assigned, apportioned. It appeared he could be doing with an apprentice.

As a curiosity, or perhaps *pour encourager les autres*, Mr. Lynch kept on his accounting desk a gag of metal, not unlike a gossip's bridle. A neat piece of engineering, this, fitting over the cranium and introducing a plate of metal upon the tongue, with an additional screw at the nose.

Mr. Lynch looked Read up and down. Sniffed. Measured the breadth of Read's skull with a pair of callipers. Catechised him. Dictated a letter. Made him add up a page of figures. Then, taking him by the shoulder, told him he could begin at two pence a week the day after next . . . and the next . . . and the next . . .

A burden now falls upon Read, heartbreaking as Christian's. All through the dog days he trudges to and from Wine Street, arriving before the watch has done calling the hours, to open the heavy shutters, light the rushlights. Thus into winter, when the wind comes moaning up the dark funnel of Wine Street and rattles at the counting house door . . . and so out into the Equinox again.

'The *John* and *Betty* arrived here on the 4th instant with 150 Bight negroes,' Read was copying. 'She purchas'd 250 and have buried eleven or more since her arrivall. They are the worst cargo of Negroes have been imported for severall years past. They were so badd Could not sell Tenn to the planters. We yesterday sold 105 at £18.10s. per head, Which Considering the Condition the Negroes were in is the greatest price that could have been given . . .'

'I am told we must direct our Vessells to the Gold Coast or Widdaw,' Mr. Lynch was dictating, 'as the Planters write me negroes from those places Especially the Latter, are in most Esteem with them. Bonny Negroes (the men particularly) are held in much Contempt many of them hanging and drowning themselves . . .'

By afternoon, even in the dark funnel off Wine Street the wind could be heard raging. 'Up wind! Up sea!' Down by the Tontine it screamed in the rigging of the jostling masts as ships ground like millstones against each other. It seemed for a wonder to affect even Mr. Lynch, who came in late. But it was not the wind. After much blowing of nose and chafing of hands, he gave Read a sealed letter.

"Tis for thy grandmother, boy. There has been a mishap. The ship was slaved to the number of three hundred and fifty, and hardly out of Lagos . . . Well, never mind, she'll read it soon enough. It caught fire, boy . . .' And he put his fingers together and pursed his mouth. 'So it looks as though I'll not need an apprentice for some time yet to come.' And he opened a drawer and drew out sixpence. 'This will have to content you, lad, till our fortunes mend again . . .'

'Up wind! Up sea!' And up and up and up and up, until it began to seethe over the iron-bolted harbour wall. Simultaneously the Frome burst his banks and, joining with the Avon, emptied into the southern quarter of the town with such a violent rush of waters that in a few minutes most of it was transformed into an inland sea.

Read slowly sharpened his pens and laid them out on the desk, shuffled his papers together and blew out the rushlight.

The flood was now gorging at the northern perimeter of Canon's Marsh. It swirled, tore, lapped, trickled and, in a sickle-shaped curve streaked with quivering moonlight, threatened the very warehouses of the Back.

In a moment it was pouring into the narrow streets. For a short while the flood carried racing reflections from the citizens' windows, from hastily lit household rushes and candles. Then, as it poured below house doors, gushed through windows and jetted through latch-plates, these lights went out. Snuffed, like old Mrs. Read's own rushlight as she was halfway up her cellar steps. The water carried her off her stout legs. Slewed her, choking and trying to scream, against the cellar wall. The frenzied black gushed into her mouth, her eyes, nostrils. Bled and flamed in her chest. Then, as if it too had suddenly given up the struggle through lack of necessity, it grew calm, hushing, as though it were some monstrous cradle, the slackening body of the old woman floating on its surface.

3

'I conceive! O thou knowest now how I conceive!' And her bell jangled, beating pitilessly on the defenceless outer rim of his consciousness.

She was sitting up in her theatre of a bed, framed by ponderous swags of worked crimson silk and topped by her escutcheon, over which a clump of ostrich feathers palpitated in the thermals created by the heat from the candles. The rest of the room was in darkness.

'Hylas, I conceive!' she cried again, her extraordinary face bereft of eyebrows, bare at last of paint and patches, in whose wizened yellow the blue eyes burnt below an enormous turban of green silk.

'Hylas!' And she indicated the writing-table where lay in readiness the half quire of gilt-edged paper, the pen, ink and sand that Read had set out four hours before when she retired for the night, leaving him to stretch himself on the couch outside her door.

'At my dictation!' And Lady Laverstock raised her hand.

'Upon a Theme of Love'

Read yawned. Through the half-drawn curtains his eyes glimpsed and caught in their tired water fiery morsels from the light of the moon, now in its descending arc beyond the trees of the park.

'The Nerves are France,' he scribbled at her dictation, 'and Italy and Spain . . .

'The Liver Britain, the Narrow Sea each Vein . . .'

The grey parrot, chained to its perch at the bed-head, shifted as though it had heard it before, then, with a kind of half-somersault, craned beneath its bar and critically examined its vent.

'The Spleen . . . And mark this, Hylas, for I find it a peculiarly apt conceit!

> 'The Spleen is Aethiopia, wherein
> 'Is bred a people of a black and tawny skin . . .'

She paused. Read's pen hovered above the paper.

'The Stomach is like Aegypt and the . . . I lack a word there, Hylas, to conclude the line, but the next will go thus:

> 'Which through the body flows, as is the Nile.'

'Bile' suggested Read after a moment, shaking the fine silver sand over the paper where it clung, smelling oddly and twinkling like frost, to the wet letters.

'Bile,' echoed the parrot.

'Why, child! Bile will do very well.'

'I thank your ladyship!'

'Thus then:

> 'The Stomach is like Aegypt, and the Bile
> 'Which through the body flows is as the Nile.'

'Bile,' affirmed the parrot.

Laverstock, where Read has been nearly a year since the Great Flood, Spring Equinox to Spring Equinox, is a writing sort of family. Even now, as the moon sets, Sir Harry, its master, is writing by the light of an early candle. The pages of his leather-bound diary are headed thus:

EBRIETAS MATER MALORUM TOTUS MUNDUS AGIT HISTRIONEM
In the Morning
Faults
Non materiall that I could observe (Sir Harry enters painfully of the day before).

Places where I was
At Laverstock at own house (writes Sir Harry) to Physick today.
Persons I conversed with
10 o'clock am to 12am My wife, Sukey, Betty Porridge, Ned Read, John Hobcraft ye Carpenter ...
In the Afternoon
Faults
Melancholick and uneasie (writes Sir Harry as the blackbirds begin whistling outside in the garden and the thrushes strop their captured snailshells against the front steps).
Places where I was
At Laverstock at own house on account of ye Physick.
Persons I conversed with
1-6 o'clock pm. My wife, Sukey. I called to our Betty Porridge in the kitchen and she answered me. But I did not see Her. Ned Read on the other side of the Spare room door next ye great staircase. But I did not see the said Ned Read ...

Lady Laverstock has for many years found Sir Harry a dull dog and does not scruple to record the fact:

> Wife and Servant are the same,
> But only differ in the Name
> For when that fatal knot is ty'd ... (she complains)
> ... Fierce as an Eastern Prince he grows,
> And all his innate rigour shows:
> Then but to look, to laugh or speak,
> Will the Nuptial Contract break ...

Lady Laverstock has friends to whom she also addresses poetry, Hecatissa, Lucasia, Althea, Clarastella, Brunetta, Amynta are all *belles esprits*, and dotted about the damp Devonshire countryside. All are subject to much the same annoyances and disappointments as herself.

To Read, however, even the hydropic Sir Harry is more comprehensible than the extraordinary woman he has to serve.

'I set no great value upon Sir Harry's partridges and pheasants, Hylas!' she cries, as they wind along the paths of her wilderness, where the rocks are shaped into artificial grottoes covered with woodbine and jasmine, and from which more paths run out, cut into shady walks and leading to ivy-twisted bowers filled with cages of turtle-doves. 'Yea, I set more store upon my larks and nightingales, for every bird of that sort killed in my ground will spoil a concert.' Then, softly murmuring the Benedicite to herself, she begins pulling to bits, petal by petal, a cowslip, breathing as she does so, 'O how marvellous are Thy works!' Flinging anthers, stamens, stigma, over her shoulder.

'The flood, thy grandma's death . . . it has all been a grievous miscarry, and thou and I, Ned, can only turn about and go back again to London,' his mother had said, Mr. Lynch's ruinous letter in her hand. 'Though it's an ill wind, as they say, for now thou canst turn back into a She again.'

Read stared at her pitilessly, hating the apparently indestructible cheerfulness which, at every change of fortune, came to her so effortlessly, making her grey eyes shine moistly and her tongue run away at a gallop.

'Thou hast fine eyes and a white skin, and art far too much in the genteel way to go on a potboy in King Street!' continued his mother, 'and besides, my conscience can never rest for making thee into a He, and all for nothing as it turns out.'

'You should have thought of that long ago, Mother,' said Read coldly.

But his mother was not listening, was pulling out

of the Indian chest, that had once been Mr. Wafer's, untidy armfuls of material, and shaking them out into crumpled-looking gowns.

'Come, Ned, to please thy mother, Ned! Off with thy breeches and shirt – come, Ned!'

He stood woodenly, in a kind of paralysed despair, a Mantegna St. Sebastian, allowing her nimble fingers to strip him, for owing to some inexplicable inhibition, he was unable to prevent her.

'Thou art wonderfully well-grown,' she clucked, passing her hands over him appraisingly, 'and thy breasts will not long be growing full. First thou wilt feel a little O like a groat, and then 'twill grow big as a penny piece ... and then ... why, it will not be long now that thy courses will be upon thee.' She was dropping the gown over his head. It smelt unspeakable. It closed down over him like evil water, in which, for a moment, he lost his breath, terrified, then tried to beat his way out, his heart hammering.

'There now, don't struggle so, child, and it will come easy, thou wilt soon get used to it again.' She smoothed and tweaked and tucked. 'Come to the glass, Ned.' Her breath smelling of cloves. 'Come!' And she led him stumbling abjectly in the unfamiliar hobble of the skirts, then stood behind him, her hands hot and heavy on his naked shoulders.

'Look up!' she cried in triumph. 'Look up and see thyself Mary Read!'

'Tis the senses, Hylas, that are the only windows into the room of the mind, which would otherwise be in darkness. Without the five senses we should have no notion of the world outside, and indeed it would not exist!' And Lady Laverstock, marking her copy of Locke's *Discourses* with a packet of face patches, turned to Read, whose eyes had been fixed on the windows, watching the raindrops course down the glass.

'How dost know of thy existence – Hylas?'

'The glass,' said Read, 'by the glass, your ladyship.'

'You well know the glass can lie!' countered Lady Laverstock. 'Yea, it can! Bring me the glass, Hylas!'

'Who am I?' asked her ladyship, peering with some contentment at the ivory cheeks touched with carnation, the corn-coloured hair of her afternoon face. 'Tell me, Hylas' – handing the glass back to him – 'does it lie?'

Read stared stonily into the mirror, seeing the face of the youth he was not. 'Yes, it lies, your ladyship.'

He had learned fast.

'And besides,' his mother had said, 'it will be infinitely more genteel at Lady Laverstock's than to go to sea.'

In the face of Read's inexpressible anguish she had gone about like a well-found ship, clapped on another wind, and was if anything more cheerful than ever. 'It will certainly be very genteel at Laverstock.'

At Laverstock all was ready for the experiment. The frogs which Read had taken from the Gizzel Pond were in moss in a wicker basket upon the Japan table in Lady Laverstock's library. Indeed Lady Laverstock's library was all Japan – and China – work, her quarto volumes separated from the octavo volumes by crazy pyramids of blue and white tea-dishes of all shapes and sizes, and that section of the library intended for plays and pamphlets and other loose papers, a recess now lined with glistening oyster shells and flanked with scaramouches, lions, monkeys, mandarins, clocks, all nodding and bobbing and chiming and ticking. To the side of them was a case wholly taken up with the best authors (albeit in wood), and to the left a bright fire in a sparkling grate of steel, and around it, taking chocolate, Brunetta, Hecatissa, Clarastella and Lady Laverstock herself who, for the afternoon, was in the character of Lucasia. There was also Mr. Vane, alias Crinkle-Crankle, and on a table beside him a primitive electric battery of his own invention.

'Not long since,' said Mr. Vane, who was in his shirt-sleeves, 'my friend had occasion to lay open the belly of his gundog bitch . . .' The ladies looked uncertain. 'She had but newly whelped, and it was remarkable that the creature in its concern for its progeny became completely insensible to her own pain, making ever little calls to her young, and seeking, flayed as she was, to reach them and lick them.' He was greeted by a ripple of approbation.

'I am all too aware that Heaven only needs to give a turn to one of my nerves,' Hecatissa (alias the vintner's wife) was confessing to Brunetta (alias the clerk's sister), 'and I should be an idiot . . .'

'And I am all too well aware,' Lucasia was saying to Clarastella, 'that the face of the Sun will by degrees become so encrusted with its own effluvia that it will give no more light to the world, and that in any case the Earth only very narrowly escaped a brush from the tail of the last comet, which would have infallibly reduced us all to ashes . . .'

Mr. Vane had by now opened the lid of the basket and removed from its nest of moss, one of the frogs . . .

'I have developed an aversion to all ways of travelling,' Hecatissa was saying. 'A chair is my terror, and even a coach and six is quite out of my good graces. I,' she confided to Clarastella, 'am reconciled to nothing but walking . . .'

With a neat flourish Mr. Vane severed the frog's head. The ladies screamed faintly and drew back their skirts.

'Hold!' cried Mr. Vane, dexterously wiring the limp corpse to the machine on the table. 'Lo! It yet lives!' They crowded round the frog, which was now vigorously kicking in time with the impulses from the battery.

'And it feels no pain?' asked Clarastella doubtfully.

'Bless you, no,' cried Mr. Vane, 'for it is without a head!'

'Then,' pondered Lucasia gravely, 'is it possible that such an experiment could be advantageously employed, say, in some manufactory?'

'Certainly!' replied Mr. Vane.

'What, then?' cried the ladies.

Read turned away, it was not his idea of entertainment. It put him too painfully in mind of the badger-baiting. He greatly preferred, when his mistress allowed him, to go down to the stables with Sir Harry and practise single-stick and throws with the grooms and gardener boys there.

'See here, Ned,' Mr. Wafer had shown him, 'place thy hand here upon my shoulder as if thou wert about to apprehend me . . .' And Read had felt a magic shift of weight. One so swift that in a moment he was sprawling on his back in the dust.

'But thou must take care,' Mr. Wafer warned him, 'or else thou art like to break thy opponent's back!'

So now in the yard Read wrestled and ducked with Nathan and Moses and William Buckingham, growing every day more certain in the strength of his arm and the judgement of his eye.

'You are losing thy pretty pale and melancholic look,' complained his mistress, 'and are grown something swarthy and less to my liking, and your suit has grown tight on thee, Ned, and were it not for thy quick understanding, and the fact that I have set myself to educate you . . .'

'. . . and I wish you was a little older, Ned, than thirteen,' confessed Betty Porridge in the hen yard. 'Thou art so gentle and quiet a lad!' She leaned against him, and he could smell the pleasant tonic smell of her meal-covered hands, and for a moment her sheer comeliness and the kindness for him in her grey eyes lit a warmth in his breast.

'I'll carry the buckets for thee, Betty,' he said, 'for thou art a kind lass.' And he stooped to pick them up, and as he did so he felt a warm trickle down his inner leg, followed by a gathering coolness.

'Lord, boy!' cried Betty, 'thy breeches are wet!' And she bent in concern and touched him, and when they both looked there was light-coloured blood on her fingers.

He was, as Lucasia would have him, composing, carrying out the lesson she had imposed.

In Singing the Lady Lucasia's Lap Dog's Praise

he wrote carefully in his best hand.

> First then her outward beauties note,
> The glossy, silken, snowy coat.
> As soft as Bactrian camel's hair,
> As the unspoiled Ermine fair,
> Marbled here and there with black;
> Gently weaving down her back;
> The comely spreading Ruff is plac'd . . .
> (the pen slurring slightly then recovering)
> Beneath her neck with ribbons grac'd . . .

Then, as if impelled by a force of its own the pen began writing faster:

> Poor stuff when I think of all the great world waiting only a day's walk from here. Bristol and the sea, and beyond our own English sea the Atlantic and the New World, Haiti, Hispaniola, the Bay of Campeche . . . for I think sailors must be happy men to have such opportunities of visiting foreign countries and beholding the wonderful works of the Creator

in the remote regions of the earth . . . my mind can conceive of nothing but pleasant gales and prosperous voyages . . . But O, dear Mr. Wafer sir, ever since you went I have so sorely missed you, and all that you could tell me for my own good, I finding myself as if alone in such a strange, unknown world. I know not even who I am nor what I must do, for you was my one true friend and could always, always tell me . . .

The pen halted. Began idly drawing circles, squares, then a rhomboid. Then began afresh, the rhomboid becoming a sloop, all sails set and running free, the sea creaming at her foot as on the model ship Mr. Wafer had once built him.

And now I think in truth you are telling me, and in your own good way (wrote the pen), that I am fit to go to sea at last . . .

4

But not quite yet, it seemed.

'They wear very long crisped hair,' Lady Laverstock was remarking of the Venetian women. 'It is of several strakes and colours which they artificially make by washing their heads in pisse, and then dishevelling them on the brim of a broad hat that has no head but an hole to put out their hair by, so as to dry it in the sun . . .'

Mr. Vane, old Crinkle-Crankle, was nodding, Read staring through the blinds of the rocking coach and seeing nothing but barren plains and mournful willows.

'. . .their petticoats come up from their very armpits,' continued Lady Laverstock to no one in particular, 'and so high, I have heard say, that their breasts flub over the tying place . . .'

They were some hours out from Maestricht on their way to Rome, the horses painfully traversing the vast expanse of sandy plain that quivered in the August sunlight. For Read, locked in the minute world of the coach that stank of Mr. Vane's attar of roses, time as he had once known it had almost ceased to exist. Minutes treacherously expanded into what seemed like hours, and then, as ambiguously, the hours dwindled to seconds, the only available points of reference being the posting-stages, the risings and settings of the sun, the gaining moon, against which Mr. Vane's toy repeater, prettily signalling the halves and quarters into the stuffy interior of the coach, had become meaningless.

Aeons ago now since their landing at Ostend where, beneath a high sky and bowling white clouds, the citizens, newly emancipated from the French by

Marlborough, had stood cheering on the harbour wall to welcome the British flag. A lifetime since Read had slipped out of the hostelry at Bruges early in the morning to climb the hundred steps of the cathedral tower.

Up and up he'd gone, first by stone steps growing ever higher and narrower, then by a swaying ladder of wood. Up and up and up, so high, finally, that even in the still summer morning the wind could be heard perpetually moaning round the parapet. He had just reached the topmost rung when it began, almost as though it were alive, to vibrate, and this so violently that he would have been thrown off had he not managed to tighten his hold at the moment the great bells began to swing. He managed to crawl to the bell platform and to stretch himself out with his hands over his ears as the first peal commenced, enveloping him in an entirely new element of pure sound, which, to begin with, was almost intolerable. His body rocked with sound. The bones of his thighs and forearms thrummed with it, the blood in his veins seeming to effervesce. Yet, as wave after wave pounded through him, ringing its wonderful music into his flesh, his blood, his bones, into the very atoms of his being, he found himself accepting its unfamiliar and mighty possession. As he did so, a silence began growing at the heart of the sound, and in the silence he imagined he heard a voice speaking, and the voice seemed to be that of Mr. Wafer. Then came a brief shift of attention, and be became aware once more of the tumbling music outside him, so that he lost the words he thought he had heard. He subsequently tried to recapture them as the horses drew Lady Laverstock's heavy painted coach inexorably towards the Alps and the passes into Italy, sought to translate the words into a picture. Then there came into his mind a great and bright light passing through a shutter pierced with small holes, so that on one side of the shutter the light was whole, while on the other it appeared as numerous small beams, and it came to him that what he was seeing had something to do with the relationship between Earth and Heaven, but further than this he was unable to proceed.

Liège, Spa, Aix-la-Chapelle, and along the valley of the Rhine. As they proceeded Lady Laverstock dictated the names of the principal buildings along with their history and dimensions, the supposed number of inhabitants, the flora and fauna, as garnish to the letters which she dispatched at regular intervals to Brunetta, Hecatissa and Clarastella – Read writing as well as he could on the small travelling-desk, complete with paper, quills and sand, that his mistress had set up in the coach.

'Let Dutchess out to piss!' she suddenly cried, leaning forward and rapping on the glass some way out of Bonn. The coach drawing to a halt, she gave a little scream of pleasure. Below them, anchored in the centre of the river, was an immense raft, with pretty cottages built upon it, their chimneys smoking, flowers growing at their doors, and men chopping wood, women spinning, and children playing among the lilies at the water margin.

'Faith, what a philosophical notion!' commented her ladyship delightedly to Mr. Vane. 'Look, sir! To be peripatetic upon an island of friends together, and floating from bank to bank of that great river! Picture yourself, sir! An island of *virtuosi*!'

Meanwhile Read, walking Dutchess, the large red chow, along the bank in the fading light, heard a sad moaning and glimpsed, walking in front of him, a woman with glow-worms flashing like diamonds in her hair.

Emms, Mayence, Oppenheim, Worms, still holding to the valley of the great river, and after, Mannheim,

Augsburg, Munich, leaving at last the trapped air of the plains and drawing up by slow degrees to the freer heights of Innsbruck. At Innsbruck Lady Laverstock took to a chair, and Read and Mr. Vane to asses with ropes tied with a loop to put their feet in in lieu of stirrups. Halfway over the pass they changed from asses to mules as being yet more sure-footed . . .

'Sure, Ned, 'tis a great Poetic conceit for life itself!' cried her ladyship as, blinded by feathered rain, they wound through rocky clefts and defiles hardly able to see a pistol-shot in front of them, the horizon everywhere closed in by rocks and mountains which seemed to touch the skies, and in many places to pierce the very heavens.

'Surely I'll compose on this! What say you to this . . .'

'"Nor dare the immortal gods my rage oppose,"' she declared, pen in hand, from her chair as they wove past thundering cataracts of melted snow that threw up opalescent mists, so that they could barely see or hear one another. At which Read was again reminded of the tumbling bells at Bruges, and the message in the still heart of their sound which he fancied he heard once more in the roar of the cataract, but still could not make it out.

At night they turned and turned again on palliasses stuffed with dried leaves that made such a crackling, and pricked so painfully through the ticking, that no one but Dutchess got a wink of sleep.

'Such a race of ogres!' complained old Crinkle-Crankle next morning, contemplating with shivering disfavour the mountain inhabitants who made it their barbarous practice to nail heads of wolves and foxes and even bears to their front doors.

'They are no doubt a goodly sort of people . . .' Lady Laverstock dictated in a letter to Brunetta, 'but have vast wens of flesh growing to their throats, some of which I have seen as big as an hundred-pound bag of silver hanking under their chins; among the women especially, and that so ponderous that to ease them the women wear linnen cloths bound about their head and coming under the chin to support it. Their drinking so much snow water,' she concluded, 'is thought to be the cause of it . . .'

Mr. Vane, however, was no longer interested in the causes of anything, but sat slumped, without patches, in his chair, muffled to the eyebrows in wool as the chair-men trudged and slithered over the shale and ice, sleet driving full in their faces. Then, on the third day, the clouds miraculously lifted and they saw Italy at last.

'At Bologna we were so pestered with those flying glow-worms call'd Luccioli,' Read took down at Lady Laverstock's dictation, 'that one who had never heard of them would think the Country full of sparks of fire, in so much as beating some of them downe and applying them to a book, I could reade in the darke, by the light they afforded.'

By the time they reached the shady lemon groves of Cardinal Aldobrandini's villa, Mr. Vane had regained lost *ton*, having, in the last ten days, been physicked to his ultimate satisfaction.

'Will stinking flesh give light like rotten wood?' Lady Laverstock asked him, her mind still running on the wonder of the *luccioli*.

'Ah yes, your ladyship, there was once a lucid sirloin of beef seen in the Strand. Foolish people thought it burned, when it only became lucid and crystalline by the coagulation of the aqueous juice of the beef by the corruption that invaded it. 'Tis frequent, ma'am, I myself have read a Geneva Bible by a leg of pork!'

They three and Dutchess were now approaching a large theatre of water, its curve reminiscent of a rainbow. Beneath, they had just discovered an artificial grot where were curious rocks, hydraulic organs, and all kinds of metal singing birds moving and chirruping mechanically by the mere force of water.

'How so?' queried Read's mistress, bending low to study a copper ball dancing mysteriously three foot above the flagstones. But before there was time to confirm that it was in fact supported by a jet of wind artfully conveyed from a secret vent beneath, there was a sudden squirt! from a concealed faucet. This catching her, she fell back drenched, but crying loudly '*Miracolo!*'

'Setting aside the fact there is no clean walking anywhere ...' dictated Lady Laverstock in her memoir to Sacharissa, 'the people here pissing and fouling the ambulatories of all their great palaces and churches, there is, Sister, nevertheless ...

Surprised by an unaccountable yawn Read's mistress sternly stifled it and resumed. 'Nevertheless Sister, there is indeed no end to the Italian miracle!'

Dutchess was panting at their feet, and above them in the wistaria arbour into which they had been driven by the pitiless sun, large black bumble bees vibrated somnolently.

'Last sennight we witnessed at Padua three dissections by the great Cavaliere,' Lady Laverstock continued. 'First a man's cadaver flayed – in particular the right forearm and the thoracic cavity – am I not correct Ned?' to Read who was blinking heavily in the overpowering heat, 'Then a woman begun ...' For a moment her voice trailed off, ' ... commencing at the *os pubis*, and extending from there to ... Ned! I find I grow monstrous drowsy in this heat ... There! for I have now spoiled thy dictation! No matter, though, it will make a draft ... Then to the hospital of San Francesco Portenari ...' Read waited, his pen poised above the paper, sweat gathering in his palm.

'Here was a trepanning we saw, a lancing ... four

sweatings . . .' His mistress's voice now erupted into a soft low snore, bringing her up sharply.

'Four sweatings . . . salival severalations, salivations . . .' She was snoring lightly now. Was asleep.

'This were an entertainment of a monstrous sort,' wrote Read (for the paper was spoiled anyway), 'and one from which I was forced from pity to turn my eyes. A poor woman secured with ropes and her thighs thrust open with a wedge to allow of the application of a styptic as a cure against the clap. At which she screamed lustily, to the shame of those among us who took snuff and looked on smiling, saying that it was a consequence of her own folly and etc., she being a whore. My mistress, I noticed, went yellow as a jonquil and turned her head, she having intended all along to brave it out, but failing. Mr. Vane, who had gagged when they began before to flay the cadaver of a little child, grew so cheerful when the woman was at last untied and carried away, that he delivered an *extempore* oration to the other tourists on the results of his recent experiments upon ants' eggs. "I have dissected their eggs," cries he, "and find that each has within it an occluded ant, which has adhering to its anus a small black speck . . ." "What does it concern a man to know ought of the nature of an ant's anus?" someone asked. "O, it concerns a *virtuoso* mightily," replies Mr. Vane, "so be it knowledge, 'tis no matter what!" '

They were now in Rome, much of it abandoned to brambles, the Circus Maximus, that had once seated 160,000 spectators, nothing now but a vast heap of confused ruins. Part of it had been converted into a garden of pot-herbs, while there were cows browsing in the Forum. As at Padua, the citizens relieved themselves without hindrance upon the marbles of Hadrian's villa, near which was a refuse dump where Read saw them dragging a dead harlot, her feet tied to a horse's tail.

At the church of St. Cross an altercation broke out between their guide and Read's mistress over his refusal to allow a woman into a side chapel where women were permitted to enter on only one day in the year. She was considerably mollified, however, by being allowed to see, by way of compensation, two thorns of Christ's crown, three chips of the real Cross, one of the nails, some of Judas's pieces of silver, and the doubting finger of St. Thomas. Indeed Read found himself scarcely knowing what to think, his mind having become quite distended with marvels. The finest so far had occurred in Piazza Navona, where a mountebank took a ring from his finger and licked the dull dark stone, at which it burst into a flame the size of a small wax candle – the trick being several times repeated.

But now, at San Sebastiano, some little way out of the city of Rome, they stood in a shorn cornfield in the September sunlight, on the brink of yet another wonder. Between the cut gold stalks a negligible-looking sort of hole, very little wider at its entrance than a badger set, ran sharply away and downward.

''Tis in a manner of speaking the whole object of our journey!' cried her ladyship. She had discarded her hoop for the investigation, and was wearing a dark overwrap secured by a crimson cord about her waist.

The guide preceded her. He crouched down, and like some stoatish beast worked his way vigorously into and down the hole, and vanished. To Read there was something so inexplicably unpleasant about the movement that it caught at his belly. For it was as though the man, before their eyes, was entering the uterine passage of a vast woman. Being sucked in. Swallowed up. Read's mistress followed him with much wriggling, uttering little cries, like a small girl being ingested . . . Her square-heeled shoes of mauve velvet kicked for a moment, then she too was gone. Mr.

Vane, who had long since resumed his full regalia of paint and patches, refrained from entering the hole, preferring instead to remain above ground sketching in a straw to protect him from the sun.

Read, in two minds whether to follow his mistress, bent and put his head into the hole's entrance. A flat cold smell came up, as though from a rabbit burrow, but tinctured by the homely smell of burning pitchpine. He withdrew his head for a moment and, searching for something to take with him, picked up an ungleaned cornstalk and rubbed the head between his palms, then sucked the grains into his mouth. They were familiar to his tongue, and when he ground them between his teeth, the bitter tonic flavour reassured him. He paused, then thrust his head into the hole and pushed. To his surprise, the sides of the passage closed round his body almost pleasantly, like a cool glove. He wormed and pushed against some sly pressure, due perhaps to trapped air. He pushed again, just managing to contain a nascent panic by pressing forward determinedly against this either real or imagined resistance, hearing his own breathing pant out muffled by the close air of the tunnel. His blood began to pound in his head. He started to count. But had barely reached seven before there was a rush of air and he was suddenly delivered into what appeared to be a smoky stone forecourt.

'Nobly, Hylas!' She was standing between two guides, who were holding resin torches high above their heads. In their sputtering light Read could see streets or alleyways leading off from the point at which they were standing.

''Tis the noblest thing I ever saw, and a very great curiosity!' commented his mistress as, slowly, their shadows leaping on the stone roof, they moved down the passage which gave on to certain square chambers which looked as though they might at some time have been chapels, since there were paintings on the walls to which the guide pointed. One, Read saw, was of a bowl of water with peaches immersed in it, like those he had daily seen in their alfresco meals above ground, and beside the bowl of fruit was a flask of red wine and a half-cut loaf.

As they regained the passage and moved forward once more, Read became conscious that the way was lined with stone shelves, and that upon the shelves were recumbent figures all appearing to be in an advanced stage of emaciation. By the light of the guide's torch Read could see that every bone was outlined, as though, nerve and muscle, they had been expertly flayed by a surgeon.

'Look!' cried one of the guides, and passed his hand, barely touching it, over a ribcage, whereupon it collapsed inwards in a tiny explosion of dust. 'Look, Signora!' And the guide held up his illumination to a shelf which, unlike the others, was closed by a course of flat stone. '*Il Santo*!' And in the uneven light Read glimpsed engraved palm leaves, and a dove flying into darkness with a fragment of palm in its beak.

'Leave us, *camerere*!' Lady Laverstock suddenly ordered. 'I have a whim to be left here for upwards of half an hour alone – in the darkness . . .'

Accustomed, perhaps, to similar eccentric requests from previous travellers, the guides smirked and withdrew, their torches dwindling to points of warm rose until the darkness closed seamlessly behind them.

They stood for a few moments, Read gritting the corn grains between his teeth, hearing nothing but the breathing of Lady Laverstock and the thudding of his own heart.

'Surely our earthly pilgrimage ends in death!' commented Lady Laverstock calmly out of the darkness. 'Were we separately alone, Ned, you and I, we would experience something like the state of the uninformed

Lockean mind, aware only of its own existence and of nothing else. The outside world would not exist, and there would be only a sense of being . . . How could we then deduce, I wonder, that we had been created at all? As it is, Ned, you and I have one another to scrape sparks off!' She paused, adding, 'It's a fine entombment, and an experiment that I shall be most happy to report to my sisters in philosophy home in Laverstock.'

Read closed his eyes and tried to see Laverstock, with Betty Porridge comfortably feeding her hens, and Nat and Joe down at the stables boxing, but he could see nothing. Nothing in the heart of darkness in which they now found themselves.

''Tis said a French bishop and his retinue, adventuring too far, it seems, into these dens, and their lights going out, were never heard of more,' commented Lady Laverstock. A moment passed. Nothing. Read began to shiver.

'I find it disappointing that Mr. Vane did not think to venture in with us,' said Lady Laverstock. 'I had thought such a phenomenon would have had his scientific interest.' Nothing.

'It is no less than immensity,' said Lady Laverstock. 'An immensity of dark . . .' Nothing. Nothing.

Moments passed.

'Ned!'

'Yes, your ladyship!'

'Just to be sure you was there.' Nothing.

'Summon the *camerere*!' ordered Lady Laverstock suddenly. 'I find I tire of the experiment.'

'*Camerere*!' The darkness swallowed Read's voice as though he had shouted into a box. '*Camerere*!'

They waited for a moment. In the dark Read heard Lady Laverstock shift her feet and displace a stone. It made a welcome, worldly sound, and Read stooped and felt for it. His hand encountered something cool, oblong and smooth in the dust. It felt like a cylinder of some sort. He straightened, and dropped it into his breeches pocket.

'Call again, Ned!' Her voice was developing a curious edge to it, sounding almost like a suppressed sob. He managed to croak once more into the darkness, '*Camerere*!' and together they waited, motionless in the silence that followed.

'Give me thy hand, Ned!' And in the extraordinary blackness he made a responsive sweep of his arm and nearly lost his balance. 'Here!' she called, her voice cracking. 'Here!' He swept again, with faith that he would find her hand, then brushed and grasped hold of it. Her palm was cold and slippery with sweat.

'We are like to be lost, dear Ned, or at best plundered . . . I am a foolish woman, Ned, and have lost my way. I hear nothing, nothing. It gives back not even an echo, Ned!'

He hesitated, his mouth dry, eyes closed, tears of fear trickling down his cheeks. Then he heard a shuffling beside him, and knew that his old mistress had gone down on her knees.

'O God, have mercy on us! Where is the way out, Ned? Have mercy upon us, most merciful Father; for Thy Son our Lord Jesus Christ's sake, forgive us all that is past . . .'

He closed his eyes tighter still, and from them moving rings went pulsing out like gold helices into the darkness.

'God have mercy, Christ have mercy!'

The gold helices went spiralling out, creating, as it were, an element of their own. They were turning through and from and over him, and he began to sweat. Then he opened his eyes, and even in the darkness the helices continued to pulse out from him, and as he watched them spinning into the darkness, he saw that a notch was indenting the outer rings at roughly the same position as eleven o'clock on a clock face . . .

'Christ have mercy, Christ have mercy . . .' Read put out his hand and closed it over Lady Laverstock's and helped her on to her feet, and together they slewed to the left and upwards, following, as he judged, the curious break in the ebbing rings of the helices which, as they went haltingly forward, appeared to be expanding.

'Oh Ned! Ned! I led thee to this!' And she halted and leaned so heavily against him that he stumbled. He recovered, and supported her half-fainting for many, many yards, his free hand groping all the time but encountering – nothing. Then he stopped, and they waited for a moment, and Read saw that the notches on the outer rings were beginning to fill in, were thickening, were turning in fact into a light, that grew, leaping and dazzling, becoming ever bigger, more roseate and golden, and disclosing behind it at last the bulky figures of the two guides. They were grinning.

Choked with smoke from the torches, they stumbled to the mouth of the tunnel, plunged upwards. Scrambled feverishly. Emerged. For a moment Read gazed about him, blinded by the daylight, gulping the perfumed evening air like water.

Mr. Vane, his hat awry, his clothes strangely disarrayed, his face-lacquer oddly smudged, was staring at Read with an uplifted brush. There was an empty canvas before him.

'Faith, boy! You indeed look as though you had been among the dead!' Then he laid down his brush and moved towards Read as he tried to raise himself from his knees, then sank to them again, his forehead pressed against the sharp gold points of the stubble, the white alabaster phial that he'd picked up rolling out of his pocket . . .

5

He wore it now, having painstakingly drilled a hole and threaded it onto a length of pack-thread round his neck. A Jesuit who'd tried to buy it off him at Naples had told him the garnet-coloured dust it contained was certainly the blood of a saint, since the phial closely resembled one in the cathedral containing the dried blood of St. Januarius. This, the Jesuit assured him, liquefied miraculously to a rich raspberry colour eighteen times a year beneath the officiating hand of the Bishop.

'God's mercy! Ned, you must keep it ever by you, for it surely saved us from the catacombs!' exclaimed his old mistress, stopping her crying for a moment, for he'd only a minute ago told her that he'd signed on with a Queen's ship and was leaving her service.

The decision, retrospectively the first important one of his life, had astounded him in its simplicity. A squadron of Queen's ships were at anchor in the roads, flying their multi-coloured pennants against the sparkling blue of the Bay, and he'd fallen into conversation with a pig-tailed seaman from a seventy-four. In the course of this he learned that six of the *Ruby*'s crew had jumped ship, and they were taking on men. Within moments he knew he was not going to return home with Lady Laverstock over the mountain passes, but was going to sign on with the *Ruby* instead.

'To be taken from me, the only child of my old age . . . and pray what is to become of Dutchess? There being no one now to walk her . . .' his mistress sobbed, while old Crinkle-Crankle, squinneying through the beating glare off the water, wrung his hands crying, 'Alack, boy! Alack! Alack!' a sparse tear oozing from beneath one eyelid and snaking slowly down his rouged cheek. 'Thou knowest it not, but thou art embarking on a life of villainous slavery!'

Read frowned, remembering it, and fingered the phial as he looked over the *Ruby*'s rail to where the smoke from the French shore batteries stained the limpid July air over Toulon.

'Damn if they haven't hauled their twenty-pounders from out of their men o'war and set 'em up on the hill above the town!' said Swan, snapping shut his glass. Swan was the surgeon's mate.

There was a puff of smoke followed by an ugly flat clap, then a wavering scream, and they instinctively ducked as a shot fired at extreme range plunged aft of the *Ruby*. Ashplant, who on the lieutenant's orders was still stapled to the deck, opened his eyes, then closed them, his yellow hair streaking with sweat.

'Sure the captain will release him before we engage?' asked Read, seeking to keep the begging note out of his voice. 'He'll surely release Ashplant, sir?' But Swan had turned away.

Poor Ashplant, a friend from that first day Read stepped warily aboard into the astonishing wooden world of the *Ruby*. A world keenly obedient to the calculations of geometry and the great movements of stellar and solar time, obedient in their turn to eternity itself. The *Ruby*, however, rendered down these massive conceptions to a time of its own, not unlike that of a monastery, and like a monastery, marked by bells and sandglasses. This was quite strange enough; what was equally strange was that the ship was alive. Being built of trees and moved by the winds, she joined within herself the elements, so that to sail her was an interpretive science.

Such uncompromising grandeur, however, was experienced by Read personally as an assault of unfathomable smells, inexplicable sounds, creakings, groanings, crackings; in being shouted at in an incomprehensible language while trying to live by a time twelve hours behind that of the shore, and with sleep limited to four hours at a stretch, so that for the first few weeks he gaped and dozed in an unearthly dream-world, uncertain whether he was asleep or awake.

This impression was further accentuated by the extraordinary ship's company. For on inspection the *Ruby* appeared less like a 74-gun warship than a Noah's Ark. Goats lay on the quarter-deck, chewing the cud and sunning themselves, or, to the fury of the lieutenant, pattered incontinently over the white planking on their polished grey slots. Coops of cackling fowl were piled one on top of another behind the steersman, while on the gun deck, noisy gaggles of white geese explored the bread bags of the ship's crew, and in the *Ruby*'s waist – for she happened to be *en route* from Messina with supplies for the rest of the squadron – thirty red cattle lowed and stank. Nor was this all, for to Read's unaccustomed eye the entire ship seemed to be pullulating with energetic and destructive urchins between the ages of six and fourteen. These, euphemistically called 'servants', were more like young apprentices, every sea officer including the cook being allowed one, and the boatswain, gunner and carpenter two each, while the captain was assigned four for every two hundred of the ship's complement. Into this world Read was assumed, and for a time the sheer pace and strangeness of it gave him little opportunity to assimilate what was happening to him.

There were moments, however, when he was sharply reminded of those first days on trial at Colston's. One being the first day when, as a volunteer, he was sent below to be passed fit by the surgeon. Someone had reassured him (it was probably Ashplant) that the examination would be a formality, the ship needing men so badly; furthermore, the surgeon would certainly be drunk. Expeditiously stuffing a balled-up rag in his placket, Read had gone below to brave out his destiny. And the surgeon had been drunk. One eye was already closed, though the other, bright as newly cut lead, raked Read up and down so attentively that for a moment his heart knocked in his throat. For his part, the surgeon, peering through a blue haze in which the candle flames wavered, saw a well set-up lad of good address with dark red hair and a lively violet eye, and though more than usually flown, marked him down as a likely boy to help in the cockpit. He nodded, dismissed Read with a wave, and returned to his brandy, after which the thought of discovery barely entered Read's head.

Thanks to Ashplant letting fall that not only did his new friend possess a caul against drowning, but also carried a Star in his hand, Read rapidly grew in popularity with the men of the starboard watch. They, like the rest of the *Ruby*'s company, were addicted to games of chance, readings from the Tarot and other mystical activities much frowned upon by the warrant officers, who discouraged such games whenever they could, though they bloomed mysteriously in the ship's dark corners. Many of the crew were volunteers, who had left the ploughtail not many months before in the search for adventure and the hope of prize-money, and they were still unsettled in the Service. While not a few of the crew were oddities in their own right. It was not long before Read became acquainted with a remarkable forecastleman who swore, to Read's amazement, that his legs were actually made of green bottle-glass that would shiver to splinters if he landed for one moment too heavily on deck. And there was another, a cooper this time, with the curious philosophy that at one and the same instant he was going backwards as he went forwards, down as he went up (though no one else could perceive it), and that it was simultaneously both dark and light. It was a cast of mind, Read was to discover, that endowed the man with furious courage, for in the course of an action he was in his own mind always undergoing its opposite, so that while running gamely to the attack, he was also running swiftly to safety, so preserving himself. On this strangely heterogeneous company the hierarchy of the warrant officers, with their rattan canes and ropes' ends, imposed an enterprising conformity, drilling otherwise reluctant individuals into the self-reliant floating commonwealth at whose head was Captain Mackra.

Read soon discovered that Captain Mackra (a tarpaulin captain of the old school, who had come up to his present position from being ship's boy) ran an immaculate ship. His artificers were skilled enough to have stripped down and rebuilt the *Ruby* as she sailed. Her tackle and rigging were in a constant state of perfection, so that in the presenting of her sails to the winds she bloomed and faded and bloomed again to the admiring eye, like some beautiful white rose of the deeps. As for her decks, they were daily holystoned to the whiteness of flour, and kept so under threat of condign punishment, of which Captain Mackra was a master (having at his command various possibilities of duckings at the yard-arm, haulings under the keel, settings in the bilboes, and being bound to the capstan with a basket of shot round the neck – among other things). In this instance, detesting tobacco as much as incontinent goats, the Captain had spitting-pans set at strategic points about the decks for the men to use. It was his humour, should a man subsequently forget himself and dirty the planks with tobacco juice, to tie the offender's arms behind his back, remove all the spitting-pans bar one, and tie this securely with straps to the man's chest. He was then forced to run hither and thither at the beck and call of any of his mates who wanted to rid their mouths of tobacco juice. Playing the part, as Mr. Tench the boatswain admiringly expressed it, of the captain's perambulating 'spitpan'.

By the time the surgeon got round to asking the lieutenant to call Read out of the starboard watch to be his loblolly boy, Read, who was physically apt, had been initiated into most of the workings of Mackra's ship. He was dashed, accordingly, to find himself about to join the company of what the ship called 'idlers'. These numbered warrant and petty officers, stewards, cooks, joiners, sailmakers and the like. The way, moreover, by which Read had worked himself up from being a 'waister', responsible with the worn-out seaman and other greenhorns like himself for sweeping and cleaning the deck, had been hard. For early on he had discovered a shocking component of his being, one of which he had been unaware at Colston's or indeed anywhere else since. This was a seemingly insurmountable revulsion for heights. Few of the crew could have been totally insensible to this particular fear, since it was frequently exploited as a punishment by the warrant officers who, on the slightest suspicion of surliness, were given to sending the offender to the masthead. Such an event, however, could by and large be avoided. What could not be avoided were the daily exercises aloft for the boys and landsmen, and Read burned in secret shame to see the young boys climbing to the topgallant and royal yards like joyful marmosets while he, invaded to the core of his being by fear and loathing, longed to slither on his belly like a serpent in the dust of the earth.

This flaw soon grew in his mind to represent the impossibility of his ever entering a cleaner element, of making the passage from an inferior to a superior existence, and whenever he pondered it, which he increasingly did, it appeared as a sentence, condemning and confining him in what he privately thought of as his tremulous woman's flesh.

It was Ashplant, one of the star foretopmen, who on a hot windless day in spring transformed him into another creature.

'It's time at last for thee to become a skylark, Ned, so that you can hand and reef the yards! So place your foot here, Ned, by my hand' – and they began to climb, with Ashplant below him guiding his feet –'always looking up, as if to Heaven' – so Ashplant said, though Read, poor earthbound creature, could feel his bowels churning and the sweat pouring icily from below his armpits.

'See here, Ned, I'm here! Feel, I have my hand on thy ankle!' For Read, the hot vomit bolting suddenly into his throat, was swaying and shaking as though he had an ague, the ratlines beginning to slither through his inert wet hands.

'Hold fast a moment, Ned, and look up like a man!' And Read, knowing that at any moment he might, like a fallen angel let alone a man, plummet thirty feet to the deck below, became conscious that Ashplant's warm still hand was encircling his ankle.

They stayed so for many aeons, encapsulated in the gentle rumbling billow of the sail through which the sun shone cloudy silver. Then they began to climb once more. Up they drew, with painful slowness, a foot and another foot. After a few minutes, it seemed to Read that the air round them was growing fresher, and he saw that they were now entering the tree-like landscape of the upper yards. As if to endorse the impression, two birds got up, then, with heads turned towards them, tilted effortlessly into the blue air.

'Rock doves,' murmured Ashplant, 'from the African coast. 'Let us rest likewise for a little, dear Ned.'

It was at this moment Read realised his hands had begun to grow dry, and that he had stopped salivating.

It was as though he were in the process of sloughing off some primal self, bred in the ooze of mud swamps; as if from out of the state of vertigo, a new creature like an imago was emerging.

'We are now all but there, Ned!'

They were now ten feet from the mast-top and about to negotiate the notorious futtock shrouds. These, by reason of their underslung position in relation to the mast-top, necessarily forced the topsman to arch backwards and outwards for a second over the seventy-foot drop below, before he could swing his leg over the top's side and drop safe into the barrel.

They started to climb once more. Ashplant had begun to sing. It was a light country song with a happy lilt to it. Read could not take in the words, but the tune, repetitive as it was, had a pleasantly mesmerising quality, and he found himself humming in time with it, climbing without apparent effort, his hands dry, his eyes fixed steadily on the top, which was by now not far above them. Then the singing stopped. There was a short silence. Read found himself remembering, with great vividness, the bell tower at Bruges in the moment before the great bell struck. And remembering, he realised that his mind was now in an almost ecstatic state of expectation. It was something he could never have put into words, but he knew he was about to experience a revelation of some sort.

He heard Ashplant talking to him. Knew that at last the moment had come. Amazed, he watched his clever hands firm on the shrouds. Felt his back arch in ecstasy as the protective blue of the sky, which was now his element, poured over him like a benison, and far off he heard someone screaming, as his leg hooked like a steel grapple over the top's side. Then he dropped safe into the protective shadow of the barrel.

It was in this way that Read became an able seaman assigned to the starboard watch of the foretop. How he joined the aerial club of young men lounging at ease against small stunsails rolled up into cushions, from where, like lazy gods, they surveyed the busy doings on the decks below. It was here Read and Ashplant first exchanged their short life-histories and, cracking themselves with laughter, yelled into the wind their anthems to the confusion of Captain Mackra and Teate, the terrible first lieutenant with the thick white face and flaming hair. It was such an anthem, overheard in some other part of the ship by a sharp-eared spy of the master-at-arms and reported instantly to the lieutenant of the watch, that had sent Ashplant to be stapled three days to the deck on a charge of mutiny. Of these he had by now endured two, fed daily on bread and water and otherwise left to lie out under the burning Mediterranean sun in his excrement, until Read, under the kindly averted eye of the watch, could get to him and swab him clean.

'They're coming within range!' observed Swan, returning to the rail as another ball shrieked overhead. Meanwhile the *Ruby*, backed by a following wind, continued steadfastly towards Toulon in company with the remainder of the squadron. On board, the crew's hammocks had already been stowed fore and aft in the nettings, to act as baffles, while below decks the galley fires had been beaten out and the bulkheads taken down to minimise injury from splinters. On the gun decks, the garlands had been stocked with shot both between the guns and round the masts and hatches, while rams, sponges, priming irons and linstocks were ready to hand to serve the firing of the *Ruby*'s guns.

'Within range!' commented Swan laconically as a creaming thirty foot column of water reared up aft of them.

'Sir!'

'Get below, damn you!' shouted Swan, intending

nonetheless to intercede for Ashplant with the lieutenant.

'We're messmates, sir!' cried Read in despair. Earlier on, while the *Ruby*, beating back and forth under grey winter skies, wore out her men day after day in the course of her guard duty against the French privateers, Read, sick for home, had looked into Ashplant's kindly blue eyes and been reminded of English skies. In snatched moments in the tarry balcony of the lee forechains, he and Ashplant had forgotten the low, rain-shrouded coastlines of Messina and Syracuse, and seen instead Myddel in Shropshire where Ashplant lived with his mother.

'If ever there was a gentleman, that is, if you could call a pig a gentleman, then Old Mose, he was a gentleman...' And the tarry balcony sounded with laughter as they saw Mrs. Ashplant's mean neighbour, Fitch, bending low to interrupt Old Mose in his essential commerce with a young gilt. ' "Two servings for the price of one!" says old He! At which Old Mose ups and with a neat turn of his head gashes Fitch in the breeches so bad, doesn't he, that they have to send for the apothecary to suture his hinder parts!'

Then Read read out from Lady Laverstock's letter that had been waiting three months at Leghorn, ' "I am sure could you see my fyreside you would laugh hartely to see Dutchess upon a cushion, the cat of another, and Pug of another lapt all but her face in a blankitt..." '

'I'd pay you to learn me my letters, Ned,' Ashplant said one day. He was showing Read the Fisherman's Bend. ''Tis the king of all knots, my honey, for when the parts be drawn together, the more you pulls the faster they holds. But see how a pull the other way disunites them, and how easy they cast off in a moment... which goes to show,' said Ashplant, turning his kind eyes on Read, 'the very great necessity of us all pulling together in this wicked world.' Then, casting aside the king knot, 'Speak Latin to me, Ned, and see if I can guess its meaning.'

'*Ubi pedunt canes?*' obliged Read after some thought. He framed the words slowly and deliberately.

Ashplant wrinkled his brow and blew out his cheeks in concentration. 'Sure it's some great matter, Ned, it sounds so grave to my ear... No, don't say, wait and let me try to answer it.'

'*Paulo supra pernas!*' continued Read, beginning to grin, 'and there's your answer!'

'Why are you laughing, Ned?'

'Why, Valentine? Because this is the grave question I asked thee, which is, "Where do dogs fart?" ' And as Ashplant's hand went out, painfully gripping his shoulder, 'The answer to which is, "A little above their hams!"'

'You snot-nosed son of a dogfish!' And for a moment they grappled furiously, Ashplant's head pressed hard against Read's shoulder.

'Why, then, to make up I'll ask you another,' bellowed Read, for Ashplant was lightly punching him in the ribs, 'and here it is, *Cur canis micturus?*'

'And pray, my dear boy, what does that mean?' And Ashplant left off punching and assumed a grave expression.

'Which is to say, "Why doth a dog, being to piss, hold up one leg?"'

'Why then?' asked Ashplant, with a look so amused and kindly that Read suddenly felt what he had never felt before, something like a shadow passing over his heart, like a cloud over the sun.

'And that is to say,' said Read, feeling suddenly ashamed, ' "*Crus alterum erigit*, Lest he should bepiss his stockings."'

But that had been back in May...

'Get below, you little swab!' shouted Swan as another shot screamed overhead, taking a portion of the superstructure on its way and sending splinters whining through the air. Ashplant was now shaking his head to and fro, whimpering . . .

Journal, August 5th 1707 . . . it seems that by this time our captain had all but achieved his first objective which, in common with the other ships of our squadron, was to get the *Ruby* close inshore as possible to commence bombarding both the fort this side, and the dockyards behind the intervening neck of land. By now it had become plain that many of the crew were viewing the task before them with trepidation, the shore batteries being so strong and entrenched, and we like to be a sitting duck for 'em. Before being sent below by Mr. Swan I heard the captain swear on the lieutenant's telling him the men was uneasy in this way . . . I was later told that on his hearing my poor friend crying, being pinned as he was to the deck, he orders them 'to release that son of a whore'. He then ordering them to pipe the crew abaft, then shouts to them through his trumpet that he heard they hung an arse – but that he'd never in his life known English sailors afraid before, in all his thirty years at sea, man and boy. 'If we must sail up to their gingerbread, which we must, then by God we will!' shouts he. At which I'm told there was a cheer from the men, then the soldiers' drums began their drubbing and the bosuns' pipes to screech . . .

Four feet below the water line on the orlop deck, Read felt the jar as the hawser ran out in a sheet of flame, bringing the *Ruby* to anchor. In the cockpit the surgeon's instruments had been brought out of the chests and laid ready, trays of wads, probes and scalpels which in time would conclude the grotesquely parallel operations taking place on the gun decks.

'By God, he's taking us right in under their French noses!' Swan was saying. 'I've heard the gunner say they'll have to depress their guns mightily at the fort if they're to fire on us, though he reckons we are facing some eighty-four great guns, and twenty more from the fascine batteries, not to mention supporting fire from their men o'war that are part submerged in the harbour.'

'Great Heavens!' cried the purser, wringing his hands. Prised out of his kingdom next to the cockpit, a kingdom that stank of putrid cheese and rancid butter, he'd been sent along with the chaplain to assist the surgeon.

'The captain released your friend,' Swan began, turning to Read, but his voice was lost in the opening cannonade from the fort.

At the first shot, the purser and the chaplain hurled themselves to the deck. The others sat rigid on the sea-chests, staring at one another. There was a short silence, during which Read could visualise the order of firing the great guns: 'Lay down your crows and handspikes – take off the apron – take your match, blow it . . .' At which the *Ruby* gave a shudder and the lantern above their heads swung wildly on its chain as her guns began, one by one, firing in reply.

Not even his wildest imaginings had prepared Read for what followed. Noise of unbelievable brutality, noise continuous and sustained, possessed him, hurting not so much the ear as hammering relentlessly through head, stomach and limbs, dulling all sense, including that of time. It was the timelessness of the operation that was peculiarly horrible, for when at last a brief silence fell, it was impossible to judge whether the guns had been firing for ten minutes or as many hours, and though the firing had stopped, his body continued to throb with it.

'Damn their blood!' commented the surgeon in a

whisper, while Read's mind, as though independently seeking to render such chaos comprehensible, began feverishly ransacking memory for comparison. The tumultuous carillon in the great tower at Bruges came first to his mind, but in the heart of that sound there had seemed a Godlike meaning, even though it was impossible of interpretation. The present sound, in its mindless repetition, was without meaning. Then he remembered the vacant darkness of the catacomb, swallowing sound itself, giving back nothing, nothing in reply – and yes, in that darkness had been some quality of brutal emptiness akin to the sound they endured now.

Tears of strain began gathering in Read's eyes, and he turned to hide his face, aware, as he did so, that a cracked voice was calling out of the darkness. A titanic shadow leapt across their faces, bellied into the cockpit, and rendered down into the neat figure of the boatswain as he stepped into the moving yellow pool cast by the lantern.

'I've come to be docked, sir!' and with his good hand he held out, like some choice offering, the crimson and yellowish bolt of flesh that had been his left hand and forearm. At that moment a thunderous explosion rocked the ship, causing the boatswain to stagger, and throwing the rest of them off their perches. This was followed by the sound of shattering glass as a shot from the French shore battery, catching the *Ruby* between wind and water, smashed its way through the purser's store next door. Even the surgeon dropped his scalpel, and Read was left holding the boatswain's shattered elbow as the surgeon plunged into the swinging shadows to retrieve his instrument.

'Cast off, my honey, and I'll hold it myself!' growled Tench, for Read's teeth had begun to chatter. 'If I'm to be docked, I'll be docked, and that's all about it!' At which the surgeon leaned forward and began to reduce the tangled warp of sinew and bone chipping which was alone attaching the man's arm to his shoulder, interrogating him meanwhile as to what was going on above decks. Read now desperately sought the darkness beyond the lit cavern of the cockpit.

Here, his teeth chattering with shock, he first spewed then slowly urinated, his water comfortingly hot, running soundlessly from his body to the deck . . .

Journal, undated . . . and I, standing there, could hear the boatswain telling the surgeon in as calm a voice as if he'd been at home, how the captain had ordered the guns double-shot fore and aft, and how they'd grown some of them mighty hot from quick firing, and then gone bouncing up to the beams and torn out their ringbolts . . . But by now more of our men were being brought in to us, having suffered sorely in this cannonade, and our guns, beginning to fire anew, caused such a recoil that the purser and I was hard put to stop 'em slithering with all their wounds this way and that, across the deck like so much dead cargo, groaning miserably.

It was now that I saw, from out the corner of my eye, that the purser and chaplain together were having frequent pulls from a case-bottle of brandy the purser had about him. The effect of this was to make the one sluggish and uncaring what he was about, whilst the other was coming to a greatly wrought-up state. But Mr. Swan at that moment calling me away to put a lock on a man, I saw no more for the time being . . .

'Where dost thou come from, then?' asks I of the man. He was vomiting, and a cold sweat was spread on his countenance. A grape-shot splinter had penetrated through the upper part of the right femur and come out under the scrotum, which was blown up like a bullock's bladder, and it had carried away all the perineum extremity of the rectum and part of the buttock . . .

'From Yarmouth,' says he in a whisper, adding, 'a wife and four little children . . .' At which his tears flowed, so that I found tears standing in my own eyes. And as I struggled with him to hold on to him (for he was a strong man and in very great agony and crying out), I thought of my friend Ashplant, and how this was nothing like the great glory we had supposed war to be. And I found myself heartily wishing an end to it. What was to become of us, if nothing was to be done about the fearful situation in which we now found ourselves, sitting duck, as Mr. Swan had said, to the shore batteries, and the captain a hard man to quit his post? At this I tried to pray, as I had been taught when a child in Bristol. But nothing came. Then I thought of the Star I carry in my hand, that people say must ever be magic, and also of the phial I have about me of supposed saint's blood that I found in the catacombs. And it was a childish thing, I know, but I took the phial and, unstoppering it, put a little of the contents on my tongue, and allowing it to rest there, set about praying for our release yet more diligently. It tasted bitter to the tongue, dissolving in extreme bitterness, so that I was frightened to swallow it. But reasoning, how could it be efficacious if I did not swallow it? I did swallow. And it seemed that in a minute or two my mind grew very clear, excessive sharp, though from what I could not guess. But that was all, and I had to confess myself very disappointed . . .

Swan, who had applied a dressing of *unguent de styrace* to the dying man, had moved on to diminish chaos in his own way, and having extracted part of a shattered blade bone from a shoulder, was now drawing together and knotting the lips of the wound, closing from sight the purple and white and curious yellow into a neat piqued ridge of near recognisable flesh.

Meanwhile it grew very hot. Not long after, a seaman bending low came in with a man on his back. He laid him carefully down, then pulling out his pouch, thrust a wedge of tobacco into his mouth. 'Death han't as yet boarded him,' said he through it, 'though they've been yard-arm and yard-arm this last two glasses . . .'

Journal, undated . . . seeing from where I stood that the man he had carried in had yellow hair, I thought instantly it was my friend. But our chaplain, bending over to unwind a crimson scarf that was about the man's neck, said it was poor Jack Trumpet that was one of the stewards. As he did this, the ship recoiling from another salvo, what we had all supposed a red scarf came away in his hands and, wriggling like a snake fell to the deck. We could see then that what we had supposed a scarf was indeed a great clot of blood which, coming away as it did, showed us all the black hole where poor Trumpet's throat had been. It was at this moment, the surgeon ordering the seaman to carry Trumpet's body up and throw it overboard (the continuing press of the wounded becoming well-nigh insupportable), that our chaplain gives a great cry and begins divesting himself of his clothes, crying out how that the Lord was gracious and full of compassion . . . 'Lay off, damn you!' cries Mr. Swan, but our chaplain continues hollering as if he'd been in a church, how good to us all the Lord is being, and how very great his mercies and etc. Then he stoops and rubs his hands in the red slime now covering the deck and, simpering all the while, makes to smear his face with it, after rubbing it over his arms and breast as though refreshing himself at a spring, being even about to lick it from his hands, at which, not being able to forbear longer, I beats him to the deck with my fists, whereat he ups on his feet again and, shrieking, makes for the upper decks. In this he would have ultimately succeeded, to the great scandal of all, had not Mr. Swan, the purser and I manhandled him to the door of the surgeon's cabin and locked him in . . .

It was now, all of us having been so occupied, that we realised our guns had for some time been silent, a sudden red fog coming down unawares being the cause of it. Now what was strange (for I later had it on good authority) was that this fog came down at about the time I was holding the Yarmouth waterman for the dressing of his wound, when I had also laid a little of the contents of the phial upon my tongue, and was praying so diligently for our delivery. Whether the contents of that phial was turned again to blood by my action, I know not, for I never did spit to see . . . suffice to say, the red fog came down as if to protect us from the great batteries ashore. So that after a fight of near seven glasses or three hours and a half, in which our guns fired forty-nine broadsides, our captain was forced to signal for us to slip our cables and sheer off, ordering at the same time each seaman a pint and a half of raw rum . . .

They were already singing fitfully by the time Read emerged on deck, to be confronted by the pinkish wall of fog that had forced Mackra and the other commanders of the squadron to raise the bombardment. Had it not been for the fog, Mackra would certainly have kept his guns with all the tenacity of one of his own red Staffordshires which he kept chained in his cabin. As it was, the boats were lowered, and the *Ruby* towed out of range, where she now lay at anchor, her horn sounding out a mournful warning, like some requiem for her lost souls, to the hidden ships around.

Read looked over the side. The fog hovered barely a foot above the surface of the water, which was smooth as milk. Waterdrops from unseen spars above were raining on to the deck as though from forest trees, and through this mist men were moving like wraiths.

Ashplant, my old mate! Ashplant, my friend!

The chain-pumps were clanking, for the *Ruby* had taken on a list, and slung out over the side, the carpenters, scarcely able to see a hand in front of them, were laboriously drawing in a square of fothered sail to plug the breach made by the shot that had caught the ship below the waterline.

Ashplant?

'Brave Benbow lost his legs, but on his stumps he begs . . .' they were roaring from the lower deck. A seaman staggered past. His underjaw had been shattered by grapeshot, but he had a can of wine in one hand and a funnel in the other which he was introducing into his mouth and, pouring in the wine, was enjoying the precious liquid as though nothing had happened.

Ashplant?

But no one paid any attention.

While the surgeon dressed his wound, thus he said,

'Let my cradle now in haste
On the quarter-deck be placed,
That my enemies I may face 'till I'm dead, 'till I'm dead.'

Ashplant, my own dear? But by now most of them were crying, their arms round one another's necks.

Twelve hours later, the effects of the rum had dissipated and a gloom settled over the company. The fog had partially lifted, revealing the already dead littering a glassy sea on which the *Ruby*, her sails limp, floated motionless. By some trick of the current, however, they came with bloated bodies and gull-ravaged eyes, slyly bumping against the ship's sides, offering themselves, as if seeking humble admission to the ship's company once more.

By mid-day a blazing copper sun had rendered everything metal on deck too hot to touch, and liquid tar was forcing up from between the deck planks. In the makeshift hospital on the lower gun deck, the more fortunate wounded hung like bats from the roof of a cave, with scarcely a gap between the hammocks. The less fortunate lay where they had been hastily lugged out of the way, or in cots in the darker corners of the hold, many of them with their wounds still undressed.

At daybreak Read, who had spent much of the night searching for his friend, followed Swan with a horn lantern into the den of the lower gun deck. Swan, stripping to his waistcoat, crept on all fours under the hammocks, forcing his bald pate up between them and keeping them apart with his shoulder, attempting as well as he could to dress the men's wounds and administer clysters . . .

> *Journal continued* . . . on the second day after this engagement which had been so woeful for us, the wind picked up, and it was put about we was setting course for Gibraltar, to refit. Our spirits lifted, but were almost instantly dashed by the squadron commander ordering us to stand by to take on board the sick and wounded from our Allied force that had been besieging Toulon all this time, but was now in full retreat before the French reinforcements under Nessé. So it was that conditions on board that were already bad became intolerable, with barely a foot of deck space not taken up by the

soldiers and their wounded, for whom they attempted to rig up what shade they could against a burning sun. By nightfall, though we swabbed the decks down with vinegar and burned sulphur, the stink of dysentery hung heavy over them, and what was still more terrible, the stench of corrupting flesh. The wounds of many of them, as with those in the hospital, harbouring a legion of maggots . . . In such a crush I began to despair of ever finding my friend, though as loblolly boy I had the chore of going round these crowded decks, ringing my hand-bell and, in silly rhymes composed for the occasion, inviting those who could yet walk, and were in need of treatment, to come before the mast where the surgeon and one of his mates would attend to them.

Good lads! good lads! come show up your sores . . .
Whether got from Mars, or caught from the whores!

So up and down ladders I went between decks, and into blind corners, thridding my way like a weevil in a biscuit, and clapping my bell. But though some I met had glimpsed my poor friend at the height of the action, when he kept his quarter, no one knew of his present whereabouts, so that halfway through the middle watch of the third day I determined to search our hospitals again, so many of those there having died and gone to a better place . . .

He was lying concealed in the hold to one side of a bulkhead, where he had lain all along unnoticed, and it was only by his yellow hair that Read, hardly able to breathe in the overpowering stench of the place, was able to recognise him. In the light from the lantern it looked as though he had already gone. His eyes, sunk far back into his head, were closed, and his nose pinched and tallow-coloured. Yet, as Read bent over him, he seemed to catch the sound of a light wheezing or squeaking, as though Ashplant, with extreme difficulty, was just managing to draw breath. Read bent closer, and hope instantly filled him, for he saw that his friend's breast was very slightly palpitating. He stretched out a hand and felt for his heartbeat. To his joy there was a sudden fluttering pulsation beneath his fingers. Then Ashplant's shirt bulged. Gaped. And as Read reeled back, an enormous rat nosed its way out of his chest cavity and thumped to the deck.

For days after, Read hardly spoke, though continuing with his duties in the cockpit and hospital, watching his hands as though they belonged to someone else, as they neatly swabbed and bandaged after the ministrations of Swan and the surgeon. Swan twice commented on his torpor, and offered to cup him, but Read refused, until the surgeon, in exasperation, ordered three ounces of blood to be taken from a vein in his foot. But it was without effect. Inwardly, Read was living with Ashplant, closer to his friend than they had ever been in life, absorbed in an intense inner communion in which he spoke wordlessly to his friend and secretly referred to him in everything he did. Then, as though his grief were like a living plant, he found that, in a way he could hardly account for, he was missing Ashplant with a terrible sense of physical loss. Finding himself both awake and dreaming, longing to touch his friend again. And, had he been able to frame it, to consummate the love he now knew he had felt for him.

By now, however, he could not even remember Ashplant's face. He had long ago exhausted those tricks, played within the memory, when the dead can be surprised into allowing their image to appear before us for a moment, whether in the turn of a head or in the lifting of a face to the light. The more he tried, the more elusive did the image of Ashplant's face become, until at last it vanished altogether, and in his despair it seemed as though Ashplant had never existed. It was then that his mind turned to what had happened when his old friend, Mr. Wafer, had died. How he had gone looking for him in their old haunts, as he looked for poor Ashplant now, and how he had tried to recall the old man's face and the sound of his voice, and how in the end, long, long after, Mr. Wafer had seemed, in his quiet way, to have returned in his own good time – unbidden.

From where he sat, holding Lady Laverstock's most recent letter, the African coast, copper in the October sunlight, curved away from him towards a gathering twilight that in its serenity seemed to deny all that had gone before.

'I had rather lost an hundred pound to have saved poor charming Dutchess,' he read. 'As she lived soe she died, full of love, leening her head in my bosom, never offered to snap at anybody in her horrid torter, but nussle her head to us and look earnestly upon me and Sukey, who cryed for three days as it had been for a child or husband – so much sense and good nature and cleanly and not one falt; but few human creatures had more sence than she had . . .' At which Read finally bowed his head, and for the first time since Ashplant's death allowed himself to shed tears. He cried for the loss of Ashplant, for their times together, and for Ashplant's wasted youth in the great Toulon siege that had ended so miserably . . . and for the songs he used to sing, which like most cheap music unbearably stirred his heart.

October 10th . . . and it came to me then, seeking to retrieve what memory of him that I could, how he had once asked me, envying it, whether I would teach him to write and speak some of the small

Latin I had brought with me from Colston's, and how I had teased him on that score. So now I resolved that for his sake, who had died and gone to a better place, I would no longer squander my life as I had done, since it was now, in a manner of speaking, also my friend's, but re-shape it instead to some good purpose... Yet my ardour for a career in the Service cooling, and finding myself every day wishing to make an end of my life on board and start afresh in some other calling, I yet had no firm notion what I should do. It so happened that Mr. Swan, leaving the ship at Gibraltar for a full surgeon's appointment, encouraged me before leaving to embark on a scheme of apprenticing myself to a barber-surgeon once I got home, since he had already taught me something in the way of his trade. I can now change dressings, administer clysters and cataplasms and the like, and also know something of the setting of fractures, besides the rudiments of pharmacy that he taught me, pressing on me, before he left, his own tattered copy of Woodall to study. Nor have I forgotten that part of Science that I witnessed diminishing the Chaos that prevailed in the orlop deck at the time of the great bombardment, and how it seemed to me that, within our small lantern-lit circle of the cockpit, our Science was in some part also reducing the greater chaos in the Universe outside of us. It is with such thoughts that I consider staying on with the *Ruby* until she returns to the Downs, this in the hope of acquiring further skill in medicine...

On the thirtieth of the month, the *Ruby*, careened and refitted, and under orders to join the Western Squadron patrolling the French ports of the western seaboard, was awaiting her new commander.

6

Journal, November 2nd . . . this had long been talked of, our old captain falling sick (some said with chagrin at the poor outcome of the bombardment), and it being accepted that Teate was within his rights in his expectation of succeeding to the command of the ship. Not so, as it turned out, he being passed over by the powers that be in favour of a lord's son . . . The arrival of our new commander was heralded, to our great amazement, by a ten-oared barge shaded by a vast green umbrella, though by then the weather had turned cool. There then steps out from the barge a being as different from our old captain as could be imagined. In place of our square-rigged man with his blue powder-burned cheeks and jutting lower lip, we have a tall, gangling young gentleman in a large white hat, with his silky brown hair tied up with a crimson ribbon behind, his coat of yellow silk lined with sky-blue, and open to display a garnet brooch glittering in a great jabot of Mechlin lace. Completing this was breeches of crimson velvet and stockings of silk, and high-heeled shoes of blue Morocco studded with diamond buckles. He had a steel-hilted sword inlaid with gold at his side, and an amber-headed cane dangling from one wrist. When this strange craft comes alongside to be piped aboard, it could be seen that beneath the hat's brim his face was masked against the sunlight, and that his hands was covered with white gloves, each secured by a ring on the little finger. He passed by us accompanied by a retinue looking more like the chorus from the Naples opera than sea-going officers, the which causing such a smell in their wake as though all the scents of Araby had been jumbled together, gave us to wonder what manner of commander it is we now have . . .

The command of the *Ruby* now passed for all practical purposes into the hands of Teate, the first lieutenant. This was unfortunate for the ship's company. Authoritarian as he had been, even Captain Mackra had been known to restrain the barbarous rule of his lieutenant, made now more Draconian through disappointment. Furthermore, where Mackra had *been* the ship, combining in himself each stage of the hierarchy through which he himself had passed, Teate had been imposed. He was a man apart, a conqueror who drew power solely from within himself.

By the time the *Ruby* had left the southern coast of Spain and emerged into the Atlantic to join the Western Squadron, the equinox had passed, and winter come to the Bay. The gales increased, those from the east bringing bitter cold that froze the spray on the rigging, rendering the sails stiff and sharp as sheets of tin, and the smallest rope thick as a man's arm with ice, and so sharp that it cut the men's hands to haul on them. Gales from the west, meanwhile, forced the ship into constant danger from a lee shore, so that the lieutenant was often hard put to find sea-room while keeping a tactical position from which he could attack the French ships venturing out of harbour.

Of the new captain little was heard or seen. Early on, orders went out to the officers on the quarter-deck to permit no one to walk on the side under which he slept, and that no officer was to appear on deck without a wig, sword and ruffles, nor any midshipman nor petty officer to be seen in a check shirt and ordinary linen. This would have occasioned laughter, had there not been anger at the injunction that only members of the captain's own entourage should be allowed into the captain's great cabin without leave. This limit on their right of access to their commander infuriated the ship's company, and it was from now, under the Janus-like command of the lieutenant and the wan woman of a captain, that a change crept over the ship.

Slow at first, it became increasingly manifest as the days went by. It began with the warrant officers sensing that the unbroken chain of authority that should have existed between them and their officers had been severed by lack of contact with the captain, and by the tyrannous and seemingly independent authority of Teate. Their implicit disaffection soon spread to malcontents on the lower deck, and it was now that the preoccupation with divination and games of chance, prohibited in Mackra's time, grew to be a regular feature of their lives . . .

> *November 30th* . . . we are now come to a strange pass, so many of the men being given over, or so it seems, to the dabbling in magic (to give it no unkinder name), and the warrant officers doing little to check it, and I caught up in it more than I would by reason of many of them thinking it was I caused the red fog to come down at the time of the Toulon bombardment, besides a number of other little circumstances since, and for which they hold me likewise responsible . . . On this point of Science and Magic I find myself much in two minds, having both seen in the surgeon's cockpit the great authority of a Science such as medicine and the Reason that promotes it (and in Reason I had a certain grounding when my old mistress and her friends sought to discuss, though somewhat broken-backed, the Lockean *Discourses*). But there is also, by way of a counterbalance, the Magic (for want of a better name) such as that which occurred in the voices of the bells in the great tower at Bruges, and later to greater purpose when I was lost in the catacombs

with my old mistress. So now, being open as it were to both influences, I find myself seeking a mean between the two for the government of my life, but know not how . . .

By December, the *Ruby* was off Ushant, wallowing in interminable grey seas, and beating to two points of the compass. Commons were by now so short that though they went meatless on 'banian' days three times a week, what passed for meat on the remaining four was hardly worth the name. Battened for long periods below the dripping decks, 'like pilchards in a cask', as one of the stewards ruefully expressed it, two hundred men were by now on the sick list with putrid fever, while the remnant were called out into the wet and cold at all hours, often with less than three hours uninterrupted sleep. For them, it was only the daily beer ration, and the divinations of Tom Gander, the self-styled Magus of the lower decks (he of the bottle-glass legs), that relieved the tedium of their lives.

The ritual of the Magus was in itself an education. He would take his place at the table rigged up in the number eight gun bay, the bay itself looking like some dimly lit confessional or side-chapel in the broad-aisled cathedral of the gun deck. He sat at the north side of the table, explaining how, in esoteric law, the hidden currents of the earth flew from north to south and back again, thus seating all true authority in the north. Then, while the men watched, fascinated, he brought out the ebony box, unlatched it, and from their wrappings of crimson silk drew out the cards of the Major Arcana, spreading them out flat on the table before him.

'Cut, my honey!' said he to Read.

It was towards the end of the first dog-watch, on a day when despair had reached infernal proportions with the news, only two hours before, that a signal had gone out from the flagship for the *Ruby* to change course and make for the coast of Spain, to intercept an expected convoy from the West Indies. It happened also to be Christmas Day, during which there had been a grievously disappointing show-up of the rum ration, which Teate, for some reason best known to himself, had failed to implement as tradition demanded. Compounding their wretchedness was the fact that the meat for this day of all days had been uneatable.

'I have it on good authority them hogs was stinkin',' said the Magus, shuffling the cards. 'The captain himself knew they was full of matter, for he was told when the butcher was a choppin' of 'em that his nose bled and he spewed . . .'

'Watch your tongue!' growled someone from the shadows.

'Cut!' said the Magus, paying no attention, and Read did as he was bid. 'No,' went on the Magus, 'they was salted down all the same, wasn't they? And taken aboard by the purser for our victuals. Cut again! Which is how they makes out of us poor lubbers, both the purser and the captain too, I'd say . . . Why, young sir, it's the Lovers! Here's a young man yard-arm to yard-arm with two tidy little frigates to either side of him, each of whom seems 'ticing him on her course, but he's caught between them in irons as you might say . . . Now, young sir, this card is telling us you've solved a ticklish one here, between loyalty to an older woman, and your desire for the younger, which interpreted, as you might say, means that Ned has made up his mind to go for independence, and a fine thing too! Though I must tell you this card here ain't all plain sailing, for as you goes independent, so is you courting the end of your independence, which is a roundabout way of saying that in the winning of thy life, thou art also faced with the prospect of thy death! Cut again! Ha! the Charioteer, seventh in the Tarot, and a prime number signifying unity within complexity, the number too, as everyone knows, of the Seven Virtues and the Seven Sins, also my dears, the Seven Ages of Mankind, the Seven Seals of the great Book of Revelation, not to forget the Seven Days of the Week. This falling next to the Lovers tells us our hero's made the right decision as regards the previous card, and will now move smoothly along his chosen road safe and sound, Ned!'

A heavy thud shook the *Ruby*, and the purser's tallow-dip burning sullenly in the foul air of the lower deck gave a sporadic leap.

'The Fool reversed! So we see that after all the Charioteer runs aground because he has gone and made a foolish and impulsive action. Steady on, lad!' – for Read was impatiently turning up the next card.

'The Hanged Man . . . though not as you might expect, seeing him dangling here with his ankle caught in that bowline, for this is a sign of renewal and salvation, but not before our hero takes his life in both his hands and casts himself many fathoms down into the very depths. You might not think it, but this knot is going to hold him up quite safe, since the rope itself is belayed to Faith, and the knot being a bowline anyway, which is one of the surest knots of all; and he's going to go on a while hanging like that which means as how he's free, totally free, and all the misery he's been through will be forgotten and turned to joy . . .'

Read was about to turn up another card, when they were interrupted by a loud clattering from the gangway, followed by the unexpected appearance of the master-at-arms with a corporal. These walked slowly forward and laid their hands on the Magus's shoulders.

'Mutiny is it, then?' asked the Magus looking up at them, at which they nodded.

'Then who gives me away?' the Magus asked,

looking round. 'Who be the Judas on this deck?' Then turning to Read, who was standing transfixed with dismay, 'Well, my honey, it seems we are to leave you to hang on a little longer!' At which he rose from where he had been sitting, and without further comment accompanied his captors towards the upper deck . . .

They stood now, watching, the *Ruby* centre of a moderate sea, the moon newly risen, her light silvering the quarter-deck as the master-at-arms tested the knots binding the Magus to the Jacob's ladder. The soldiers were stationed on the quarter-deck, the men watching from the main deck, and the officers, among whom could be glimpsed the unfamiliar figure of the captain, observing from the spar-deck.

The drums of the soldiers rolled. The master-at-arms stepped forward and tore the Magus's shirt to his waist. As he did so a wail went up from the men close enough to see that, tattooed plainly across Gander's shoulders and some way down his spine – was a crucifix.

> *December 27th* . . . this was a cruel thing we were forced to see, and in my view little enough cause, which was a charge of mutiny for the complaining against our victuals, which was all too well founded and against which (the time-honoured complaint of the voiceless at sea) shot had many nights been set rolling about the decks.
>
> Here was the butter stinking, and all the colours of the rainbow, and the meat, rusty old salt beef lain in pickle eighteen or twenty months, not to speak of the pork which was rotten . . .

The boatswain's mate ordered to execute the flogging, seeing there was a crucifix drawn on poor Gander's back, stood back with his mouth open and the cat dangling down by his knee, unable to raise it, till the master-at-arms shouting out that it would be the worse for him if he did not proceed with his orders, he moves his arm a little way. Then, continuing to stare as if turned to a block of wood, he brings it down in a slubberly fashion across Gander's back as though some force unseen was preventing him.

'I'll deal with thee!' shouts the master-at-arms, raising his cane to beat the man over the shoulders, at which the man taking fright, he raises the cat a second time, then a third, and all to no purpose, at which the master-at-arms catching him a sharp cut below the ear, he begins at last to flog Gander. And then to flog him with increasing force, Gander screaming out his legs would break with these blows, until the master-at-arms had counted the customary three dozen lashes. It was now we saw Captain Gallivant (for such matters are always left to the captain's whim) signalling a further dozen strokes, which being at last accomplished (Gander taking it very sore), the executioner left off, leaving our poor friend with the surgeon, more dead than alive (though had he been made the subject of a court martial, he could have sustained nigh on three hundred strokes which would have killed him).

A brooding inertia now settled upon the ship, as though the men, too exhausted to act for themselves, were waiting for some external force to move them, though for some this waiting was accompanied by dread at what such a force was likely to be, considering the act of blasphemy they had just witnessed.

What for many was to provide an indication of what was in store, occurred towards the end of the second dog-watch, when a man came stumbling to the officer in charge crying out that he had seen the boatswain's mate who had flogged Gander turning a knife on himself: '... all at once his breast became red like a robin redbreast!' he blubbered, 'and he crumpled, and his throat was cut!'

As if to give substance to this doomful omen the wind, which had been rising steadily all day, now began to gust at gale force. By 3 a.m. in the middle watch it had become a tempest.

Read (whose hammock was slung in the cables) was woken by the play of gun-carriages on the deck above, mingled with the cracking of the cabin bulkheads and the screeching of the bosun's pipes calling up all hands. When he gained the pitching deck he saw that the sea had whelmed up into raging waves, mountain high, on the peak of which the *Ruby* appeared to hang suspended. Both officers and men were running about with distracted faces, a few of the topsmen were clinging like greenfly to the yards, attempting to unbend sails that had been ripped to shreds by the screaming wind, while others were seeking, too late, to strike the topmasts which were quivering and bending like hazel twigs. Across the chaos of white water separating them, Read glimpsed three others of the blockading squadron driving under bare poles through a creaming race that submerged their decks.

At this moment an exhausted topsman came slithering down a backstay and landed at Read's feet, shouting that his mates had gone below to drink their deaths, supposing the events of the last twenty-four hours to have been of so shocking a nature that no power on earth or in heaven could save them now, adding that he himself was about to join them. Many had seen an unknown man of bull-like strength working the decks alongside them. He himself had run into him, and breathed his hot stench which he could testify had been like the stench of a he-goat. 'But when I looked into his rolling eyes, I knowed him for who he was!' And the topsman turned on his heel.

Read hesitated, momentarily at a loss. There was now hardly a man left on deck, and none at his accustomed quarter, so he turned into the yelling wind and, following the topsman, clawed his way along the lifelines as far as the main hatch.

They had no sooner gained the companionway, than above the noise of the labouring ship could be heard sounds of shouting and of wood being ripped apart, and of heavy blows being struck on metal, and a white-faced boy thrust past them crying that the men were breaking up the officers' chests and drinking their liquor, while others were making their way forward to fire the magazine.

On reaching the gun deck, there could be seen at its further end, and through the thick smoky light that hung over it, figures violently locked together. Then above the tumult came the sound of a pistol shot, followed by silence, in which for a moment the figures unknotted, and only the groaning and creaking of the ship could be heard.

Read, pressed against a bulkhead, watched uneasily, his eyes smarting from the smoke of the charge in the confined atmosphere. Then the hubbub broke out again, followed shortly by a second shot and a further silence. Then a great wailing arose, wave upon wave of anguished sound, and from where he stood Read saw that the knot of men was parting, as though, being long in labour, it was about to give monstrous birth. Then out from the very matrix strode Teate, followed by four seamen dragging two dead men by the feet, while a fifth was clubbing a man forward who, covered in blood, was dragging himself along as best he could on hands and knees. Even in the weak light Teate's orange hair was flaming, his pale face covered in blood like some avenging angel, and he was smiling . . .

Journal, undated . . . such was the extraordinary power of this man (nor do I know from where he had it) that not only was he able to subdue an uprising all but single-handed (our captain not stirring from his cabin during the whole course of the storm), but his influence appeared to extend even to the elements themselves, for by the end of the middle watch at four in the morning there was a miraculous shift in the wind (this time no thanks to my Star, it would seem) so that by the day following, the *Ruby*, our malcontents securely ironed, was proceeding under jury-rig for the Downs . . .

7

By the spring of 1708 the *Ruby* was lying off Ostend. The troops she'd taken up to Tynemouth and back in pursuit of the French invasion fleet had no sooner disembarked than, like colts scenting new grass, they began to kick up their heels and dance:

> 'Two times our horse was put to the worse
> Which Mallberie weel did see . . .'

sang a grating Scots voice. To Read, leaning against the harbour wall watching, the accompanying fiddles had a melancholy sound, and he sensed that the apparent abandon with which the soldiers' women and their children were dancing was more despairing than celebratory.

Their men, lean and gaunt-cheeked, had pulled off their heavy boots and were smiling into the white sunlight with half-closed eyes. One of them, yellow-footed as a duck, had picked up a starved dog and was solemnly partnering it:

> 'With good hearts and our screwed baguinets
> We advanced on a deal of rye . . .'

Then, as the song drew to its close, one of the women accidentally brushed against Read. She turned her head, smiling into his eyes by way of apology, then impulsively held out her arms. The gesture was so open and generous that without thinking he caught her hands and sprung on to the grass beside her. It was grateful to his feet, too long used to the pitch and roll of the *Ruby*'s decks, and he suddenly felt his spirits rising as they had in the old days before Ashplant died. But the last chords were already playing, and in a moment the jig turned down in a blare of triumphant sound, at which Read found himself being swiftly run to one side of the gathering, where a leathery little sergeant in full regimentals was already dispensing generous measures from a stone jar of brandy that lay between his feet.

'Ah!' – seeing the brightness in Read's eyes – 'if only the sailor had been in *that* great battle! (Down with it, sailor! And here's another.) If the sailor could have but seen how the great Argyll tore open his shirt before the engagement that day, to show his boys he was wearing no protective steel against his heart! And after! How he chased those butterbox-arses of Frenchmen out of Ramillies on the point of his sword! Whee! Whoo! Wham!' shouted the sergeant, growing quite red in the face. '(Show us poor landlubbers how a sailor stows his liquor!) Not but that the great man received three shots upon him, luckily all of them blunt. Here! And here! And here! Which would have snuffed any mortal man. (Damn my blood, but the sailor's a great sponge!) The Art of War, my dear,' continued the sergeant smoothly, 'is of all professions the most honourable. Without which Trade cannot flourish, the Penal Laws be put into execution, our Religion, Liberty, Property, and all that is dear and valuable to us secured! Eightpence a day if you cast your lot with us and the great Duke of Marlborough!' suddenly yelled the sergeant, for the fiddles were sharpening up for a reel, 'and all found! (One last can, sailor!) For the invaluable honour of wearing the yellow facings of Argyll's!' And the sergeant turned up his pale blue eyes in simulated ecstasy and squinted wickedly into the clouded silver of the sun. '(And here's to another! And promotion all but certain!)'

This last, however, was drowned in the opening chord of the reel, signalling the moment when all restraint, mercy, order, sanity, is dropped; that moment before the wave topples, the hound is unleashed, the charge fired. Then they were possessed by marvellous sound, which separated them from the world outside. For in the leaping cadences so much that had been experienced was magically translated for a moment into music; glorious acts of courage and passion and laughter, tender beginnings and terrific partings, and sometimes there were quiet glimpses into the landscapes of childhood, homely dunghills steaming under red winter suns, quiet hillsides scattered with moonlit sheep still as white stones.

Read was already light-headed, as Sergeant Davidson had all along intended. He spun like a dervish, and as he spun he concentrated, as though his life depended on it, upon the quietly smiling face of the woman whose hands he was grasping. Her face was the still centre of a world whose sun, sky, sea-wall and anchored shipping flew crazily time and time again over his left shoulder. He soon discovered that if, for so much as a second, he took his eyes off that dreamily smiling face, the sun stood deathly still, and it was the woman's face that began to spin. From far off he heard her call out, and with an effort he drew his eyes (tending to see double now, triple even) back to her face. Then he shut one eye, and for an aeon and an aeon and an aeon, they spun on together through vastnesses like a planet. Then he sensed rather than heard the fiddles moving down into a Strathspey. Someone collided violently with them, he was flung headlong against his partner and, his foot encountering a slide of bruised turf, the Charioteer, heart thundering, plunged (as the Magus with the bottle-glass legs had correctly predicted) from a superior world where hopeful young men become apprentices to barber-surgeons, to a nether world, where he lay sprawling and winded on the greasy turf.

He was heaved slowly to his feet, and as he stood

swaying against his partner, noticing how fast she was breathing and that she smelt lightly of sweat, he was put in mind for a moment of Betty in the fowl yard back at Laverstock, with her clean grainy hands and her kind eyes. Then his partner, her hair sleeked black over her wet temples, turned her tired face to him, and in a surge of pity Read bent and kissed her thin cheek.

Later this seemed his last conscious act for many a long day to come. The fiddlers' elbows had hardly stopped their jigging, it seemed, before Read, in company with the enterprising sergeant, found himself saluting the tight mauve face of the sergeant's captain. The captain, in what appeared to be less than a twinkling, ordered Read instantly accommodated with a cadet's uniform, appropriate accoutrements and a crown to drink – not many days after which Read, with hardly time to collect himself, set out by water for Brussels along with the reinforcements for Marlborough's army.

This was to prove a strange interlude between one life and another, during which Read exchanged that familiar world divided rationally enough between land and sea, for one dreamily amphibious. For long days and afternoons the heavy black barges, loaded to the gunwales with sacks of flour, shifting horses, cannon, limbers and singing children and women, their men drinking and playing cards, slid along beneath a vast pale sky. Into this arose, as they passed, the glittering gold wind-vanes of Bruges, Ghent, Dendermonde, which in turn sank back into mist behind them as the locks took them neatly into the slow-moving waters of the Schelde, winding them for a time between its marshy banks of reeds and yellow flags, before giving way to the formality of the poplar-edged canal along which they slid smoothly into Brussels.

They arrived to find the town in uproar. Only the day before news had come in that Vendôme, the French commander, stealing below Marlborough's guard, had appeared in force outside the walls of Ghent. Another day passed. Ghent capitulated, followed almost immediately by Bruges.

'The States have used this country so ill,' wrote the Duke to his friend Godolphin, 'that I no ways doubt but all the towns will play us the same trick as Ghent has done...' Struggling against habitual depression, he was now alarmed for the fortress town of Oudenarde on the Schelde, forty-five leagues to the west, towards which Vendôme was already reported to be hurrying. To counter this he had ordered troops to force-march from Brussels to Lessines, fifteen miles south of the fortress, with the aim of building pontoon bridges over the river to take his main army when it came up. 'My blood is so heated...' he complained in his letter to the Duchess...

As his commander was sanding his page, Read, by now two-thirds of the way to Lessines, was coming to grips with one aspect of a soldier's life never experienced on board the *Ruby*. While having some notion of the hunger and thirst he might be expected to endure, he had been totally ignorant of the frightful effects incessant marching could produce, so that by the time they were passing the small town of Herfelingen, his thighs were so raw with chafing that he could barely walk without agony.

> 'Full twenty miles we marched that day,
> Without one drop of water;'

a man tough and brown as a strap who'd fought at Almanza, was softly singing beside him.

> 'Till we poor souls, were almost spent
> Before the bloody slaughter...

'You got too much juice in you, my fine cock!' he grunted, winking at Read, but when they halted briefly towards evening, he gave Read goose-grease to rub into his burns before they rose to continue their march through the night.

They now entered a seemingly boundless tract of country striped vividly black and white in the moonlight, and so dazzling, that after a time it confused the sight and Read found himself closing his eyes in protest against it. Immediately he did this he felt his knee or a shoulder painfully jarred as, semi-conscious, he stumbled and struck the stony ground. Otherwise it was that the man from Almanza would fetch him a restorative blow to the side of the head. Pictures began to swing into his mind. His old mistress smiling, with Dutchess at her heel and a basket over her arm in which was a steaming pasty. He began to smile at this as the ground came up once more and struck him viciously on the jaw.

'Bet that made your eyes water!' chuckled the man from Almanza, though a few minutes later he passed Read a sliver of tobacco to chew. Read took it and slipped it beneath his tongue, then transferred it between his teeth, chewing until the bitter juice began slyly trickling from the corners of his mouth. He immersed his tongue in the liquid and presently began to experience what felt like an increasing clarity of mind, as though the faculty had been fully awakened, much as when he had placed the contents of the phial upon his tongue. His legs, machine-like, were now carrying him without apparent effort along paths that led deeper and yet deeper into the rustling night woodland. As he went he found his mind insisting that now was the time to confront himself, it was now that he should contemplate without fear the extraordinary fact of his existence.

What kind of creature was he? By what ruled or guided? Were the intimations he had experienced in the past of significance? For what must he hope?

At this his attention shifted capriciously, and he found himself remembering with affection the *Ruby* and her kindly wooden walls. It now seemed that with all her faults the *Ruby* had been a tight, well-founded commonwealth of brothers, in which each man (if only in terms of his prize-money) had a stake. It had been a life externally ruled for them, in which orders were obeyed without debate; a life removed from too great a commerce with the rest of mankind. It was a life such as might be met with in a monastery, or perhaps in a besieged city. Was life then a question of being either attacker or defender? Which was as much as to say, being a He or a She? For which, pondered Read, was he fitted? For he was discovering that the qualities of a foot-soldier were those of the hunter as well as the scavenger. A foot-soldier had to travel light like a thief, practise an often criminal resourcefulness. It came to him that such a life might not after all be for him. The thought was now there. Some alteration taking place in him at this very moment. Was he possibly turning womanish? Here was a shift of mind he had been able to isolate but not yet make use of. The awareness, once established, began to increase in importance. Hard-won, it had to be held fresh and undiminished against the onslaught of irrelevancies that now began besieging Read's suddenly fagged mind. All at once, as he hobbled below the out-jutting roofs of Lessines, it rendered down into a splendidly simple decision. This was that, at the first opportunity, he would resign from the foot and seek to become a trooper in a regiment of horse.

He slept where he fell, was still dreaming when the man who'd fought at Almanza roused him with a shake, around two in the morning. Of what followed ('Not so much a march,' as one of the French generals lightly commented, 'more of a run!') Read retained only fragmentary impressions. Of leaving Lessines still bathed in white moonlight. Of all the dogs barking as they set off to march through the night, and the dawn of the following day. Of reaching Eename at ten o'clock where, rocking with fatigue, he gazed down on the Schelde winding lazily through its butterfly-haunted marshes. There were herons fishing on the bank, he noticed . . .

There was to be only a temporary respite. Scouts not long before had reported the French already crossing the river six miles up, over pontoons constructed in the night. At this the English were instantly set to build their own pontoons, over which the main army would cross when it came up.

They set to work under a hot white sky in which even the birds had gone silent, and Read noticed that even the water forget-me-nots at the river's edge were wilting in the heat. He was to remember the vegetable stench of the river mud, its almost irresistible suck and pull, as, up to the thighs in the treacherous stuff, they lurched unsteadily to and fro, securing the cockling line of tin boats against the current, after which they lashed the cut pine-lengths across to make a firm platform. The pine-lengths, being recently cut, were weeping resin which caked on their hands, making the business of lashing the ropes and fixing the breeching slow and cumbersome. The man from Almanza all the time whistled battle tunes below his breath. Read, himself pouring with sweat, saw that in spite of the heat his friend's brow stayed dry, as though any juice that might once have been in him had been pressed out long ago.

They toiled on until just before noon, when they heard a thunderous roll of drums, and looking up saw the main army cresting the hill above them.

The torrent of cheering had barely died down before they were again at work, manoeuvering the larger field-pieces on to rafts. By now working had become dangerous, since the French on the opposite hill had brought up their twenty-fives and were finding their range. Little by little they eased the heavy limbers on to the rafts, then chocked and secured them. The current at the point where Read and his friend were working was slow but insistent, and the men alongside had just eased the limber a third of the way on to the raft, when the ropes temporarily securing it to stakes driven into the ooze of the bank, stretched suddenly, then parted with a crack. The raft yawed round into the current, listing with the weight of the limber to which, for a fleeting moment, the men hung grimly. Then the weight tore it out of their hands, and Read had a second to fling himself aside before the machine plunged like a mad creature over the side of the raft, taking with it the man from Almanza. As though in slow motion, the raft reared up out of the water, then clapped back in a cloud of spray, neatly shearing off the face of a corporal who had been attempting to avoid the murderous downswing of its arc.

Read had barely time to shake the water from his eyes before his friend surfaced beside him. The man from Almanza was grinning like a snared fox in his agony, and as Read caught him by the collar he gave a cough, flung up his arms, and the water closed over his head once more. The current had by now swept them within reach of the opposite bank, and striking through the clogging pads of the water lilies, Read attempted to feel for his friend amongst their fleshy stalks. But, his strength giving out, he was able to try this for only a few minutes. And before he was properly aware of what he was doing, he had fumbled his way to the bank and, grasping at the flags by the water's edge, drawn himself out. Lying there, he became aware that the cavalry were already clattering over the pontoon, that one of the riders had halted, was looking down at him. At which, opening his eyes and looking up, Read found himself staring into the red high-fed face of his commander.

Had Read been able to see it, the array of battle, like some gigantic crimson organism, was spreading out fanwise, its 60,000 men closing in to an engagement that would last until nightfall, its scattered units fighting savagely yard by yard for isolated cottages, small orchards, cabbage patches...

Read now entered an extraordinary and fractured continuum. A flint firelock was thrust into his hands with the order neither to fire a shot nor bring his bayonet to the charge until within actual pistol-shot of the French. Almost immediately he was aware of the bubbling snout of a mild-looking rusty boar into whose sty he had apparently jumped (presumably to recharge his musket), spattering his gaiters with green filth as he did so. And now, as in a dream, an old man appeared, hoe in hand, and leaping furiously into the sty beside him, flung away his hoe and commenced battering Read's head, with all the force of which he was capable, against the pigsty wall. Read fended him off, half laughing, half sobbing, shouting in English that they were friends, that the whole of the English army was on the old man's side. And as he shouted, one part of his mind was considering what a fine prize the boar would make should he come that way again. Roast crackling began to engage his mind painfully, for he was now obsessed with hunger. This found him hours, or it could have been minutes after, standing in an abandoned cottage garden attempting to bite off the top of a bullet in order to load his musket, and all but swallowing it because he'd crammed his mouth with small onions, which was all that was growing there...

It was growing dark, beginning to spot with rain, and over the intervening hedges the flashes from the fusils tore vermilion rents in the thundery air. So great was the confusion by this time that no one could any longer tell who was a Frenchman or who an Englishman, save by getting near enough to catch the stink of garlic. As the rain drove into their faces, the English officers, afraid that their men might begin firing on one another in the mêlée, ordered a ceasefire. It was at this point that the Huguenot officers who were serving under Marlborough began simulating the orders of the officers of the French King.

'*A moi Picardie!*' they shouted. '*A moi Roussillon!*' And the French soldiers, running out of the darkness thinking that it was their own officers calling, were taken – hideously.

Read found himself stumbling away into a night that groaned with unseen wounded, making for a pale light that shone to the left, and which he took to be the baggage-train. As he did so, he stumbled against something yielding that lay in his path, and stooping, saw by the same pale light that it was the body of a half-naked woman, her skirts rucked up round her waist. Rain was beating into her open eyes, and he recognised her at once for the girl he'd danced with back at Ostend in the spring. Her arm was encircling what looked like an old blanket, under which something appeared to be quivering. For a moment it went through his head to leave both the woman and her burden where they were, then he raised the corner of the blanket and saw the white shocked face of a small child. As he stooped towards her, the child screamed and shrank from him, but with his last vestige of strength Read picked her up and, binding her tightly to him, tottered on towards the light.

'In hedges and dykes they lay like dead tikes . . .'

they sang later of this engagement.

'As the dark night began to draw near,

> For fear of alarms we stood to our arms
> Until the daylight did appear . . .'

But by this time Read had already been dead to the world three hours in a dry nook of the baggage-train, the child's hot arms wound tightly round his neck. Shortly after daylight, still hugging the child to him, he sought out Mother Ross in the sutler's tent.

She was a Scotswoman, still passably young, though with few teeth and a lean brown face, and over her left eye a black patch which in moments of indecision she habitually smoothed. It was said she'd put on men's clothes and gone to war to look for her soldier sweetheart, ending up by fighting in Hay's charge at the battle of Blenheim, where she'd lost an eye, her sex being discovered later in hospital. After this she'd met up with her sweetheart and turned sutleress, supplying the army with its bedding and provisions. She was reputedly skilful at seeking out booty, and a woman who enjoyed driving a hard bargain.

'What am I to do with her, Mother?' asked Read, drawing back the blanket and disclosing the child, who was beginning to whimper.

'It's surely Calmette's?'

'Yes, Mother, the French had her . . .'

'One of the other women'll no doubt take her,' ventured Mother Ross, stroking her patch and looking consideringly at the struggling child.

'I'd rather you took her. She'll have enough to eat with you.' And Read remembered the boar. It might be an added inducement.

'How much can ye pay?'

'I'm seeking to go for a cadet with Cadogan's when we're out of this scramble.' And Read suddenly noticed that the hazy morning was reverberating with the sound of crowing cocks.

'That way ye'll get half-a-crown a day,' rejoined

Mother Ross thoughtfully. 'Good money!' She was staring at Read with her one good eye, blue as a washed-out rag beneath the heavy black eyebrow. She was staring at Read's face, at his feet, and with particular attention at his hands, rubbing her patch all the time and beginning to smile.

'Christ's blood! You're sure not a lass going for a soldier?' As the cocks, catching fire from one another, screamed triumphantly across the wakening countryside. From where they were standing at the tent mouth the mist could be seen winding off the river glittering below them.

'You're surely not on with yon fool's game?'

'How much?' demanded Read, staring into the hazy depths of Mother Ross's good eye.

'I'll take this, then,' said Mother Ross, indicating the phial round Read's neck. 'It's a pretty thing and may bring me luck ... I'll take it so I'll always have something for my pains should ye not get into Cadogan's, or lest they get to find out who ye are ...'

One day's rest, and the great organism began reassembling out of its own guts, slowly moving into yet another set piece.

'I have acquainted Prince Eugene with the earnest desire we have for our marching into France,' wrote the Duke to Godolphin on the morning of July 26th (the day on which Read got his transfer to Cadogan's). 'He thinks it impracticable, till we have Lille for a *place d'armes*.'

So Lille it is, and the great siege-train that since the French capture of Ghent could only be taken by water as far as Brussels, began to set out overland on the seventy miles separating Brussels from the fortress of Lille. 160,000 horses dragging 60 mortars and 100 siege guns. 3,000 supply wagons creaking laboriously through the flat landscape in a convoy stretching over fifteen miles of roadway.

Read accompanied the convoy on a grey, riding now in the distinctive uniform of Cadogan's: red coat faced with green, broad silver lace at its sleeves, green waistcoat, green shag breeches, laced hat, and armed with breastplate, sword, two pistols and a carbine.

By now he had gained some insight into the idiosyncrasy of Marlborough's cavalry. Shoot they may not, the Duke being so little a believer in cavalry fire-power that he restricts each trooper to three rounds only, and these solely to be used to guard their mounts while baiting. The main feature is the charge itself, a new and lethal conception peculiarly Marlborough's own, presenting as it does a rippling wall of intelligent steel to the oncoming enemy, the pace of the charge neither gallop nor canter but a fast trot, each man knee to knee with the next. In this case, Read's right knee against that of Piert Gerhardi, a young man with primrose-yellow whiskers and eyes like azure wasps, seconded from the Flemish.

He first came to Read's notice in memorable style during a cavalry exercise in the Brussels Grand Place, an exercise put on with the object both of impressing the citizens and dissuading them from withdrawing support from the Allied war effort.

The right wheel, perfectly executed, had just been completed, and was about to be followed by its counterpart, when an enormous blue roan with a plain, fiddle-shaped head suddenly broke ranks and, impervious to every effort of its crimson-faced rider, bored mutinously across the Place towards one of the town dignitaries who was observing proceedings from the back of a handsome mare. The alarmed councillor had time neither to flee nor to slip from his mount before the roan, snorting like an enraged bull and by this time displaying a prodigious marbled zab, leapt rider and all upon the mare, embracing her plump quarters with his forelegs and covering her.

The roan and the mare, thus curiously locked, now carried their bellowing riders for some considerable distance at an ungainly waddle, much to the enjoyment of the entire square, before being finally persuaded to desist.

'How could I know,' confided Gerhardi in his pleasantly flawed English over a bottle of schnapps, 'that they had left him with but half of his bollocks!' Though he ever after showed peculiar affection for his singular mount. Read for his part was to retain a vivid if confusing impression of laughter mixed with sexual puissance and dominated by Gerhardi's striking good looks.

On to the summer and into the autumn of the siege of Lille, which will cost fifteen thousand lives. Meanwhile Read and Gerhardi became friends; the suns and winds of the days spent covering the siege-trains coming overland from Brussels, browned Read's cheeks and etched shallow wrinkles at the corners of his eyes, and he grew almost as tough and lean as the man who'd fought at Almanza, though he, by now, was almost forgotten . . .

> *Journal, undated* . . . it was confirmed here today that the enemy had been successful in closing the main highway between Lille and Brussels, so that we are now obliged to fall back in order to protect the ammunition trains that must now come direct from Ostend, a circumstance that must greatly add to our difficulties in the execution of this siege . . .
>
> . . . rumoured amongst us that the French, having cut the dykes round about the neighbourhood of Ostend, our commander is to fit out a fleet of flat-bottomed barges, so that by this means he may move his siege-train over the flood water . . . though pity is it to see so much reclaimed land put to waste again, likewise many tens of fine cattle and horses

lost by reason of their owners not having been warned . . .

. . . the French having countered by increasing the volume of floodwater, so enabling them to launch galleys capable of waylaying our flotillas, this to our very great nuisance . . .

. . . engagements being fought in freezing sleet, the weather turning monstrous cold and many of the horses dying from lack of victuals and exposure, and the men, some of them, suffering frostbite. I found yesterday my sword, when I took it up, stuck to my hand, and unthinking pulled away two inches of skin from my palm, which was owing to the steel becoming so frozen it was like a fire . . .

. . . we today heard that by God's grace the city of Lille fell three days back. But it is said the Duke has set his face against going into winter quarters until both Ghent and Bruges be recovered for the Allies, thus protecting his lines . . .

It grew colder and colder yet. It became the coldest winter in living memory, so that Read and Gerhardi, with iron pitons screwed into their horses' shoes, went skirmishing over the dykes and moats that were locked in deep black ice. By the New Year of 1709 first Ghent, then Bruges at last opened their gates.

'This campaign,' wrote the Duke to his old friend, 'is now ended to my heart's desire . . .'

It is only the beginning, however, of Read's and Gerhardi's campaign, or more properly Gerhardi's, as they fly across the ice pushing sleighs carved like swans, leopards, dragons, full of laughing, screaming girls, for no girl is safe with Gerhardi . . .

'At last I am inside the house,' Gerhardi was saying as he vigorously cleaned out the roan's hooves. 'Three weeks of very great preparation. First, my friend, I am every Sunday in the church. This is not normal, but I seek to please the Mama of Dimples in all things. Oh the Mama!' and with a crash Gerhardi threw aside his knife into the tack box. 'This lady is ever snuffing with her big nose like a pig all things out! Well, three Sundays of church, my friend, then expensive blossoms to the Mama sent, then I call with blossoms to the house for the Mama, but really to see the adorable Dimples . . .' He picked up the curry-comb. 'This time I am not even let in, so full of rigour is the Mama in the guarding of the character of her daughter Dimples. But the time after that, yes! So here I am with my heart beating very much, and the frightening Mama has just gone to the window to peer out with her great nose from the curtains to see what it is that her neighbour is doing, and it is at this moment that I move a little closer to the sweet Dimples, and I allow for a second the sleeve of my uniform to brush lightly, thus, across the bodice, so that in that second I am in a Paradiso of imagining all things!' – Gerhardi turned up his blue eyes in ectasy – 'Then instantly I am horrified, for the Dimples give a little snort, and down she go on the floor in a heap like an animal. And she is lying there before me senseless, senseless, my friend, with feeling emotion for me! Then Mama she come back from the window crying, "What you do to my Dimples!" and alas it is now all over, and it is the end of many weeks of work and preparation, and we must be patient all over again.'

'You'd better try the *Open Bible* next time!' said Read shortly, putting away his tack.

'Let us have little drinks first, then let us both go to the *Open Bible*, dear Numps!'

Swaying slightly, they finally reach the *Open Bible* which is situated in one of the intimate narrow ways leading off the Grand Place. But Read stays below, quietly drinking with two of Madame's girls, when his friend goes upstairs – to return not all that long after with a puzzled expression.

'?' asks Read, looking up.

'You come and try, Numps!'

'Not I,' says Read, laughing, 'I'm content where I am!'

'Then,' says Gerhardi, rocking on his heels and hiccuping ruefully, 'this must be a case I think of what the Scottish call "the cocks of the usquebaugh!"'

This, however, in no way deters Gerhardi next time, blue eyes concealed by a wimple, giggling and farting as Read shoulders him over the high wall of the Begynhof in pursuit of the pretty widow in the ruby dress; Gerhardi confronted by a hissing cob swan –'I tell thee it loves thee, Gerhardi! Pray buss it!' – and Gerhardi smooths his primrose whiskers and offers to asphyxiate it with his schnapps-laden breath. Bawling and drinking, they yaw through the narrow wynds of Bruges, drinking and bawling anthems in celebration of their youth and wickedness, as once long ago with Ashplant, Read all but rupturing himself with laughter. So that they hardly care a fig when Corporal Tolley removes their swords and locks them in the guardroom, because it is never long before they are out and off, pelting ecstatically the moon, the gold steeples, the swans, the pretty girls, with bread rolls and china oranges and flowers . . . Gerhardi! Dear adventurer, fool, love, friend, rueful and sweet blunderer . . .

'My ink is fros,' complains Lady Laverstock in a letter delayed weeks because the messenger ships are iced into the port of Harwich, 'and tho I writ with it as it comes boiling from the fire, it's white. If I might tell you all the stories are daily brought in of accidents occasioned by the Great Frost, I might fill sheets, as children drown upon the Thames, postboys being brought in to their stages frose to their horses stone dead, and we are obliged to the horses for having our letters regular . . .'

Read turned from the window where the skies were at last clearing and the ice beginning to melt. 'If the French King signs the Peace, the war will be over in a month, and what then, Numps? Shall we then ride together no more?' And looking at Gerhardi's pleasant face as he stared into the rosy light of the stove, Read felt suddenly desolate. The sensation took him by surprise. It was as if another self, of whom, until now, he had been hardly aware since Ashplant's death, had stirred. Gerhardi turned and smiled up at him, rubbing his hands together over the flames. Appalled, Read found that his heart was beginning to hammer, and that his ears were filling with a menacing gold hum, like the sound of swarming bees. So insistent was this disturbingly sweet sound that his mouth filled with saliva and he felt that at any moment he might vomit. Totally unaware, Gerhardi appeared to be saying something which Read, in his extremity, couldn't hear, he could only watch Gerhardi's beautiful mouth moving soundlessly as the room, growing frighteningly dark, tilted, and his knees buckled . . .

In the event they were not to be parted.

'God's blood!' Gerhardi was moaning through a mouthful of pork crackling at just about the hour in late May that the Dutch, Austrian and English were pressing their Articles of Peace upon the French King. 'For it is only, God knows, that I must see her again!'

'You tire me with your whoreson amours!' commented Read sulkily, for he was struggling to come to terms with what he now knew – that he was in love with Gerhardi.

The discovery had been attended by disconcerting symptoms, jealousy for one, jealousy quite painfully physical, and as disturbing as the uncalled for love that had suddenly given rise to it. For another, the pressure of Gerhardi's knee against his in their seemingly perpetual drillings for the charge, was now enough to send Read mad. At such times warm air, pungent as ether, seemed to enter deliciously his lower bowels, expanding shamelessly the nervous shrunken maps that he'd forgotten about of the royal regions located there, expanding them into a soft, insistently swelling landscape. A sweet country (the one perhaps vouchsafed Read by virtue of his violet quadrant), of hazy water-meads, swooning willow and fat, slow-moving cattle engulfed to their bellies in pools warm and green as at Clitumnus, which spilled again into welling streams moving down to the deep river which, inexorably flowing, caused Read's legs, inert marble as they had become, to sag apart to admit of its enormous dark sweetness, so that he all but lost his grip on the saddle.

By the same iconography, however, an adverse word or gesture from Gerhardi converted this scene to an ashy wilderness where bears drank and owls screamed with maddening fitfulness. Added to this was anxiety without let. Wherever Gerhardi went Read, never frightened before, was now deathly afraid. Read had, in fact, become womanish, and this bound him humiliatingly to his friend's side, gelatinous with terror lest Gerhardi be captured or killed, to prevent which he found himself making absurd efforts either to head off his friend from possible danger, or else, where he could, to get between him and the enemy. Gerhardi, dashing as ever and absorbed by yet another girl, saw nothing, though Corporal Tolley reproved Read three times for his folly on the march from Tournai alone, making disparaging remarks, furthermore, about the condition of Read's accoutrements.

'Where's thy intellects, thou poxy son of a whore!' he yelled. 'God's blood! I'd not recognise thee for the same spark we took on last springtime!' And Read could say nothing. Nothing of the abhorrent weakness that came over him every time he looked into Gerhardi's eyes. Nothing of the ever-present dilemma, which was whether to reveal himself to his friend or not.

'Should peace not come about,' Gerhardi was saying as he cut another fid of roast pork, 'and war break out anew...'

'Let it break out!' thought Read mutinously...

'So plaguey handsome!' moaned Gerhardi pushing aside his plate and reaching for his pipe and tobacco...

April 27th... in spite of the Duke's success it seems we are shortly to be again at war, the French King refusing to sign the Articles *in toto*, though I heard it on good authority that the great Duke himself expressed the opinion that he should rather venture the loss of his country, were he the French King, than be obliged to join his troops for the forcing of his grandson, which is what the Allies were asking of him... people speak of our going forth to take Tournai...

September 3rd... Tournai at last taken, this after a siege of two months – the finest and strongest fortification in Europe, and the Allies like to have lost upwards of four thousand men, with the enemy's continual fire of small shot underground making it impossible for the miners to roll bombs into the galleries and so dislodge them. For there was not a foot of ground that was not undermined and casemated, and all fought in the dark...

September 6th... the Army is now set to begin a siege of Mons... we remaining at Tournai for the time, under General Withers...

September 7th... Nothing

September 8th . . . Nothing

September 9th . . . Nothing

But on the ninth, Marshal Villars, waiting in the vicinity of Mons for an opportunity of raising the siege, makes a sudden southward thrust to threaten Marlborough's Dutch and English encamped in the nearby village of Blaregnies. The Duke has in his turn now to consider whether to continue with the siege of Mons or turn and engage Villars. He has to consider further whether to attack the French commander at once, or wait one more day for eight battalions under General Withers to come up from Tournai. He decides to wait.

Between the rival French and English armies ran a deep screen of forest, passable either through the gap of Boussu to the north, or Malplaquet to the south. The Duke now sent orders for Withers to come up by way of an undefended track to the north of the main battlefield from where, bypassing the village of La Folie, he should fall on the left flank of the enemy encamped behind the wood of Sars.

Late on the afternoon of September 10th, Read and Gerhardi, both riding with Withers' battalions, entered history once more at the outermost and north-western corner of the tapestry.

By nightfall they were moving cautiously through thick mist, that hung swathe upon swathe over the boggy osier beds of the Schelde, the vaporous air absorbing like damp wool the sharp chinking of steel as the company moved forward, figures of men and horses vanishing, then reappearing out of the murk. To Read it seemed they were riding into a cloud that might trap them in limbo for ever, and he found it hard to believe that hidden somewhere in the formless tracts in front of them were two huge opposing armies. The knowledge made his senses unusually alert. In his mind's eye he began constructing the concealed landscape through which they were moving, scenting river mud on the heavy air, rotting cabbage stalks, streaks of fox, and hearing the ratchetting call of disturbed pheasants, all indicating the farmland and interspersed woodland through which they would have to fight when daylight came.

By three in the morning, caught up in the mist ahead of them, the Duke's main army was at prayers. Not long after, taking advantage of this cover and as yet unmolested by the French cannon, they began moving into position. Shortly after six the mist lifted, to reveal, in the gaining September sunlight, one of the Duke's finest set pieces. Line upon line of his army were standing in perfect order, the infantry three deep, the cavalry behind them in the same formation, and over their heads the enormous standards of billowing silk belonging to some of the proudest princes and states in Europe.

'...hardly seven o'clock when we marched to attack,' noted one of the Duke's commanders briefly. '...it really was a noble sight to see so many different bodies marching over the plain to a thick wood where you could see no men...'

From earthwork batteries constructed overnight, the Allied artillery now began its opening bombardment of the French positions, and in the rapidly dispersing mist, the French guns commenced their reply...

Read and Gerhardi heard the exchange as their horses approached the wood, in whose gold depths the leaves were falling. Hearing the guns, Gerhardi kneed in his charger close to Read's, then drew rein, and for a long moment they turned and smiled at one another.

'Well, Numps!' And Gerhardi drew off his glove. 'Thou and I have had great sport together!' – and he held out his hand. But before Read could take it,

Gerhardi had reached swiftly over his saddle-bow and kissed him on the mouth.

It had just gone nine when Read, reconnoitring a large spinney, looked across an intervening stretch of meadow and saw a large dog-fox break for cover at the margin of a small wood. He hesitated a moment, and then, from where the fox had come, caught a flicker of movement. For an instant the blood beat in his throat, for if a French scout had seen them he would conclude that reinforcements might be heading by way of the track through the Sars wood. He was about to spur forward in pursuit when Gerhardi brushed past on his roan with a squeaking of leather, galloping flat out across the gap. Read wheeled and followed, and as his beast swept under the low branches on the outskirts of the spinney, he cannoned with full force into the quarters of a horse whose rider had just paused to relieve himself from the saddle.

Recovering, Read tore out his sword and lunged. The man, his mouth slack with incomprehension, backed and attempted to wheel. Read slashed at him, missed, swung his horse around and swung his sword again, coming down savagely on the tendons of the man's sword hand, so that he screamed and dropped his sabre, his frightened mount pivoting and making off under the dripping trees with his rider clinging to the saddle by one hand.

There was a pistol shot, and turning, Read saw that a second man had come up and was firing directly at Gerhardi. Gerhardi swayed with the flash, and as he did so the French scout hurled his pistol in his face. Read wheeled again, flung his own pistol at the man's head, and in a sudden transport of rage closed with him, thrusting his sword-point into the man's mouth, enlarging it to the ear. As he did so the Frenchman struck out, slicing into the cloth of Read's coat, and Read felt a long line drawn swiftly up his inner arm to the right armpit where it detonated in a sudden freezing gush of air.

He turned then to look for Gerhardi, who was nowhere to be seen, slid heavily off his horse, and holding his arm, walked slowly to where the Frenchman was lying on the ground, and unsteadily kicked him. The man, eyes open, had blood gushing from his face, but was unmoving, and Read saw that his stroke had severed his windpipe.

Above, in the warming air, the trees dripped like alembics, the drops raining noisily on to the fallen leaves, though somewhere there was a more relentless and faster dripping that Read could not locate. He looked up, swaying, and through a rent in the leaf-canopy saw sunlight spinning downwards in a shaft of chalky light, and could hear, very distinctly, a blackbird singing, and from the depths of the woodland to the east, rapid and intense fire.

He turned, staggered, and almost fell, then with difficulty went down on his knees, and half crawled towards a small clearing through which a stream ran. His fingers encountered, then sank into, the cress growing at its margin. He laid his head down, and allowed the cold water to sluice through his dry mouth, managing with his good hand to pull the enormous weight of his stiffening arm into the chill of it, his blood smoking into the water.

Gerhardi found him seven minutes later. The second Frenchman's pistol had misfired, blackening his face and deafening him as he turned to pursue and finally cut him down.

Gerhardi dropped to his knees, raised Read, and with difficulty dragged him back from the water's edge. Then, apprehensively, he slowly turned back the tattered sleeve. The wound, caused by a strike which had just missed the brachial artery, confronted him like a creature in its own hideous right, and his bowels lurched. He began feverishly clawing up handfuls of sopping cress, pressing its beautiful greenness into the greedy leaking mouth. Then, changing his mind, he tore away the remnant of Read's shirtsleeve, and with shaking hands bound the wound lip to lip and closed it, knotting the remnant as securely as he could.

Read himself appeared to be unconscious, his face grey as wax, then suddenly Gerhardi saw the great artery in his throat begin to pump, and colour began coming into his face. Gerhardi raised his friend once more, and one-handed began to unbuckle his breastplate, his fingers fiddling clumsily with the straps. Read groaned and stirred in his arms, but his eyes remained closed. The buckles gave at last, and Gerhardi began to unbutton his undershirt with the intention of taking his friend's heartbeat. His fingers fumbled stiffly at the fastenings as his mind raced, but took in the extraordinary whiteness of the young man's skin, recollecting as he did so that he had never seen him shirtless. Halfway, his fingers seized altogether, and he slipped his hand into the bosom of the young man's shirt. As he did this his thoughts were violently arrested, for his fingers encountered an unexpected softness. A softness that was like the breast of a dove or a drift of flour. But his mind still running on wounds, he took this to be a contusion of some kind. Though when he moved his hand over his friend's breast and immediately encountered another such softness, he at last tore open Read's shirt to its fullest extent and was appalled to see that his hand had lain over the breast of a woman.

Even now he was unwilling to believe the evidence of his eyes, and he gently slid his hand below the waistband of Read's breeches. It met with a mournful nothingness. Then came to a familiar wound. A cloven wound, in the past delightful to him, but in the present context stupefying. Alarming to him in its own way as the wound he had just bound.

To his horror he felt a fierce momentary lust, repelled instantly with shame and outrage. Followed by a flood of tenderness, angrily rejected. Succeeded in its turn by an overwhelming sense of loss and betrayal.

8

For a moment there was total silence, then Read realised the blackbird was singing. There was the noise of water trickling, and the minute sound of leaves disengaging and falling softly to the ground. The firing had ceased momentarily, and the morning was beginning to grow warm.

Read lay, eyes closed, listening to these sounds which some mysterious power had stripped of familiarity, so that there seemed to be an almost religious revelation in the tenderly repetitious gurgling from the stream which, without effort, he could separate into individual jewels of arrested sound, kind to the ear as the green of leaves to the eyes.

Gerhardi, gazing down in pain and awe, heard only confused background noises of no consequence, for he was momentarily stunned. He bent lower, studying Read's face intently. Only the smooth cheeks could have denoted a girl, for in spite of his new knowledge, the face remained a boy's. Framed in straight, dark red hair, it was sunburned with her summer's campaigns, which had also hollowed her cheeks and drawn lines round her eyes. The narrow-bridged nose and the deep caverns round the eyes were in any case too pronounced, the mouth, momentarily stained with blood from a bitten lip, too long and thin and compressed for a woman's. But the knowledge that she was a woman in spite of this, both repelled and, in a way Gerhardi was unwilling to admit, frightened him. He took Read's good hand in both his own, and, as if beseeching his friend, waited for her eyes to open and reassure him.

Read's hand was cold and heavy, and Gerhardi felt

in his pocket for his flask, intending to force the spirits between her teeth, but at that moment Read sighed, and Gerhardi saw that her eyelids were flickering.

But only a few moments later he was aware that Read had once more fallen back into some kind of night, and the spirits trickled wasted out of her mouth. Time passed. Then Gerhardi, still staring down at her, thought he could hear words, breathed out with extreme difficulty from perhaps a pierced lung; breathed up from far down, from along grey corridors of the empty castle-like place in which Read now lived. The structure itself was barely inhabited, for she'd shrunk inside it to a mere thread, pale and dangling, caught by some mercy on the roughness of the stone coping of the well.

Gerhardi carefully unbuttoned his coat, rolled it up and pushed it beneath Read's head, then, going to the stream, half-filled his three-cornered hat, and returning, raised Read, letting the water run drop by drop into her mouth from one of the tarred points. Then at last he saw Read's eyes open.

'Why, Numps, here's a fine do!' Read whispered and tried to smile. Then, catching the unmistakably altered expression in her friend's eyes, 'Hast thou found me out at last, then?' And she closed her eyes in weariness.

She lay, curiously without pain, but possessed by an ever-growing euphoria. In the course of this, behind closed eyes and in a secret but radiant ritual of the spirit, she dedicated all her hard-won skill and strength and independence to her friend, everything that had once made her a man, as well as the precious but only half-understood intimations she had experienced in the bell tower at Bruges, in the catacombs and in the engagement at Toulon.

'Alas, Numps!' cried Gerhardi, guessing none of this. He bent, forcing himself to kiss her white lips, at which moment his charger suddenly threw up his head snorting, and out of the corner of his eye Gerhardi could see men running out from the trees on three sides of them. He scrambled to his feet, fumbling for his sword as the first man ran at him. Then, when he was almost on top of him, Gerhardi hesitated, let out a wild whoop, and in hoarse chorus with the man himself, gave vent to expletives of relief and pleasure, for the man, like the rest of the detachment, was wearing the yellow facings of Argyll's.

On their toilsome way back to the lines, Gerhardi found opportunity enough to reflect on the implications of his friend's extraordinary transformation, which both had kept concealed from the soldiers. Shock had been succeeded by a kind of restless excitement, then given place to puzzling feelings of regret and worse still, melancholy. This was so painful to one of his cheerful disposition that he at once set about persuading himself that the discovery need make no essential difference to their relationship, provided always that Read's sex were kept a secret. Yes, they would continue as before. As friends. As drinking companions. As for the rest . . . this Gerhardi resolutely put from his mind. So that by the time they reached the lines, he had grown almost cheerful.

It was a mood destroyed instantly by the red-faced surgeon briskly cutting away Read's shirt to dress the wound.

'Lord Almighty! What have we here, young woman? Is this your whore?' Turning to Gerhardi, who had been instructed to sit on Read's hand to keep the arm still for the suturing.

'There's something I'm set on never being!' swore Read as the stitches went in from wrist to armpit. 'Christ's blood, Gerhardi! Either we break an honest shilling or we go our own ways!'

So on to tonight. A laborious time this, as autumn

ground down to winter, and the men went into quarters, and the wound caught cold, leaving Read with a persistent low fever. After which, barely recovered, she started out on the unaccustomed trial of acting the woman.

'The first thing you must learn to do is to keep your knees together!' said Mother Ross with a wry smile (Calmette's child had been seven weeks dead from the enteric, she told Read), 'and if you don't, you'll make a right gowk of a woman even though you do have bonny eyes!'

'God help me, I can't breathe in these slops!' cried Read. 'I can't swing an arm, Rose Ross, nor yet walk a full pace!'

'Wheesht!' growled Rose Ross, mixing a brown and brandy for a can of flip. 'It'll maybe turn out worth it in the end . . .' adding brown sugar and stirring it with a hot iron so that it foamed, ' . . . tho' I doubt it!' She smacked her lips, her one eye turning philosophical. 'It's strange for us, Soldier, who've been both man and woman you might say, and yet neither. Certain it is an awful lot depends on the clothes ye wear . . . fine feathers make fine birds, or so they say, and that's true, but it's marvellous the way the simple wearing of a pair of breeches can put heart into a woman! For to be sure, it's something of a glory to be a man!'

'What about your man?' asked Read.

'I liked him well enough to go for a soldier and lose an eye for it.'

'And now?'

'Now is now!' replied Mother Ross shortly. 'But to tell the truth, Soldier, I find myself relishing my freedom too much for my own good. And that even though I have a fine business built up out of my own hard work. But to this day the whiff of a discharged flintlock goes straight to my head, so that I'm crazing to get through that door and be off with the rest of them.'

'I don't know that I can stomach it,' groaned Read, 'this acting the woman . . .'

'Do you not love him, then?' asked Rose, raising her good eye from a critical appreciation of her second can of flip.

'Well enough,' replied Read uncommunicatively.

'It's a strange thing, Soldier, how not knowing, women will sometimes give their hearts to a woman in men's clothes . . . There was a lass I knew with a great heart. Such a roaring girl she was, ran away to make her fortune in King William's wars, and sure enough came back a corporal. She took up with a widow woman in her home town, and sure, Soldier, if the laws of the land had permitted it, I think the widow woman would have married her more cheerfully than she had her deceased husband by whom she had six children. As it was,' went on Mother Ross into her flip, 'they who concern themselves with such matters had midwives examine the corporal. Her royal parts, they found, was prodigiously grown, and when rubbed up, it was said extended half the length of a finger.'

'?' asked Read.

'Yes, and they were minded some of them to hang her, but in the end she was only whipped with rods and banished from her partner in crime, which I consider a cruel thing when all is said and done!'

'Sure it was either a marvel or a consummate folly,' commented Read, smiling, 'and not to my taste.'

'Ah, that you can never say,' replied Mother Ross.

Silence fell. Outside the sutler's tent it had grown dark, and in the spring night a hunting owl gave a thin shriek as it worked the picket lines.

'Well, listen to this, Soldier. I will own I like you! And I wish, Soldier, as you was a man . . .'

But tonight is tonight, and after their great wedding,

Cadogan's officers, who have bought them out of the regiment, are huzza-ing fit to bring down the roof, and passing round a hat slopping over with gold and silver pieces . . .

'. . . which will be enough for us to get to Breda, Numps, and set ourselves up in an ordinary to serve the garrison!' said Gerhardi. He was still in his shirtsleeves, sitting in a chair in the furtherest corner of the room, looking into his glass.

'For the dear love of Christ, Gerhardi!' called Read from the enormous feather bed. 'Come and put me out of my misery!'

Gerhardi rose, and walked slowly over to her, unbuttoning his shirt. He made to snuff the candle, but Read caught him by the wrist in her strong grip.

'Look at me, Gerhardi!' And Gerhardi found himself wishing like the devil that she'd let him snuff the candle, since all she would see in his eyes would be a confusion of lust, regret, contempt – a great pity. Above all pity, that she was no longer a man. Regret that never again would they go riding together and exchange their gross but affectionate insults.

'Ah Gerhardi!' – (laughing) – 'have courage!' And she took his weight ardently in her strong arms.

They clasped, but without tenderness, like furious wrestlers, and commenced their battle. Toiling in angry passion, with bruised lips and aching tongues, their skins sloughing. Grappling ever more fiercely in their terrible insistent searching of one another in a war that ultimately knew no sex. Still at last, they looked at one another. Then, in the calm candlelight, turned to stare appalled at the pleasured ruin of Read's strong body. Then with aching throats, and near to tears, they began to laugh.

Such nights and nights again, to eighteen months later in the upper room of the *Valiant Trooper* in Breda's main square. Breda, strongest fortress on the Dutch frontier, built on the banks of the river Merck which surrounds the castle like a moat. Breda, never mind, where every door looks as though it were studded with diamonds, the doornails being so zealously polished by its scrupulous housewives who do not hesitate, for propriety's sake, to shut up the fire-irons in net-work, and disguise the vulgarity of warming-pans in Italian velvet.

To dine at the *Valiant Trooper* costs twenty pence, with wine ten pence the pint, though at seven pence there is a popular white worked up with lime so as not to be too heady. There are always generous fires, and pepper plants wreathe the windows, giving the sense of drinking in a happy ever-blooming spring, no matter how the ice growls and cracks outside, or the wind goes flaying across the polder. The *Trooper* is as popular with the men as with the officers of the garrison. Waggons and coaches setting out from Brussels each day stop there, as does much of the water traffic from Antwerp and Delft. In a word the *Trooper* is beginning to pay, his takings already outstripping those of the once popular *Blackamoors*, and even challenging those of the *Orange* across the road.

People respect the Gerhardis, the Soldier in particular. Men enjoy the easy way she has with her, and their women, though affecting to be shocked by her history, know very well she will never make off with their husbands or seduce their sweethearts. She keeps, too, an admirably orderly house. That is, until one night . . .

'By God!' bellowed a drunk dragoon suddenly holding up his glass and squinneying into it, 'he's served me short measure!' The dragoon in question was well known to be one of those for whom war was a very heaven and peace hell. The taproom raised their heads and took their pipes out of their mouths.

'I'll run him through the lungs for this business!'

roared the dragoon, indicating Gerhardi and rattling his sabre. Gerhardi, who a month before would not have brooked such an insult, made no move, merely stared at the dragoon and rocked slightly.

'Pox! He's a raw fellow,' shouted the dragoon, whipping out his weapon and confidently slicing one of the pepper plants in two. 'Someone who don't know what it is to have a towel drawn through his body!'

The taproom looked towards Gerhardi. He was still swaying, and sweat was breaking out on his forehead, and his lips were pale.

'He shall not only blow out a candle with his wound, but the sun shall shine through him!' boasted the dragoon, and hit Gerhardi across the buttocks with the flat of his sabre.

Later the taproom only remembered the rush of skirts, the sound of two swift blows, and the clatter of the dragoon's sabre as it fell to the sanded floor.

'Stay where you are!' groaned the Soldier from between clenched teeth. 'I'm as strong as a man,' they remembered her saying, 'and I can break your back!'

It was after this that the *Trooper* forsook his early promise and began to go downhill.

But tonight . . .

'You've failed me, Numps!' she said sadly. 'See how you made me love you, and then went away.' She was lying naked beside him, the candlelight soft on her body, turning it the colour of *Rosa Indica*, the Persian Rose.

'Come back to me,' she said, and held out her arms. But he was unable to touch her.

'By my heart, it was you left me, Soldier!' he replied miserably, moving away.

'Don't call me Soldier!' And her beautiful eyes narrowed.

'Why not? For you was a soldier, and it was a soldier I loved.'

'I'm Mary, and I am your wife . . .'

'Perhaps I have a wife, but I've lost my friend . . . Ah Numps, if we could go back to that time before the wood of Sars . . . Could you but put your uniform on again, Soldier, and let me see you as you was then . . .' And his eyes softened.

'I am Mary.'

'Soldier! Please, Soldier!'

'I'm Mary, I tell you!'

'Put on your jacket and hold me in your arms . . .'

'I cannot!'

'Please, Soldier . . .'

One night five days later, on her way to the chest for clean linen, Read saw a light wavering below the door of their room. She tried the latch, but it was snagged on the inside and wouldn't open.

'Gerhardi!' But there was no answer.

Seized with foreboding, Read set her shoulder to the door. The hasp snapped and the door flew open. Gerhardi had set down a candle on a small side table. His back was towards her, and he was gazing motionless into a glass. As she hesitated on the threshold, he turned slowly, and in the light from the candle Read saw he had shaved off his moustache. His face was painted, and he was wearing her clothes. They gazed in silence at one another for several seconds. Then slowly he held out his arms to her . . .

'Please, Soldier!' he said.

And out of love and pity she does. And she does again. And together they begin moving into a bewitched landscape which never could have been, recreating the consummation again and again and again and again of a suspended moment on the autumn day shortly before entering the wood of Sars . . .

They gave themselves up to this on the short autumn afternoons when the sun, like a red cannonball, slipped down into the white evening fogs, and on into spring when the same sun, growing warmer now, came searching for them through the veined leaves of the peppers that screened their window. Long before this they began drinking to extend time, steeping themselves like drowsy wasps in Schiedam, so that their hours grew confused and they forgot the dividing line between day and night, between what was real and dreamed. Through the secret negotiations between the English and French that autumn, to the withdrawal of the English troops and the signing in April 1713 of the great Peace for which they had both fought, Read and Gerhardi barely left their room, and Gerhardi often did not leave their bed. For their room had become a timeless cave in which all motion, all life, were arrested as they lay watching their shadows and the shadows of the pepper leaves flickering like black flames against the walls. Four months later Gerhardi, without protest, slipped into a tertian fever.

'Tell me again, Soldier, tell me again . . .' And Read would describe how the leaves had been falling, and the mist rising from the osier beds, and the early cocks crowing, and how they had ridden out side by side into the sunlight in the direction of La Folie, and how just outside the wood of Sars, with the French guns already beginning to sound, Gerhardi had turned and taken his friend's hand and kissed him.

'Again, tell me again . . .' As the late spring turned into summer, and the people came and beat on the closed blistering doors of the *Valiant Trooper*.

'Soldier, tell me again . . .' as beyond the windows the great bells of the cathedral rang in the New Year of 1714. 'Tell me again,' and closing his wasp eyes, 'dear Numps . . .' he said, and died in Read's arms.

Even before Gerhardi's death she had grown negligent in the running of the inn. The floors of the *Valiant Trooper* were no longer freshly sanded, nor the tables scoured frosty white as an eighty-gunner's quarter-deck, and the beautiful jungle of peppers languished unwatered in their pots. In the last days of Gerhardi's life the *Trooper* did not even open his doors which, like the window shutters, remained locked and silent as the black ice which imprisoned all nature outside.

Read drew the curtains and lived by candlelight like some sorrowing Empress, eating hardly at all, and seeing no one but the old man who was the only remaining potboy. It was he who went out to the market to get what little she needed, and kept the stoves in, occasionally opening a side door to let in an old customer who had not forsaken them, and it was he who nightly brought up the Schiedam gin which she and Gerhardi had habitually drunk together.

Flown, she spent much time before the glass, perplexed at the extraordinary nature of a mind still able to ask questions of itself. 'What am I?' it might demand of the still face before it, knowing it to be its own. 'How do I know who or what is myself?' Then in seeking for points of reference, it performed a sideways step into more familiar regions, areas of its own history (where else to look, saving even the philosophers?) and would at least find there a proposition to consider. Gerhardi had loved her as a man, had taken her to be one kind of person, while all the time she had knowingly been another. What she had revealed to him, feeling this to be her true self, he had been unable to recognise or love.

When, in the mournful weeks that followed, Read tried to ponder what had really happened since leaving off being a soldier, it came to her with increasing conviction that she had in fact killed Gerhardi. She had killed him with her greater strength and her demanding passion, and in seeking to have her passion answered, she had gone with him into a fevered world, hazardous as a tropical jungle, to whose fevers Gerhardi, being the weaker, had succumbed. Gerhardi, her own age, and at his death scarcely more than a boy, brave and once happy and foolish as a boy. By loving him as a woman she had killed him.

The torment was her youth. She had still her life to live, providing always that she chose to, and what form could this life take? The notion of continuing on at Breda was intolerable. Even when Gerhardi had been alive she had had to struggle against the revulsion she experienced in the sole company of women, for they had brought back to her the coarseness, and untruthfulness, the terrible preoccupations of her mother. The obsession with the textures of stuffs and meats and hair and flesh. The life of stifling confinement. Of concealment revealed in the pursed lips and averted eyes, the faint sighs and injured silences. Above all there was the terrible battle with time. Time as dust, as rust. Time gobbling and tearing and spoiling and wasting. Time who was master of the humbled existence of a subject race.

She consoled herself with the thought that she might put on men's clothes once more and join one of the foot regiments at present quartered in certain of the frontier towns. Then dismissed the idea, knowing too well the tedium of such a life during a peace. Then in her search for guidance she began pondering the main influences directing her life until now, and one late afternoon she lit a candle and took out pen and paper and began to list them.

Providence, she wrote, underlining it, and beside it, as she pondered, absently drew a moon in its declining quarter, with black-stroked clouds partially obscuring it. Then below *Providence* she finally wrote, 'Deliverance from the catacombs, from the Toulon bombardment by means of the red fog, from the great storm off Ushant.' But there was also the operation of possible Magic to consider. Magic which was when a person acted in co-operation with evil spirits, or was guided more likely by an irresistible influence. So what place in this scheme of things had the caul, or the Star she carried in her hand? Or the reliquary she'd given to Mother Ross? And what of her destiny seen in the Tarot cards? For had not the Charioteer indeed fallen as bottle-glass-legs had predicted? And was she not now come to the card of the Hanged Man, surely one of the strangest of the Major Arcana? The card, she remembered poor Tom Gander telling her, that can either signify the Seeker who, rejecting the laws of man, takes his life in his hands and casts himself into the depths in order to discover his soul; or who else lives in a dream world, located neither in heaven nor earth, but suspended somewhere between the two in a place of his own invention, his eyes turned inward, blind to the world about him.

Read shivered, and hurriedly wrote *Science*, by which she understood a clear and certain knowledge that was grounded in demonstration and self-evident principles. Beneath *Science* she wrote, 'Seamanship. Apothecary. Innkeeper.' But as she wrote, covering the paper with what in the candlelight looked like cabalistic signs, it seemed that this exercise in self-discovery was already changing its character. It was as though the very act of questioning had already initiated a process of answer.

'The bells of Bruges,' she began writing, 'the Alps, the catacombs' (a second time). Above these she wrote the word *Intimations* and underlined it. After which, for no particularly good reason, she found herself rapidly writing down the names of Lady Laverstock, Ashplant, Mr. Wafer. As she was writing the last, she experienced, quite perceptibly, the lifting of a heavy cloud. He, after all, had always known who she was.

She now began to run over in her mind and with intense pleasure the skills he had taught her, surely with some foreknowledge of the life she was to lead.

How to read the winds, how to knot and splice and sharpen knives – how to throw a man. She recalled the precise manner in which he had described the making of a canoe (doubtless should she ever be stranded), the skinning of a manatee, the splitting of a coconut. Then, in her half-drunken state she heard the sound of water. Not the sluice-directed water of the Brabant canals, nor, if she understood it correctly, the waters of the Mediterranean (for when all is said and done, this is an inland sea). No, the sound came to her as the waters of the far wider seas on which Mr. Wafer had himself sailed. Then, almost as though he had spoken, she knew that it was time to put on men's clothes again and go west. For it was of the West he had told her, where the green turtles could be seen browsing on sea-grass fathoms below, and nimble black monkeys coming down at low water to dig out periwinkles from among the mangrove roots, and where, as in Hispaniola, they blew on conch shells to summon the slaves and the small black pigs who had been browsing all day in the woods.

Read got up and went to the window, and lifting the hasp that held the shutters, threw them open. The air already smelt milder and more tender than it had for many weeks, as though the ice imprisoning the water-plants all this time were melting, allowing the plants to bud again.

Read turned back into the room, and setting the candle on the floor, bent and lifted back the heavy lid of Mr. Wafer's Indian chest, rummaging down through the neatly folded contents that were like aromatic layers of her previous existence, and drawing up at last a pair of green shag trooper's breeches . . .

So it was that a long nightmare came to an end, and Read put on her men's clothes once more, and three days later took the small boat sailing every fourth day between Breda and Amsterdam.

Berthing at the Singel by the Jan Roon Porstooren near the Bergstraat, she made her way to the *English Bible* in Warmoes Straat, hoping to pick up news of an English ship that might be sailing to the West Indies. For it was now in Read's mind to take ship for Jamaica, and to seek out, if she could, the small sugar estate that old Mrs. Read had reputedly purchased there.

Walking about this small town with its pewter canals and houses of plum-coloured brick snugly held below the huge arch of its skies, Read felt her spirits rising. With the Amstell at last free of ice, the canals were crowded up to the city's heart with shipping, and in the bustle of the quays she found herself thinking of Bristol once more; Christmas Steps, Rope Walk, Wapping Dock, and Mr. Wafer in his blue-grey coat with raisins in the pocket to reward Read for learning her letters.

Three weeks passed, however, with no sign of a ship. Read grew impatient, left off looking for an English ship, and at last decided instead to take a Dutch ship reported already waiting in the roads. This was the *Virgin*, 240 tons, Captain Blaes, Master, bound for the Guinea coast and after for the New World.

On April 10th 1715 Read, now twenty-two, was about to step from the iron ladder in the quay wall into the waiting tender that was to take her out to the *Virgin*, when a sudden shouting, breaking out from over her shoulder, made her turn her head, so that she all but crushed her leg between the tender's side and the stone of the quay.

A knot of men was running down the quay, pushing at arm's length before them a stumbling man. The man, whose clothes were in tatters, wore an obstinate rather than terrified expression, Read noticed. When the mob reached the end of the quay near where Read stood, they fell back an instant, uncertain what to do next. Read saw the man draw himself up with an air of defiance, a gesture that only served further to enrage his persecutors who, with a roar of fury, knotted together once more and, with a rush, butted their victim clean over the quayside, from where he fell with a loud splash into the murky waters of the harbour. The men, their work accomplished, turned away, and in the diminishing babble Read twice thought she distinguished the word 'catamite'.

Their victim, who appeared unable to swim, was sinking for a second time when Read, still standing on the weedy bottom rung of the iron ladder, bent down, and seizing him by his hair, drew him to the surface. The man, spouting water like a triton, shook himself, then gripping the iron rung on which Read stood, and just managing to grunt, 'Either thee or me must use this, brother,' gave Read a sharp push which sent her flying into the scuppers of the tender –at which the man, drawing himself vigorously up the iron ladder, attained the quay once more.

The tender had by now cast off, and Read, picking herself up, turned to see the man, arms crossed over his breast, water running in rivulets from his collar to the skirts of his plain blue coat, staring intently at her. Then Read, sufficiently close, saw the man smile, then deliberately close one eye in a wink, before turning back into the crowd.

But the *Virgin*, riding the waves, was already making to cast her cable. Read had no sooner got aboard than a bell clanged and, standing at the rail, she saw the great boom that closed the river swing back, allowing them to slip out into the Amstell for the coast of Africa.

9

'The Cormantees, coming from the Gold Coast, though firm of body and mind, have a ferocity of disposition that makes them unable to submit to bondage,' the captain was saying. 'The Minnatos, on the other hand, tend to do away with themselves...' He was lovingly slicing the dark garnet-coloured sausage before him with a delicacy not infrequent in big-handed men. 'Our friends the Mundingos, as those from the Gambia are called...' here he paused to pour a measure from the flask of Hollands at his elbow... 'tend to worms.' He pushed the flask over to Read. 'No, for my money give me the Paw-paws as we call those from Wydah – docile, cheerful – not but that they're mighty thieves and dedicated gamblers... but they have this advantage, which is that, unlike any of the others I have mentioned, they will become absolute slaves...'

Fourteen days out the *Virgin* was butting her way through squally weather westward and windward of the Madeiras so as not to lose the North-East Trades. A cow and her calf, together with a number of chickens in coops, were penned in her waist, her holds filled with a motley cargo of linen cloth, basins, copper plates, kettles, rings of copper and brass, knives, Venetian beads and looking-glasses.

In the light from the lantern swinging above their heads the captain's forehead, round and smooth as a green apple, glistened with sweat.

'The economics of it go something like this,' he continued. 'A Paw-paw costing some £9 or £10 in your money, bought on the coast, can make £29 to £35 in the colonies.' He drew the rapidly emptying flask towards him. 'And you would really wonder, my good young sir, to see how those slaves live on board, for even on this small ship their number can sometimes exceed three or four hundred. They can be so scientifically regulated in their loading as for it to seem almost incredible – the way they lie so close together, I mean . . . and I'll tell you this, my young friend, that our nation far exceeds all other nations in the regulation of our slaving cargoes. You must pardon my saying this, young man, but the French, English and Portuguese slave ships are always foul and stinking while ours on the contrary are for the most part clean and neat . . .'

Caught by a cross wave the *Virgin* rolled suddenly, absorbing the shock with complaint, the lantern, in a kind of womanish pique, flinging itself to and fro at the end of its chain. The captain, paying no attention to such vapourishness, turned and slowly drew a round-bellied blue china tobacco jar towards him, removed the lid, and bending his large nose, breathed in deeply from its aromatic interior, his thick-lidded grey eyes half closed.

'In short, I can say no more, my dear young friend,' said he, withdrawing his nose for a moment, 'than that it is possible to return from a voyage like this a rich man. Yes, my dear sir,' as he thrust and turned his thick fingers in the delectably scented material preparatory to filling his pipe, 'a rich man, I say, for in the country where we are going a man may get an estate with a handful of beads, or his pocket full of gold for an old hat. It is a country where a cat (you must know the people are persecuted by rats) can buy you a nice cottage and garden, or a few foxtails the equivalent of a manor at home; where gold is sold for iron and silver readily exchanged for common brass and pewter . . .'

Read's eyes, already heavy with the slumbrous rolling of the *Virgin*, the heat of the cabin, and the dense blue clouds issuing from the captain's thick, rounded lips, not to mention generous draughts from the flask, began to close. As she fought against sleep she thought she heard the captain beginning to sing. The voice was deep and creamy, honeyed to Read's ear which through inertia had missed the essential introduction to the captain's lullaby. '. . . but I should be lacking in my duty towards you,' the captain said, 'did I not also include a word of warning . . .' And then he began to sing, though only the comforting cadences penetrated Read's infatuated ear, rather than the words which went like this, sung softly, time and time again, as the captain, with half-shut eyes, puffed contentedly at his pipe:

> 'Beware, and take care of the Bight of Benin . . .
> There's one comes out, for forty go in. . .'

Read, however, was no longer in the cabin of the *Virgin*, but lapped once more in the heated somnolence of Lady Laverstock's coach as it swayed over the sand lanes from Maestricht on the way to Rome. Read was sitting knee to knee with Mr. Vane, old Crinkle-Crankle, though old Crinkle's conversation seemed oddly changed. He was discussing how a dozen of parakeets might be got for a half dollar where they were going, and how at St. Vincent's, under the 4th degree, the women's breasts were so big they were able to lay them back over their shoulders. At which, in that strange limbo of sleep, Read was puzzled, knowing the delicacy of Mr. Vane, and wondering how he should come to speak so indecently, Read being, after all, a young woman. And then, while Mr. Vane went on to describe how the keel of the *Virgin* was so overgrown with winkle shells that were two inches long and so big that a man might literally thrust his finger into their mouths, Read sought to surface, willing herself to the right sex, and to awake. And wake at last she did, to find herself a he after all, safe in his crib in the cramped quarters he shared with the *Virgin*'s completely silent first mate.

> *Journal, May 20th.* First twenty-four hours dirty weather and squally, keeping well windward of the Madeiras... (writes Read, who has kept his journal since leaving the Amstell).

> *May 25th.* This twenty-four hours small rain with a great swell from the west. Past the Canaries and heading for the Cape Verde Islands. Moon on its back above the sun's exit...

Could such curtailed, even desiccated entries have been somehow moistened, allowed to chit and leaf, and then branch like the mustard seed, it would have been apparent that Read was in fact charting the initial stages of a strange voyage. Of this he was to some extent already aware, for the *Virgin* had by now entered the tropics, waters unknown to Read, which spread below night skies marked by disturbing realignments of familiar constellations, and accompanied by natural phenomena that could well have been interpreted as a presage of change. Once, pinkish fire was seen crackling from the ends of the *Virgin*'s stubby crosstrees. Another time, luminous portions of a substance resembling glistening manna were seen to slither from the shrouds and roll eerily about the deck, forecasting, as the sailors said, a storm of some magnitude.

Had Read been able to give expression to his deeper perceptions, he might have offered that he now sensed himself to be voyaging towards some inward Antipodes of his own. To a world in as outrageous opposition to the one with which he was familiar as black to white, dark to light, female to male. And promising a potential universe of misrule.

Thus for Read, as the ugly rake-masted *Virgin* made the Cape Verdes, touching in at St. Jago for eggs, plantains, a couple of bullocks, a score or so of turtles and water, the Captain regaling himself on numerous dishes of flamingoes' tongues, which were a local delicacy.

May 30th. This twenty-four hours, the first very dirty, the middle and latter clear with a strong breeze. Stood away to the southward with the wind at ENE at Lat. of 10 degrees N. Met winds at S by W and SSW and stretched away for the Guinea coast . . .

Although, under the influence of love, it had taken little more than a moment for Read to change into a woman in the wood of Sars, he knew now, as the *Virgin* thumped her ungainly way into the tropics, that it might take weeks in limbo before he truly regained his lost sex.

A week after, due perhaps to the increasing heat, Read missed menstruating for the first time since leaving the Amstell. In his present state of mind, this event presented a welcome stage in a necessary transformation, and for a time, freed from considering who or what he was, he allowed his mind to turn instead, as minds readily do, to the making of pelf.

June 13th . . . and if I could seek to make an honest fortune I should be mightily content. The Captain intends trading along the African coast to Wydah, or Fida as some people name it, where he intends slaving in good earnest. He intends shipping 'em over to Pernambuco with a balance of gold dust, grains of heaven (or pepper as we call it) and elephants' teeth, and disposing of them there for the mines. For although the Dutch are denied commerce with New Spain, he knows of planters along the coast willing to do business. Failing this, he will take the small risk of spoiling his cargo by carrying 'em yet further to Montego Bay. And suppose I should make my fortune in this way, what then? Why I'll settle for a neat little sloop of my own, and do some trading on my own account . . .

Oh, approaching world of infinite possibility, when even a poor Jack Tar may become overnight a Prince.

Six degrees North, twenty-three degrees forty-five West in the Doldrums, towing the mutinous *Virgin* through thick hazes in which the sun glowed like melting wax, and the tortoises, weeping in their pens and regretting the cool under-sand of their own beaches, wretchedly laid their eggs, which then rolled this way and that with every movement of the ship, upon the tar-oozing deck. Extended limbo. Tempers rose. The mate smashed a man's nose in with a marlin-spike. The Captain addressed himself unconcernedly to a dish of turtle and a pint of Hollands. Meanwhile, in the gusting tropical showers, flying-fish landed on the deck, and the sea became alive with fleets of medusas, and once, by moonlight, a whale surfaced and blew and Read glimpsed a rainbow in the spume . . .

June 28th . . . under the 5th degree Northern latitude, the Guinea current bringing us in towards Cape Palmas . . .

July 14th . . . A.M. several canoes brought some small and old slaves, bought two, the small so dear could not buy them . . .

August 3rd . . . Breezes with thunder and lightning. At 6 p.m. the pinnace came from Cape Coast and brought a woman slave and eight jars of palm wine . . .

A week after, Read set eyes on the long flat coastline

where he was to make his fortune. It was all but hidden in a shroud of mist and rain. Through the Captain's glass he was able to make out the high-hooped roots of the mangrove trees, a green-black wall of their foliage marking the shoreline where, startlingly white against a leaden sky, the bars of angry water boiled at the river mouths. As they eased slowly along, they could see the low sand-bar from which protruded the gaunt ribs of old hulks like the skeletons of prehistoric beasts, and over all hung the stink of fish.

'They lay out their catch to putrefy four or five days before eating it,' remarked the Captain, raking the desolate shoreline for the three mangrove trees marking the fort of St. Françoise. 'The best indication will be the boats drawn up on the bar.' As he said this, the fog thinned suddenly and shipping emerged, and along the bar itself could be seen the pitched tents of the traders.

'My friend, Nicholas Pole, the factor, will be expecting us,' said the Captain as the *Virgin*'s culverdine exploded in a roar of salutation. It seemed to Read that the thick air absorbed the report as though it had been muffling wool, and he found himself recalling the Captain's stories of how in the unseen hinterland were forests so impenetrable that all light was excluded, the sound of voices swallowed, and in which the pitch torches of explorers were dimmed and extinguished. Far from presenting the energetic commercial scene he had expected, the Wydah roads seemed rather an extension of that state of limbo in which he had lived throughout the voyage, and had it not been for the sturdy figure of the Captain beside him, Read might have believed himself as insubstantial as the ghostly landscape into which he now peered.

'They are a decent, industrious people,' said the Captain, 'not like their brethren on the Golden Coast, though I fear they believe in a deity who has unfortunately lost all interest in his Creation – referring it in his boredom to a cruel and wicked deputy called . . .' here the Captain broke off, screwing up his eyes in an effort to pierce the mist which had again fallen '. . . yet even in such places as this, there are those given over to whoredoms of every kind, and against these, my young friend, I must warn you. As you value your health I counsel you to eschew them . . .'

August 12th . . . I had never imagined such a God-forsaken place . . . (wrote Read in his journal which had now taken the form of an extended letter to Lady Laverstock).

> Geographers in Afric maps,
> With savage pictures filled their gaps,
> And o'er uninhabitable downs
> Placed elephants for want of towns . . .

This I remember reading to your ladyship, and your ladyship laughing, but we are come to no laughing matter here. It has rained without cease since we was first brought to anchor in the Fida roads, the sullen roar of the downpour competing with the endless thunder of the breakers on the beach. Yesterday the Captain and I were carried in a conveyance some way between a wheel-less coach and a large chair to pay our respects to the officers of the European factories at Xavier, their capital. This is a poorish sort of place (but for the palace of their King and the European *comptoirs*), mud-coloured, because raised from mud, and their people likewise, seeming created from mud as our first father from dust. They dig out this all-pervading substance, leaving great holes everywhere into which they throw their stinking refuse without let. One curiosity for the European is the number of little mud cabins scattered about, in which live the spotted snakes which they count holy, treating them absolutely as gods, so that should anyone inadvertently kill or maim one of them, he is in danger of losing his life . . . The French *comptoir* is the grandest, with a good house for its director and sous-director, also a wine magazine, together with a flower garden and potager; the Dutch, which abutts on to the English factory, is nearly as superior. We drank with the factor who is the Captain's friend. I find him an artful-looking sort of man, much given to taking great quantities of brandy against the yellow fever, but never mind, with some useful information for my purpose, which is to sink what I have left of my money in the purchase of upwards of fifty slaves by way of increasing my fortune. He has drawn up for me a rough and ready exchange rate, sic:

Gunpowder......................	3000 livres for a man slave
Eau de vie......................	4 to 5 ancre for a man slave
Toilles platilles.................	40 or 50 pieces for a man slave
25 ordinary guns.............................	for a man slave
16 Pondicherry handkerchiefs.........	for a man slave
8 Pondicherry handkerchiefs.......	for a woman slave
20 gross of Dutch pipes.............	for a man slave etc.

This is as yet only a scheme, for I have not yet seen any of my possible purchases. I understand that any man trading must first buy twelve slaves of the King, and at his price, before being permitted to treat with the black slavers from the interior who trade at a better price for us. These, I am told, purchase their slaves as far as two hundred miles inland at the slave markets, which are regularly held there after the manner of our cattle markets at home . . .

August 20th . . . The rains continuing we have employed our time awaiting our consignment of slaves in studying the other commodities this coast affords, as well as in a certain degree of exploration . . .

Sometimes, when he gave it thought, Read found himself wondering what could be expected to come out of such a country, this extraordinary region in which he now found himself. As the *Virgin* lay at anchor in the roads, the very air came in heavy with the effluvia of the mangrove swamps, the mist that carried it coiling up from the side creeks, gliding from between the tortuously arched roots of the trees, stealing up and over the bulwarks of the ship and slyly covering everything it touched with a soft green mildew.

One night when there was a moon, an old Foin hunter took Read out into the mangrove swamp in his canoe. The night was full of its own sounds, the sand in the bay sparkling in the moonlight from the mica fragments which gave out a soft musical humming as Read walked across it. Once they were in the swamp, he could hear the mild groaning of the mangrove trees, and the sound of fish jumping, and a peculiar whirring sound caused, the old man told him, by the rushing of small mud-crabs. From all around arose the stench of decaying vegetation, to which was added a musky smell accompanied by an odd whining, followed in its turn by a kind of sighing cough, which came, the old man assured him, from the crocodiles which surrounded them.

In the course of the night Read several times found himself drifting into sleep. Once he woke, and the canoe was moving smoothly into what appeared to be a great inland lagoon, the moon shining softly over its wide silky expanse. Then he slept again, and when he next woke, aeons later, it seemed, the landscape had changed not at all, and it came to him in his dreamlike state that he and the old man had entered a region that was behind the known world, and which perhaps supported it, being the material upon which the Demiurge had not yet got to work. This primal region they were now in had always been thus and, for ever, was always going to be so . . .

Another time the old hunter took him into the rain forest. In the twilight beneath the heavy top canopy, all Read could see were the grey columns of a thousand trees stretching back into an immensity of darkness in which nothing appeared to live or have its being. It was the same when the old man led Read to the better-lit regions of the forest where the vegetation was more formed and luxuriant. Still, to Read's European imagination, it was just as impenetrable, closed in with thick networks of creeper, heavy unstirring curtains of lycopodium, and soft, immeasurably deep walls of climbing grass.

> *August 24th* . . . On our second venturing into the lighter forest the old Foin hunter that I took as my guide presented me with a little half-moon in ivory, whose especial property, he told me, was to enable 'Man see Bush'. I, not liking to wound even his savage sensibilities, took it, forbearing to tell him no European (depending as we do upon the exercise of Reason) would contemplate such a silly story, viz. being enabled to see something not seen by the eye of Nature. Then I began considering of such matters further, and was put in mind again of the great storm at sea on board the *Ruby* subsequent to the flogging of the man with the crucifix on his back, and how, a good time after, I had abandoned belief in all magic of this sort, having seen before my own eyes that it was more useful to be able to suture a

wound or fother a sail to stop a leak, or use, as Lieutenant Teate, a rope's end to subdue a mutiny, than to put faith in such passive objects which were akin to the ivory moon the old Foin hunter had now given me.

From there, as we made our way into the forest, I began considering also the magic I had been told resided in the curious coloured quadrant of my eye, in which for a very long time I could not help but believe, it having saved us, as I thought, in the catacombs. And yet, was not an eye merely an eye? An organ to see with whatever its colour – and without the colour of that organ conferring further properties? The gift of seeing alone perhaps being miracle enough? At which the old hunter suddenly closed his hand round my shoulder and motioned me to look up. At which I did look up, and saw nothing. Then, on his persuading me to look again, I did indeed see the Bush, as he had promised. And it was marvellously alive, in the person of first one, then another great creature treading wondrous softly, which creatures were elephants. So that I was put in mind of that passage in the Scriptures, about the Darkness being no darkness with Thee . . . and also of that pregnant phrase, 'The evidence of things not seen . . .'

Three days later Read was to find himself in a somewhat different cast of mind.

August 29th . . . to resume with the commodities that this coast and its hinterland affords. Besides elephants' teeth (to be purchased at not near so cheap as at one time, owing to the massacring of them for their ivory), there is prodigious amounts of gold washed out by their rivers from the inland hills. This in such quantity, they tell me, that the natives here take it up by the spoonful after heavy rains like those we endure now. I am told that, measure for measure, common salt may be bartered here for gold with certain negroes that are deformed. These, for shame, will not let themselves be seen, so that you must leave your salt in a field where the negroes take it away, and leave gold in its place. I am told these negroes are the truest-dealing men in the world and never fail of their word, which is more than can be said of some of us . . .

There is also to be had here all manner of curiosities, or so we'd call 'em at home. I speak here of the bearded monkeys, little creatures with white beards and black moustachios, there being no kinder little creatures under the sun, and in consequence much in favour with the ladies. There is also the product called Agalia, made from the royal parts of the musk cat, as well as blue parrots which, being taken by the negroes out of their nests, are tamed and made so teachable that they out-prate the green parrots of Brazil. So too the parokton, a pretty red-spotted bird with a black tail that would delight us at home. These the negroes, as an entertainment for the Europeans, eat alive, and I have seen 'em do this for an old hat or horsetail to keep off the flies – feathers, bones and all . . . There are also commodities more useful, such as cotton yarns and hides, not to speak of the marvellous palm-wine tree, which the negroes bore into to get at the sap which is like milk, making a cool and fresh drink. This is sweet when first drawn, but grows vinegary with standing, yea, seethes and bubbles when standing, as if boiling, and I believe if it were put into a corked bottle it would break it . . . Yet I must ever return to that commodity which the people here most prize and sell at the dearest rate, which is the slaves . . .

August 30th . . . There is now daily expected a fresh consignment of slaves from the interior. These will be kept in the King's prisons until such time as the European factors pay their dues to the King and his men to examine them . . . I quote here the markings peculiar to the different breed of native, and this was told me by the Dutch factor who is a mighty skeely man, being able to discern the worse from the better slave, for the black traders are like our horse copers at home, and they will pass off the worse if they can . . . One trick of theirs is to pumice the beards off the young men slaves to make them out younger men than they are (for a negro does not get a beard till he be twenty-four or so, and the traders prefer them young, around fifteen). Poll tells me the way to smoke this is to press your lips and then your cheek next the cheek of the young slaves, and that this way the sensitive skin of the lips will discern even the lightest trace of a beard. He lists the following families of negro:

The Tebon — worth nothing. They are to be known by the deep scarifications on cheeks, chest and belly.

The Aradas — the best slaves, and to be known by the little incisions solely on their cheeks.

The Foins — not to be bought, for they eat earth to suffocate themselves that they be not enslaved — to be recognised by the scarifications of their temples.

The Ajois — good — to be recognised by the painted lines that ray out from their eyes and finish at their ears. These people are very brave and fearless.

The Aqueras — excellent for slavery, and to be known by the little images of animals, lizards and serpents raised upon their chests and upper arms.

The best slaves are children, I am told by Poll, between the ages of ten and fifteen, and indeed the Portuguese take only slaves of this age.

September 2nd . . . Today a consignment of upwards of eight hundred slaves were taken out of the King's prison into a large plain, where they were thoroughly examined by our surgeons, whose province it is . . . examination that reached even to the smallest member, and that naked too, both men and women without the least distinction or modesty . . .

They worked quickly towards that suspended moment of the day when the sun lay directly overhead, and when the breeze they called the Basone from off the land exchanges for the Agem which comes from the sea. It was as yet early. In the square formed by the buildings of the European *factoires* the sugar had just been brought in to be sold, and the women were arriving from their gardens with oranges, lemons, bananas, maize, rice and chickens, and assembling around the great excavation in the centre, from where the mud for the municipal buildings of Xavier had been taken out. They chattered cheerfully and volubly before the return to their yam gardens at midday, leaving the place empty until evening, when the men brought in the pots of palm-wine. Several yards away the strenuous activity in the King's courtyard was accompanied by an incessant thin wailing, heightened from time to time by piercing lamentations from the new slaves coming in. A number of these were still attached neck to neck by twisted withies, secured ankle to ankle by thin chains, while others were bound to the bamboo staging which surrounded the King's compound, or standing apart in small disconsolate groups.

Early as it was, the surgeons of the European Companies were already soaked in sweat, their wigs crammed into their breeches pockets, their shaved pates steaming. They passed with expedition from group to group and, where indicated by the black traders, swiftly and with accustomed expertise peered into the ears, up the noses, down the throats of the men and women before them, running their hands swiftly over their breasts and rumps, probing expertly their groins, royal parts, and anuses. The groups so examined were then competently processed.

> *September 2nd, continued* . . . they put on one side the lame and faulty, those that have lost a tooth, are grey-haired or have films over their eyes, or are affected with venereal disease. These invalids are called Mackrons by the factors . . .

The wailing increased in tenor as the overseers separated out individuals from the groups with the butts of their whips. Taking out a man from his woman, perhaps, or a brother huddling close to his sister.

'Some of the cause of that,' commented Poll, who was standing at Read's elbow, 'that wailing, I mean, is that they fear we white men are going to bear them off to fatten them up for eating . . .'

Read stared ahead, glimpsing out of the corner of his eye that a group of Mackrons, consisting of a woman, an old grey-haired man and a small boy of about seven, were being herded by one of the overseers towards a gate in the Palace wall. A black trader was gesticulating towards one of the surgeons.

'He is chagrined that they don't qualify for the market,' said Poll. He reached into his pocket and abstracted a flask of spirits, and Read noticed that his teeth were chattering.

'What will become of them?' asked Read. In the pit of his belly, what felt like a small snake was stirring.

'Ah' said the factor. 'These are a highly ferocious people, my dear sir. Do you know what they do when one of their own women is taken in adultery?'

'No,' said Read, feeling the snake within him stir and stir again, almost like the onset of desire. 'No?'

'Why, they carry her to an ants' nest, my young friend (ants' nests in this country hang in trees like bees' nests at home), then they tie her there, and shake down the ants' heap and leave her there half an hour until she is almost stung to death. Then they carry her to a great fire, my dear young sir, and holding her close, cut ten gashes in her back. If she commits this fault a second time they sell her, as they do all thieves on their second fault . . .'

'So what will happen to them?' persisted Read.

'My young friend,' sighed the factor. 'In a word they will be slaughtered, and I have known this to happen in sight of our own shipping. But you must remember that the greater part of these people are born slaves to the great men of their country, are reared as such, held as the property of their masters, and as property sold, and if they were not bought by the Europeans they would most likely, as these unfortunates here, be killed anyway.'

> *September 2nd, continued* . . . after being rubbed with sweet oil a negro looks like a Spanish leather pair of boots that have been well liquored . . .

They were just finished rubbing the girl with sweet oil, but when they began to draw her towards the surgeon who was heating the small silver branding-iron over the flame of spirits of wine, she writhed and screamed, and broke loose from the men holding her, and ran towards the main gate of the compound, with the three men running after her. Read turned his face away as the screaming, terrible to hear, broke out again, rose to an agonised crescendo of despair, then died to an even more terrible whimpering like that of a frightened child, as the obscenely appetising smell of burning flesh assailed and clung to his nostrils.

September 2nd, continued . . . I doubt not but this trade would seem barbarous to you and our fellow countrymen at home, but since it is carried on solely from the necessity of supplying the New World with labour, it must go on. Nevertheless, today, in answer to some movement of my own spirit that I scarcely understood, I made myself a fool in our Captain's eyes, by exchanging three-quarters of a small keg of brandy for a slave boy of eight or thereabouts, who had been set aside by the surgeon as too young for the market. I only got him in the nick of time, as the barbarous black devil of a trader who owned him had already caused the throat of his mother to be cut, and she so heavy with child that the poor babe was still moving in her belly after she died. The old man that was with her, who was grey-haired, they had already clubbed to death. I shall call the boy Scipio Africanus after that same black servant of your Ladyship's whose place I took when he died, and when I was little older than this child by me now.

September 3rd . . . We are slaving today, since the Captain tells me that otherwise they are kept in the King's prison at our charge, which costs two pence a day *per capita*. This serves to subsist them, like our criminals, on bread and water, and so to save such charges captains prefer to ship slaves as soon as possible. The Captain further tells me that some shipmasters, the English and French in particular, buy more negroes than they can fairly carry: e.g. a ship of the same tonnage as ours, which is 240 tons, would carry 520 slaves, this allowing only 10 inches of room to each individual, which could occasion, through wastage, a loss of upwards of 15 per cent on the voyage, and as much as $4^1/_2$ per cent in the West Indies harbours before sale. For this reason, although the Captain is of the opinion that 7 slaves to every 3 tons is a preferable computation, he in fact is to carry them on this voyage in a ratio of 300 to 240 tons. Yet he still reckons to cut his losses considerably, though he admits that slaving somewhat late on in the year exposes his cargo to the risk of epidemic fever and the flux, which breeds notably in these marshy off-shores . . . This evening I began to instruct Scipio in the fundamentals of our language as a preliminary to inculcating the principles of the Christian religion, offering him from my own hand gobbets of the food he especially likes, viz. maize, cassava etc., at which he for a little time ceased his weeping and gobbled, appearing like some puppy-dog wanting to please me for my kindness . . .

10

'You will be well advised to bring a number of their musical instruments on board, in especial their drums and strum-strums,' Nicholas Poll was saying, 'so that by their playing of them they will be made content.'

The day was lowering and oppressive, causing sweat to run at the slightest exertion. In the torpid air the fetters of the slaves clinked monotonously as they came off the lighter and filed in to the *Virgin*'s hold.

'It makes a poorish sort of music,' commented Read, for the incessant chinking was accompanied by a low wailing, a melancholy sobbing, like air issuing through a blow-hole in a rock.

'If the Captain apprehends no danger the irons will be taken off during the passage,' said Poll.

'I think it unlikely . . .'

'Well,' said Poll, returning once more to his flask, 'they'll be lodged on clean boards and be brought up on deck every morning and evening time. Their apartments in the meantime will be washed, scraped and sprinkled with vinegar, they'll moreover be instructed to wash their hands and faces each day before breakfast of Indian corn, rice or yams, and before noon they will be hosed down with salt water. Then there will be a dinner of beans or barley or biscuit, boiled soft in steam and mixed with a sauce of meat or palm oil . . . so what's amiss with that?'

There was a deep growl of laughter from behind them. 'Come, sir!' broke in the Captain, coming over. 'You'll no doubt be telling our young friend here that there'll be drams for them when they take cold, and pipes of tobacco into the bargain, not to mention the

Captain's own cabin made available to them when they go sick.' He turned suddenly. 'Damn me, look at that!' – as one of the men standing in the lighter waiting to come aboard suddenly threw himself backwards, his oiled black body arching over the gunwale, and all but taking with him, as he did so, the screaming man to whom he was shackled, who began clawing in terror at the lighter's sides.

'Come up with the hatchet, Mr. Ferris, or we'll lose them both!' shouted the Captain. 'Two to one it's a Foin bastard. One should always eschew a Foin . . .'

September 5th . . . the Captain acted expeditiously, and I think rightly in the circumstance, though it was a cruel thing to see the man fall back into the water with the blood smoking away from the stump where the foot had been severed . . . Only an instant or two later we saw the white belly of a shark come up, and in a moment the man was dragged down to the sea bed before our very eyes, all that was left being a bleeding foot still fettered to the ankle of his companion. This event had a greatly sobering effect upon our other blacks, and we finished slaving without further incident, though our lighter was twice nearly capsized in the heavy surf, or burns as they call it, that foams along the shore-line. It was shortly after this we heard a report, and we turned to see a ship coming into the roads. She was flying her St. George ensign, but she had also a black silk flying at her mizzen-peak, together with a Jack and pendant of the same. The flag had a Death in it, with an hour-glass in one hand and cross-bones in the other, a dart by it, and underneath a heart dropping three drops of blood. At this time there were eleven sail in the road besides us. The French were three stout ships of 30 guns and upwards of 100 men each, yet to our amazement they, with other ships, struck their colours and surrendered to the pirates' mercy. Being only a small ship, and with but 6 guns together with the culverdine, our Captain, though unwillingly, struck also, shortly after receiving on board two of the pirates' representatives, one Barth Symson, and one Harry Sutton, demanding as ransom for discharging us 8lb. in gold dust.

We were loaded altogether with 200lb. in gold, 30 butts of grains of paradise, or pepper as we call it, and 150 of elephants' teeth, as well as our slaves; so the Captain, looking to make the best of a bad job, parted with the dust, but asked for a receipt from the men that he might give satisfaction to his owners back home. I subjoin a copy of this for your interest:

'This is to certify whom it may or doth concern, that we Gentlemen of Fortune have received 8 pounds of Gold dust for the ransome of the *Virgin*, Captain Blaise commander, so that we discharge the said ship. Witness our hands this 4th September 1715.'

I could hardly repress a smile, however, on seeing our Captain, who understood no English, gravely taking and folding this document and putting it in his pocket, for at the bottom of the paper these two waggish countrymen of ours (viz. Sutton & Symson) had signed themselves Aaron Whifflingpin and Sim. Tugmutton . . .

 . . . but there was something so singularly cruel and barbarous done here to the *Porcupine*, Captain Fletcher, as must not be passed over without special remark. This ship was lying in the road almost slaved, when the pirates came in, and the commander being on shore settling his accounts, was sent to for the ransom . . . But he excused it, as having no orders from the owners, and that the ship, separate from the slaves, was not worth the sum demanded (the English employing only run-down craft for their slave trade). Hereupon the pirates sent boats to transport the negroes in order to set the *Porcupine* on fire, but being in haste, and finding that unshackling the slaves cost much time and labour, they actually set fire with 80 of the poor wretches on board, chained two and two together, under the miserable choice of perishing by fire or water. Those who jumped overboard from the flames were seized by the sharks, a voracious fish in plenty in this road, and in our sight (for we were observing this action all the while through our glass) were torn limb from limb alive . . .

The ship blazed in the glass like a liquid sun, burnt swiftly to her waterline, the greasy black smoke from her ruined cargo hanging heavily in the still grey air, so that Read would ever associate the Wydah roads with the shamefully delicious smell of flesh burning.

'Do not fear if at first you hear a great groaning coming up from below,' Nicholas Poll had warned shortly before the *Virgin* weighed anchor. And indeed there was a groaning. But as the days went by there was also a singing, a singing that surged up from the great canvas ventilators running nine foot below decks and six foot over the top decks to carry away the ghastly stench arising from the crowded tiers below. It was a stench causing anyone unfortunate enough to catch it on a cross wind, to gag uncontrollably. It was a stench with which Read was already familiar, having experienced it when the *Ruby* once passed two Venetian galleys on her way through the Gibraltar Straits.

To begin with, the accompanying singing was inchoate, some way between sobbing and praying. Then the resonances slowly but perceptibly changed. It was as though the souls below were resolving their separate agonies, their difference of tribe and village, as if the Ajois, the Aqueras, the Guramba, were framing in the terrible maw of the *Virgin* a new voice, a common language. This was at first lumbering and slow (the sailors calling it 'Ta-Ta' in affectionate derision), primal in its necessary simplicity, but none the less telling, for it was accompanied by music of courageous certainty.

In the music, had anyone listened with understanding, could have been discerned not only echoes of the wild and passionate energy of the *corana* and their other dances, but holy psalms to the night creatures of their mangrove swamps, and above all, to the beauty and savagery of the rain forest. Here were evoked in thrilling ullulations the great bombax trees, the sensitive mimosa that when touched retracts in shame, the great tree ferns and arboreal orchids; as also the leopards, panthers, buffalo, wild hog and softly-stepping elephant . . . lizards, pythons, butterflies, parrots, fireflies; as well as the ever-thundering sea, on the holiness of which all their promises to one another had been sworn – and kept.

The *Virgin* butted stolidly through mild dark waters over which the stars hung so low that it looked as if a hand need only be stretched out to pick them, carrying in her hold meanwhile these never-to-be-forgotten memories of the great forests that the slaves had left for ever. She carried also their immensely precious fetissoes, or fetishes, that could be created from anything to hand, be it feathers, leaves, glass beads, blood. So that along with the slaves went, inescapably, their Gods; the Snake God, a fathom long, streaked white, yellow and brown; the God Ajah, coal black and two-and-a-half feet high, capable of turning himself into anything at will. It was Ajah, after all, who had promised his people they would go into a far country where there would be all necessities, all riches, and that once they got there, they would live like kings and have everything they desired, such as clothes – and enough to eat.

Under the untroubled regime of the Dutch Captain, the deck hatches were opened thrice daily to let in food barrows, guarded by two men with whips. These went clanking up the narrow aisles between the manacled slaves, and from them the men doled out the palm-oil mush that had been exchanged back at Wydah for fishing hooks, old hats and clay pipes. With almost equal regularity, the slaves were brought up into the waist of the ship. This had been barricaded with bamboo for safety, and the old culverdine trained on them as an added precaution in case of trouble. Here the slaves refreshed themselves in canvas buckets of sea water, and, for their health's sake, were encouraged to dance.

It was now that Read saw the wisdom of Nicholas Poll in urging him to take the blacks' musical instruments on board. For long periods of time beneath the *Virgin*'s shaking sails, both the cargo and the crew of the ship played music and danced together. With a brave breeze at east, the blacks, playing their strum-strums and thumping their log drums, danced tirelessly, their fetters clinking. They danced hunting and war and victory and laughter and love. Then out came the crews' fiddles, and to their leaping cadences the men sang of drinking-blinds, and one-eyed sailor heroes, of grey-haired mothers waiting for their sons, of betrayed sweethearts, of clever dogs, while all the slaves, with the exception of the Foins (who sighed and moped) clapped and grinned and boldly shook their manacles by way of accompaniment...

Read instructed Scipio beside the turtle pen. Thirteen days out and Scipio could say, 'Massa', 'good boy', 'eat', 'Massa God'. Meanwhile the sun glowed through the hazy air above them like an unobtainable golden fruit.

By the middle watch of the thirteenth day the wind dropped altogether, and there was nothing for it but to get out the longboat and row and tow the *Virgin* along. As they rowed, they noted that some way to the south-west of them was another sail, similarly becalmed.

As always in those latitudes, night fell suddenly, rapidly shearing off the day, by which time the Captain had hoved to 5 degrees South of latitude in a quiet carapace of hazy silver moonlight.

At around the change of the twelve o'clock watch (when there was always more than usual fuss and hurry), a longboat with muffled oars slid in swiftly and lashed itself to the *Virgin*'s bowsprit. Three minutes after, the watch sank to his knees, his breath sighing out through a severed windpipe. And but a few minutes after that, Read, sensing a covert movement beside his cot, woke to feel the cool snub of a pistol pressing against his throat.

'Cry out, and by the eternal Jesus I'll blow your brains out!'

Read opened his eyes, and in the shaded light from the lantern saw what he at first took to be a woman bending over him. Her head was half-turned towards the first mate, who was sitting up in his cot, staring ashen-faced. Read had only time to glimpse the intruder's quarter-profile before she turned back with a glance that almost deprived him of consciousness. A savage down-cut with a cutlass had at one time all but excoriated the entire right half of the face, leaving a raw cleft stretching from the empty eye-socket to the glistening membrane of the lower gum. This creature now wound its hand into the slack of Read's shirt and with prodigious strength half-lifted him from the cot, nearly throttling him as it did so.

'Get up, God damn you!' And by the light of the lantern Read could see that the act of speaking caused saliva to run incontinently from the corner of the puckered mouth.

Under this grim surveillance Read and the first mate commenced a wary shuffle towards the after-deck. As they proceeded they became conscious of a rhythmic thumping, like the palpitations of a giant heart, and realised that it was the slaves beating their manacles against the ship's side. They also heard the restless throbbing of fiddles, so that as they moved along the empty deck, the whole ship seemed to pulse.

The after-deck was a blaze of light cast from candles hastily spiked about the mizzen. Round the mast, a group of some twenty men were standing, the object of their attention being a tall, youngish man dressed from head to foot in black, with long black hair tied back in a string from his pale face. He had an unsheathed cutlass in one hand, and a bottle in the other from which from time to time he took a long pull. With the aid of the cutlass he appeared to be seeking to persuade the *Virgin*'s captain to enter the circle formed by the watching men.

'There is Captain Bellamy,' said Read's frightful gaoler, 'your new Master!' And through his wounded mouth the name, Bellamy, came out in a sigh that sounded hideously ecstatic, 'Vellamy!' And as he spoke he screwed his pistol painfully into the small of Read's back.

'It's a devilish conscientious rascal, to be sure!' Bellamy was saying, 'a sneaking puppy!' And almost tenderly he touched the Captain in the buttock with his cutlass. 'Sneaking, I say, as all are who submit to laws which rich men have made for their own security, for,' said he, pinking the Captain rather less gently in the calf so that a crimson star formed and spread on the Captain's cream wool stocking, 'the cowardly whelps have not otherwise courage to defend what they get by their knavery!'

The Captain winced, then grunted, staring doggedly into the gold nimbus of candlelight. From where he stood, Read could see that his face was impassive, though whether from defiance or indifference it was hard to tell.

'Come, then,' continued Bellamy in a wheedling sort of voice, 'and admit that people vilify us when the only difference between you and us,' and he pinked the Captain's other calf for good measure, 'is that *you* rob the poor under cover of the law, and *we* plunder the rich under the protection of our own courage. What do you say to that?' Once again the Captain merely grunted.

'Had you better not make one of us?' persisted Bellamy, resolutely pointing his weapon at the Captain's left ear, 'than sneak after the arse of the villains who employ you?' The Captain grunted a third time, his forehead glistening in the heat of the candles which were burning almost without motion, so calm was the night.

'Then I fear he must dance!' cried Bellamy, and as though in approbation there welled up a rumbling sound like distant thunder as the slaves once again hammered their manacles against the *Virgin*'s sides.

'Come boys, give him a tune!' There was a round of applause as the fiddles started up. It was the old tune, 'You should have told me before you left me!' and the candle flames wavered in the draught from appreciatively clapping palms. Read now saw that the outer circle of pirates had armed themselves with penknives, tucks, forks, compasses, and were closing in upon the Captain to goad him, with well-aimed jabs to the hams, calves and upper arms, into a lumbering dance about the mizzen. His breathing had already become stertorous and his eyes begun to bulge.

At this point in the proceedings Bellamy turned and saw Read.

'Alright, Miss Nanny, you can cast him off and leave him to me – and his brat!' For poor Scipio had run after Read, and was now clasping him round the knees and sobbing.

'They tell me you can dress wounds,' said Bellamy, absently inserting the point of his cutlass into the bosom of Scipio's shirt and making a slight upwards tear. 'Not but that I wouldn't prefer an artist up to caulking neatly and handy at joinery, but had you also better not make one of us?'

Read nodded slightly, catching Bellamy's hot breath, which was so generously fortified with the Captain's spirits it made his eyes water. He pressed Scipio's shoulder, and searching Bellamy's eyes, saw that the irises were black as jet, and that below them were lunatic slips of almond-white.

'Can you read, sir?' demanded Bellamy, laying down his weapon and thrusting one hand into his coat, while catching Read's shirt with the other as he did so, painfully nicking the skin of Read's nipple. 'Because if you're going to make one of us, my good sir, you will be required to sign Articles!' And he abstracted a much-folded piece of paper from his pocket.

'Article One' – cocking his head on one side and fixing Read with his black eyes. '"Every man shall obey civil command" – for even us gentlemen of fortune must respect the rules. Agreed?'

'Agreed,' echoed Read.

'"Agreed," you say? Then what about this? Article Two. "If any man shall offer to run away, or keep any secret from the rest . . ." Oh, damn my blood, read it out yourself! I was never one to waste time on letters . . .'

'". . . or keep any secret from the company,"'

Read read out by the steady light from the candles, '"he shall be marooned with one bottle of powder, one bottle of water..."'

'Aye, aye, cut the cackle and get on with the next one!' And again, as if in corroboration, the *Virgin*'s hold thrilled to the frantic rapping of the slaves.

The fiddles had now moved into a reel, and looking across, Read could see that the Dutch Captain, blood running down the side of his face, was in the act of hurling himself at one of his tormentors...

'"Article Three,"' he read out, his mind fighting to concentrate. '"That man that shall strike another whilst these Articles are in force shall receive Moses Law..."'

'Ha! ha!' laughed Bellamy, 'Moses Law, do you know what Moses Law is?' And he appeared to be all but suffocating with laughter. 'Why, Moses Law is forty stripes, lacking one, on the bare back...'

Read could see they had now secured the Captain. Leaping before him was the apparent cause of his outburst, a young man yelling with laughter, and slung round his neck, a bobbing string of the Captain's favourite red sausages. 'Saskia beloved!' howled the Captain, 'My Saskia!' Then he dropped his head and blubbered.

'"Article Four,"' Read managed to get out. '"If any man lose a joint in time of an engagement, he shall have forty pieces-of-eight..."'

'Let him free!' suddenly shouted Bellamy, referring to the Dutch Captain.

'Aye, aye, let him free!' they shouted. They had already tired of the sport and, draping the sausages round the Captain's neck, cried out, one and all, 'Three huzzahs for the Captain!'

A sailor, beside himself with either drink or laughter, now came lurching into the circle of light, cannoned into Read, drew himself up with a supercilious expression, then bent and vomited scaldingly over Read's leg.

'Why hang an arse, then?' Bellamy was shouting above the hubbub. 'You of all people must know that in an honest service such as the Queen's ships, there is thin commons, low wages, hard labour . . .'

But Read, trying to keep his hand steady, had reached the final article. '"If at any time you meet with a prudent woman, that man that offers to meddle with her without her consent shall suffer present death."'

'Ah!' said Bellamy, narrowing his eyes and staring quizzically at Read. 'A prudent woman. What do you make of that one, eh? Is there such a thing possible, do you think?' And laying his hand lightly on Read's shoulder, gently rocked him back and forth, smiling into his eyes as he did so.

The glance was at once so searching, so caressing, that Read's heart gave a wild leap. Then his throat closed. The man had smoked him . . .

'God damn!' cried Read, fighting for time, confronted as he was with the choice of declaring himself or becoming a pirate. 'Was ever such an unconscionable number of cranky rules! Why, even Moses knew he was making a fool of himself by the time he reached the tenth commandment!' He looked up, racked with indecision, and saw Bellamy was laughing. It was a laugh of such malicious amusement that for a moment Read could not breathe for terror.

'God's blood, Soldier! What's snagging you?' Silence followed this. The fiddles stopped screeching, and the slaves, as though in sympathy, were also silent. The men waited. Their faces were expectant in the candlelight, and Read knew quite certainly that it was touch and go whether he'd be allowed to go free or have the shirt ripped to his waist and his breeches torn off.

'Swear on it!' cried a voice out of the crowd. Something cold and heavy was thrust into Read's hand, and he realised with a shock that it was an axe-head.

'Aye, swear!' they shouted. 'Swear!'

There was a further hot silence. Fighting an insane desire to hurl the axe-head into the nearest face and run to the side and throw himself over, Read raised his head. The night sky arched over him, radiant in the soft light from the careless moon. Read dropped his head despairing, then, as he had once sworn away his hard-won independence for love of Gerhardi, so now he quietly swore away four years' honest service to the Queen.

At this there was a whoop of triumph. 'Oh, you'll be a free prince, my dear!' cried Bellamy, seizing a pannikin of spirits and pouring it over Read's head. 'Let me christen thee, my joy! Thou hast now signed on for a life of plenty and satiety, pleasure and ease, liberty and power! For thou hast now as much authority to make war on the whole world as one who has an hundred sail of ships at sea, or an army of 10,000 in the field! And though this be a young man's calling, as the saying is, there's many have established their own commonwealths and made their fortunes by the time they was thirty. And if they haven't,' and Bellamy, the pannikin halfway to his lips, winked, 'why then, my dear, a merry life and a short one is my motto!'

The *Virgin*, renamed the *Willing Mind*, now came back on course, crewed by two-thirds of the old Captain's men who had signed Pirates' Articles. The remainder, along with their Captain, were kept for the time being in irons below decks.

Bellamy kept company in his own sloop, his intention, like the Dutch Captain's, to sell off the slaves not needed to man the ships along the small inlets north of Pernambuco.

Twenty days out from Wydah, Scipio could now pipe, 'One two, three...' in a sweet treble, and when

Read catechised him, asking, 'What art thou made of, little man?' he would yell, 'Dirt!' and run giggling off to sink his face in the warm flank of the monkey who, chattering her annoyance, sought to bite him.

It was only when Read came to write up his journal one evening, that it struck him with a shock that part of him had already grown accustomed to his new situation. Then he remembered with a flash of shame that the old Captain was still languishing below decks in irons, at which he determined secretly to plan a rescue. For the moment, however, this had to be set aside in favour of more immediate concerns.

September 29th . . . owing to the loose command of Bellamy's replacement for our old Captain, we are like to lose upwards of 13 per cent of our slaves with the flux. This resulting from lack of care in cleaning their quarters out, and poor commons etc., and this a great pity in the last stage of our voyage. Yesterday died one man of mine, number 10, and three women, numbers 45, 67, 89, which was mighty vexing to me having paid so much of my substance for them, and besides hard on them, for with proper care it need not have been so . . . Yesterday we made a landfall at Ferdinando, 4 degrees South of the line, from where Bellamy designs sending out his scouts to contact planters on the coast. It is now rumoured about the ship's company that he purposes putting our old Captain on the maroon along with those of his crew who have stayed loyal to him . . .

Read stood at the ship's rail watching as, with a kind of bulky dignity, the old Captain, his hair disordered and his face unshaven, stepped down into the longboat to join his first mate. Then he turned and looked straight into Read's face as though imprinting it upon his memory for ever.

September 30th . . . but he knows not what I stand to lose, and might think differently if apprised of my true situation. Yet for all this it was melancholy seeing him rowed ashore with his five companions, to what kind of place no one knows, though through the glass it appeared well wooded, and I doubt not there is water too, though not the good red sausages that are so dear to his heart . . . God pity him . . .

11

Journal October 1st... Sure this coxcomb Bellamy must be out of his mind, or else very whimsical. On the eve of sending the mate and quartermaster with the *Willing Mind* to trade our slaves along the coast north of Punte Redonda, he gives orders for the longboat to return to the island of Rocas and fetch back our old Captain, Bellamy having examined closely the bills of loading, and convincing himself our Captain has somewhere concealed a great quantity of gold dust about his ship . . .

The interrogation had lasted almost an hour, Miss Nanny, the quartermaster, being bent in apparent solicitude over the Dutch Captain. The Dutch Captain's teeth were still chattering with the ague that had been on him ever since being landed on Rocas. Miss Nanny now encircled the Captain's throat tightly with his arm.

'I've seen him,' said Miss Nanny, carelessly indicating Bellamy, 'have a man's ears off and put in a pie for him to eat with pepper and salt . . .' At which Miss Nanny lightly pressed the razor to just below the Captain's left ear-lobe, and began very gently sawing to and fro, so that the blood started.

'Very true, sir!' cried Bellamy, his black eyes snapping with amusement. 'I've had 'em served up before now in a fine dish of Solomon Grundy, and very tasty I found 'em!'

In a moment blood was trickling then running down the Captain's unshaven chops, so that Read, ordered by Bellamy to be present, felt his stomach clench in revulsion.

'A little and a little...' persuaded Miss Nanny in his caressingly watery voice, as the Captain, his eyes rolling like a stricken heifer's, attempted to move his head away.

'In God's name!' cried Read, 'tell 'em what you know, sir!' But the Captain only ground his teeth.

'... more?' wheedled Miss Nanny, 'a little more?' A few moments later the Captain gave an inarticulate howl, and instinctively Read's arm shot out to restrain the quartermaster's hand. Miss Nanny looked up sharply at this, then smiled deliberately into Read's eyes, and spat.

''Tis hid in a jar,' the Captain groaned, and almost inaudibly, 'beneath a board in the cow's stall.'

'Then why the Devil didn't you say so in the first place!' cried Bellamy, 'for then I'd not have returned you to your Paradiso as now I fear I must do. The Soldier (with a smile at Read) and the quartermaster will take you back...'

October 2nd... so out comes the longboat once more, and back to Rocas goes our unfortunate Captain, still shivering with the ague, his lips bloodied, as well as his ear, with the clenching of his teeth upon them so as not to cry out. Though he would address no word to me, and though Miss Nanny fixed us most of the while with his one good eye, I managed to contrive it that I slipped the old Captain my tinder-box before the longboat beached. Further, I had words in the Dutch language (in which for safety's sake I also wrote this journal) with the five other men. They told me how they had managed to subsist so far by feeding on berries and shellfish such as cockles and periwinkles, and sometimes catching a stingray. It must be observed that, having no means of striking fire until now, their way of dressing this fish was by dipping it often in salt water, then laying it in the sun till it became both hard and dry, and then they ate it, but that the stomachs of three of them had fiercely disagreed on it, so that the men were much pulled down after with the flux. They told me Rocas was well provided with fresh water, and that a species of small hog runs wild there. I promised I would seek to speak with Captain Bellamy to get them necessities such as small-arms and shot, which was, after all, agreed on in the Ship's Articles in the case of marooning. For though they say they are free and self-governing like princes, I find the pirates are as plagued with rules as anyone else . . .

October 5th . . . His whimsicality feeds on itself! Our slaves being now gone six days in our old ship that sailed in command of the first mate and Miss Nanny, Bellamy thinks to chance his own hand in the shipping business, causing me to join his ship and giving me the temporary post of quartermaster in the absence of Miss Nanny. A position I was not ambitious of, though he greatly pressed me with his hand on my shoulder and with compliments as to my seamanship etc. And I will own that there was so great a quality of persuasion in his touch and in his manner of speaking, that a man might well against his better judgement follow him into mad dangers.

As it came about we chanced on a turtler, and without more ado we took him for our own use, and her master having two useful artists (a gunner and a caulker) with him, we persuaded them to join our company. Three days after, we engaged with a ship flying the Portuguese flag which she struck without ceremony when we flew our Black. When we boarded her, we found to our joy that besides being loaded with 120,000lbs weight of cacao, she had also 20,000 pieces-of-eight, and among other things six good horses for the use of the Governor of Sao Limsof. Our men, being young, got mighty drunk at the prospect of sharing in this great prize, and some of them mounted the horses and, to the scraping of our fiddlers, rid them like madmen about the deck, backwards and forwards at full gallop, cursing, swearing and halloing at such a rate that they made the poor creatures wild. At length two or three of them throwing their riders, the drunkest of 'em fell upon the Portuguese ship's crew, whipping them and cutting them in a barbarous manner and telling 'em it was for bringing horses without boots and spurs, for want of which the pirates were not able to ride 'em as gentlemen should – we that are now all become gentlemen scorning even to drink the ship's beer.

This, and the fine prize we had, put our new Captain in such a good humour as led him to play the part of Almighty Providence with our old Captain. For what does he do now, but make again for Rocas, ordering out the longboat under my command, loaded with a cask of flour, a bushel of salt, two bottles of gunpowder, several bullets, besides a quantity of small-shot and a couple of muskets, a very good axe, a pot and pan, and three dogs which he took in the turtler. Which dogs are bred to hunting and very useful, they say, in tracing out the wild hogs. Besides all these were a dozen horn-handled knives of that sort which we had carried to Guinea. I left these items on the foreshore of Rocas, for the poor fugitives, fearful of our intentions, were hidden up, as I guessed, among the woods of the island. But on returning to Bellamy's sloop I looked through the glass, and was contented to see 'em come down to the water's edge to examine what manner of goods we had left them . . .

November 3rd . . . yet, like some malignant fate, he has played cat-and-mouse with these poor souls. For during this long time that we have been awaiting the return of the *Willing Mind*, he has made several times as if to sail away from Rocas for ever, only to return in a few days to plague the life out of them again: such as landing and burning the canoe they had constructed with such pains over the days as a means of escape from their captivity, and shooting two of the dogs, and destroying the dam they built as a means of conserving water . . .

Yesterday the *Willing Mind* returned from her business about the creeks near Punte Redonda, though having carried not near so well as Bellamy had hoped, so many of our slaves being much worn by reason of being kept below so long, and as a consequence of poor commons since leaving the Wydah roads. This likely miffed him, for he orders out the longboat again, and approaches Rocas once more, and hailing our old Captain through his trumpet, tells him he intends returning his ship to him so that he may sail safely back to Amsterdam and see his old wife again and eat her home-made sausages once more. Meanwhile he had caused the *Willing Mind* to be towed into the little bay of Rocas, and there anchoring her, he and his men returned to his own sloop to watch them through the glass.

We saw 'em running in hope and joy down to the water's edge, two of the men instantly wading into the sea and striking out towards the ship. But they had not got far when there was a sudden loud explosion of gunpowder, and their ship took fire, and in a little time burned right down to the water and snuffed it. After this new piece of cruelty, the Captain prepared to sail, laughing and telling us it would give 'em a renewed relish for surviving. This cruelty being much compounded in my mind, since

I have it on good authority that you may never see a ship in three years along this part of the coast. As to our share from the cargo of our ill-fated ship, I suppose I must count myself fortunate in receiving something to offset what I spent on acquiring my slaves... Along with the turtler and the Portuguese ship, the Captain now determines to stretch over to Port of Spain, and from thence to Tortuga where he designs disposing of his cargo to the factors there...

November 17th... Since joining this ship the Captain, as he styles himself, has gone out of his way to declare himself my friend, calling me 'Soldier' by way of being familiar; but Miss Nanny, since returning to this ship from Punte Redonda, appears much miffed, as though I had supplanted him in the Captain's favour, which I am very far from being ambitious of. Rather, it seems to me that Bellamy, being of a malicious temper, acts in the way he does to goad Miss Nanny, who is of a notoriously jealous and savage disposition, and much feared in his place of quartermaster. Indeed, if truth were known, I am hard put to decide who really is master of this ship, the Captain or his quartermaster, for Miss Nanny seems at all times to encourage the Captain in his whimsicalities, and in so doing becomes, I believe, the secret master of them both.

The crewmen, divided now between our three ships, are complaisant enough, being in the main green boys, or ordinary seamen, turned pirate more by compulsion than free choice, and on this ship Miss Nanny is held so much in awe by them, he is obeyed to a man. Three days ago, in a slatch of still weather, by way of amusing the men, I fancy, Miss Nanny, among other such diversions agreeable to these sorts of folks, encouraged 'em to play-act. To this end he appointed a mock Court of Judicature, for us to try one another for piracy, he that was a criminal one day being made Judge the next. And this I believe he did to diminish the fear of the Law in us.

The court and jury being appointed, as also Counsel to plead, Miss Nanny, who had appointed himself Judge, got up on a box on the poop with a dirty tarpaulin over his shoulders, a thrum cap on his head and a large pair of spectacles on the end of his nose. He had the fiddles play a fanfare, then Bellamy in the part of the Attorney-General opened the charge against the prisoners, of whom, for some reason best known to himself, he appointed myself the principal. I give it here by way of a dialogue.

Attorney-Gen. (alias Captain Bellamy, and so high on Black Strap he had much ado not to burst himself laughing): 'An't please your Lordship and you gentlemen of the jury, here is a fellow,' indicating me, 'that is a sad dog, a sad, sad dog, and I humbly hope your Lordship,' indicating Miss Nanny, 'will order him to hanged out of way immediately.' (They that were looking on cheered mightily at this, but I noticed, in a way I much misliked, that the Captain stared often at Miss Nanny, especially when speaking of me, as though to confront him with my presence.)

'He has committed piracy on the high seas,' he went on, 'and we shall prove, an't please your Lordship, that this fellow,' again indicating me with a wink, 'this sad dog before you, has escaped a thousand storms, nay, has got safe ashore when the ship has been cast away, which was a certain sign he was not born to be drowned; yet not having the fear of hanging before his eyes, he went on robbing and ravishing man, woman and child, plundering ships' cargoes fore and aft, burning and sinking ship, bark and boat, as if the Devil had been in him. But this is not all, my Lord,' continued the wag, giggling, 'he has committed worse villainies than these, for we shall prove that he has been guilty of drinking' – and here he hesitated, adding in a great voice – '*small beer!* And your Lordship knows that never was there a sober fellow but was a rogue! My Lord, I should have spoken much finer than I do now, but that, as your Lordship knows, our rum is all out and how would a man speak good Law that has not drunk a dram? I hope your Lordship,' he concluded, 'will order the fellow to be hanged.'

Judge (alias the quartermaster, Miss Nanny): 'Hearkee me, sirrah!' Looking not to me but at Bellamy, with all the force of his one eye. 'You lousy, pitiful, ill-looked dog; what have you to say why you should not be tucked up immediately and set a-shindying like a scarecrow? Are you guilty or not guilty?'

Prisoner (alias Ned Read): 'Not guilty, an't please your Worship!'

Judge (alias Miss Nanny): 'Not guilty!' staring fixedly at Bellamy, (and to tell the truth there was something in this play-acting that put me in mind of a lovers' quarrel . . .) 'Say so again, sirrah, and I'll have you hanged without trial.' (Loud cheers from the men, who seemed not to understand the intricacy of the situation . . . and I liked not the look in his one eye, though it were supposed to be in jest, and I saw how he had suddenly begun to tremble as though with suppressed excitement . . .) 'You must suffer for three reasons,' he wound up, and he stuttered as he spoke, and I caught Bellamy laughing openly. 'First because it is not fit I should sit here as Judge and *nobody* be hanged, secondly you must be hanged because you have a damned hanging look, and thirdly you must be hanged because . . .' and at this point I could see he hesitated for a fraction and tried to adjust his face to a smile '. . . because I am hungry!'

Then amidst the laughter and whistles of the men the fiddles started up, but Read could see that the quartermaster was not laughing, and that the good side of his face, when it was turned away from them, had on it an expression that was something like grief . . .

November 24th . . . I came below with the object of catechising Scipio, as is my habit, and to write up my journal, and was alarmed to find Scipio gone, and only the monkey left jangling and in a bait on her wooden bar. Thinking the boy might be with the ship's cook (a Yorkshire man who has young sons of his own, and the boy, as all boys, being a great one for his victuals), I was about to make for the galley when Scipio returned of his own accord. He came in slowly and with an air I liked not, halfway between a smile that had in it something triumphant, and an expression of shame that again I liked not, he being until now, if a rogue, an honest rogue. It was as if the very air about him stood back askance. I now seized him by the ear and, twisting it so he howled, asked him what he meant by not biding in the cabin as I had bid him. For a moment he would say nothing, until, on my giving his ear another turn, he gave out that earlier the quartermaster had come by, saying the Captain wanted him, and that if he would be a good boy and do what he was bid he should have a handful of sweetmeats and a new little shirt for himself, and be allowed (which he was never allowed otherwise) to walk on the quarter-deck alongside the Captain himself.

At that I shook him, and then let him go, saying he was to do no such thing. And as I did so, he being close to me, I noticed a sweetish smell coming from him as though he was rubbed over with cocoa oil, at which a sudden thought came into my mind concerning Scipio and the Captain. But I put it instantly from my mind, though I must own it left behind an impress that will take time to be rid of . . .

By the thirtieth of the month the ship was making the 4th parallel. It was an oppressive day with very little wind, the sun greasy and ray-less, yet giving out a suffocating leaden heat. Towards evening the sea turned the colour of shimmering grey silk, the sky took on a hue like tarnished copper, and there was a heavy swell. Read, passing by the Captain's cabin, noticed that the door was hooked back for air, and as he passed he heard a woman singing. For a second it went through his mind that Bellamy, true to form, though contrary to his own Articles, might well have a girl with him in his cabin, and he glanced in briefly, and thought he glimpsed a girl sitting with her profile turned to him. Almost at once, however, he corrected the impression, for what he had taken to be a woman was, in fact, Miss Nanny. Miss Nanny's face, presenting his good side, was raised, the nostrils dilating, and from his mouth came a song such as a forsaken merman might sing, sad and plaintive, with a dying fall so nakedly wretched that Read's heart shrank within him, and he hurried past.

Several steps on, however, something made him turn and look back, and as he did so a form that must have been lurking on the inner side of the Captain's door detached itself and ran off into the shadows. But when Read reached his cabin, Scipio was asleep in his cot, his thick lashes lying without so much as a quiver on his smooth cheek.

By midnight the sky was swarming with wavering stars, preternaturally large and unusually close to earth, while the swell had considerably increased, and a wind was getting up. The sloop was now heading towards a northern horizon of such profound blackness, beyond the intervening empyrean of stars, that Read was instantly put in mind of what he had seen in the mangrove swamps with the old Foin hunter. For the darkness towards which they were making, almost solid to look at, partook of the same impersonal immensity, the same inexorable unchangingness beside which all else, including the stars themselves, was mere afterthought. From the empyrean itself great spots of rain began to fall, and for a moment Read was surprised that they too were not black.

Half an hour before dawn the expected storm hit them. The foresail, which alone had been left (Bellamy having ordered the rest of the ship down to bare poles), filled like a monstrous balloon, then split suddenly across with a sound like a pistol shot, its tatters hurled away into the darkness, as with a shudder the sloop met the first of the thirty-foot waves.

Read and the ship's carpenter, who were at the helm, clung to the kicking tiller as the boat plunged her bows into the white-streaked sea, sending cascades of water over their heads and shoulders. Another wave, and the sloop, thrown on her beam ends to starboard, shook like a dog, at which moment the near intolerable strain on the tiller eased minimally and Read, in the moment before the next wave swept over them, became aware that another pair of hands had joined their own. He turned and saw Miss Nanny, his good side towards him, and then, as they all three struggled for mastery over the wildly jerking helm, the ship rolled, fell headlong on her side, and Miss Nanny was hurled against Read. At which instant Read felt a stunning blow against his lower ribs, the pain of which filled his mouth with acid.

December 4th . . . This was like to have cost me my life, the wind blowing so hard I was near going overboard, though this was perhaps the least aspect of the dreadful time that was to follow, and which I now feel compelled to record. As it turned out, another member of the crew coming up at that instant, he took my place at the tiller, and discretion being the better part of valour (for I was still not sure whether it had been an accident or no), I left the helm and went below. When I came to examine my body by the light poor Scipio held, I found some sharp weapon had flayed at my lower ribs, having first ripped open the side of my pea-jacket, the wound it made bleeding freely. This I managed to staunch with a sponge, and when the bleeding had abated somewhat I applied a styptic I had about me, and went to venture back on deck, determined to tell the captain of what had happened. But I had no opportunity either then or later, for the sloop was taking in at the seams, and the chain-pumps going, and a sail being thrummed to get under her bow.

Towards morning the storm moderated, and by midday had blown itself out, though leaving us in something of a poor way – though not near so poor as the remainder of our little fleet that was quite scattered, the turtler being either totally lost or else blown far off course. By now Captain Bellamy, who acquitted himself throughout this business with boldness and spirit (though it sticks in my gullet to say so), had given orders to stop the pumps, we having gained sufficiently on the leak. Much of the night's damage, moreover, was on the way to being made good by the excellent artists we had with us, and I, still not sure whether my hurt had been due to the malevolence of the quartermaster or some other cause, had made up my mind for the time being to remain silent. So for the next twenty-four hours, peace reigned.

At the beginning of the afternoon watch on the following day, the look-out came slithering down a backstay hollering out there was a sail to windward, and that he was claiming his cutlass and two pistols, this being part of the Ship's Articles. It turned out to be a ship, very much crippled by the previous night's storm . . .

'Damn my blood, Soldier!' cries Bellamy when he comes up from below (he had been in his cabin all morning) 'if she ain't a Spaniard!' I suspected he was on the drink again, for he was in a mighty cocky mood, much disposed to joke, especially with me. And whether it is being wise after the event or no, I think it seemed his eye was upon me, though with what purpose I didn't then know.

Well, he gives his orders in the same jaunty tone and dives below, coming up again not long after to present an extraordinary figure. He had arrayed himself in a rich crimson damask waistcoat and breeches, with a red feather in his hat, a gold chain about his neck with a diamond cross hanging to it, and his pistols were hanging at the end of a silk sling flung over his shoulders. If it were possible he was in even more excellent humour, hardly able at times to move for laughing. Had I then known the cause for it! Our sloop was now within gunshot of the unsuspecting Spaniard, Bellamy, by rowing and towing of his own ship, giving them the appearance of coming to the Spaniard's aid. This pretence was kept up to the last degree, even to Bellamy neglecting to baffle the nettings lest the Spaniard, regarding us through his glass, might see signs of us being ready for action and so take fright . . .

It was shortly after that Bellamy fired his chase-gun,

at the same time unfurling his Black Ensign from the mizzen-peak where, tumbling leisurely into the blue air, it billowed out. Meanwhile he sent men to get out the spritsail yard under the bowsprit, in preparation for boarding . . .

'She's struck her flag, Soldier!' he shouted gleefully to Read as the sloop came about to fire another round at the Spaniard. Then, 'Damn my blood, they've starboarded their helm!' At which moment there came a thunderous roar from the Spaniard's ports and Read flung himself to the deck as the mizzen-topmast fell over them in a tangle of cordage. They were flung painfully together, but in a moment Bellamy, wriggling like a terrier, was up and running swiftly along the deck to re-form the men at the gun position.

December 4th, continued . . . after a fight of thirty minutes the Spaniard struck her colours and called for quarter. This in an evil hour, for had her captain known the confusion that we ourselves was in, being totally taken by surprise at her firing on us under cover of striking her flag, he might have taken heart. Had they but known, too, that a shot of theirs, taking us in the superstructure, had carried away also our Captain, the entire rim of his belly being shot away. But such was his grip on this world, and so great his determination (God forgive him!) that for a short time he held up his very bowels in his hands, trying with all his might to walk, before sinking to the deck in the arms of his friend the quartermaster. It was this I am sure which drove the quartermaster to such a pitch of cruelty when we came to board the Spaniard, not to mention the brandy which fired their wickedness, for I never in my time in the Queen's Service saw such cruelty at work. What chiefly galled them was the action of the Spanish captain in tricking us by pretending to strike his colours and then after firing upon us, so killing our Captain.

Misfortune was it that this Spanish Captain had his wife with him, a quiet dark woman, not very young, who was forced to look on while they tormented her husband before her very eyes, Miss Nanny ordering lighted matches to be tied between the poor man's fingers so as to burn all the flesh from off the bones. When they tired of this, they took the unfortunate woman and, before her husband's eyes, repeatedly ravished her, some twenty of them, one after another, though not Miss Nanny, who looked on biding his time, he standing there like a butcher, in blood up to his elbows, the whole of his shirt dyed with it where he had held our dying Captain to him. And all this time, they told me, he trembled with excitement as though he were in an ague fit. But most of this was reported after to me, since these proceedings so sickened me that I early left that scene. Besides I feared greatly for Scipio, having for some time kept a continual watch over him, thinking him to be in imminent danger from the jealousy of the quartermaster, who I knew sought to damage me in any way he could.

It was for this reason that earlier in the day, and well before the action I have described, and being much occupied with repairs about the ship, I had earnestly enjoined Scipio to stay quiet in the cabin. At which he grew sulky and inclined to defy me, whereon I cuffed him, and then and there turned the key on him. And thus he remained in the hours prior to the action, and thereafter until I should choose to go to him. But not in the safety I had hoped for . . .

When Read reached the cabin he found the door lolling back on its hinges. A glance inside showed him the place was deserted, and both Scipio and the colubus monkey gone. For a second Read hesitated, then immediately the remembrance of the smell of cocoa oil and the manic behaviour of Bellamy came to mind and fused into understanding and he ran back along the deck to the dead Captain's cabin. It was locked. Read kicked open the door and forced his way in. The Captain was stretched out on his cot, his naked torso still swathed in blood-crusted linen. His eyes had not yet been closed, and his lip was hooked over a glittering eye-tooth, giving him a vulpine look. Beside him, naked and tethered by a collar and chain to the bars of the cot, was Scipio. His eyes were rolling, and he was whimpering. There was a small pool of drying vomit on the floor, and beside him lay the colubus monkey, its head at an odd angle.

Anguish never before experienced now possessed Read totally, and for the next few minutes he was turned into a grieving woman. On later reflection he knew that he had perfectly known what it was to be a mother. He knelt down, and with tears running down his cheeks attempted to take off the collar, but it was drawn in so tightly round the child's throat that for a moment his shaking fingers were unable to unfasten the heavy buckle.

'They hurt yo poor boy!' cried Scipio, casting himself into Read's trembling arms, where he lay like a bruised flower as Read covered his face with kisses. 'They hurt yo poor boy so!' And in the light from the doorway Read could see there were liver-coloured bruises covering his rump and belly.

There was no sign of the Spanish captain nor yet of his tormentors when Read, in his search for the quartermaster, gained the deck. At first sight it seemed totally deserted, all having gone their way drinking or pillaging. Then Read heard moaning, and saw the captain's woman lying where she had fallen. She was on her back, her thighs parted, and Miss Nanny, his back to Read, was at work between them. Then Read saw the quartermaster slowly rise up, the woman's head caught in his arms. She groaned, at which there was a convulsive movement from the quartermaster, accompanied by a sound Read had heard before, like a stick snapping.

December 4th, continued . . . the Devil suddenly looked up. Then got off his hams and began running low towards me, taking his knife, which still had the woman's blood on it, from between his teeth. My pistol being already primed, as he came at me I cocked it, and as he threw his knife, fired it full in his face . . .

The quartermaster lay there. Read stared down at him for several seconds, his heart thundering, then still holding the smoking pistol he went over to the woman. But she was dead. Read turned, the blood from where the quartermaster's knife had snicked him spattering to the deck, as he walked slowly back to where flies were clustering about the quartermaster's pashed head. One of the crew lurching past halted for a moment, then aimed a drunken kick at the body

'She-devil!' he said.

Read knelt down. Then, unable to resist a terrible compulsion, he began slowly unbuttoning the quartermaster's blood-soaked shirt. Then he unlaced the placket of his canvas breeches, the flies clotting unnoticed on his bleeding arm.

December 4th, continued . . . one side of his body was like that of other men, the belly hard and lean, the pap flat, that side of the chest marked by an arrow of fine black hair (the quartermaster being a very young man). The other had a line of woman's paps almost to the crutch, like to some sow or she-dog. Below this the royal parts were both those of a man and a woman, but in themselves useless for either office, the generative member being no greater than a child's finger, with an orifice behind in which was exposed, like peas shrunken in a pod, the remaining parts of the member, the whole making a kind of monster – though the skin was very white and blue-veined, for Miss Nanny had ever kept his shirt buttoned. I looked long on him, my head spinning, and my stomach, for all I had seen some unwholesome sights in the course of my life, like to void up its contents. Then, just as surely as if I heard a voice speaking, it came to me that I and the dead monster before me yet shared something between us. This was that Almighty Providence had decreed we two should endure always the pain of not knowing perfectly who or what we were. Us both, in a manner of speaking, being half-creatures, unfinished, and not as others are. And then it came to me also, the truly terrible thought that lying before me was a figure of my inner self, and moreover shown me by my Maker as a warning and a fit object for contemplation. At which I found myself growing faint . . .

Becoming aware that the heat from the sun was beating down on his unprotected head and that he was bleeding from the arm, Read stooped and covered the quartermaster. Temporarily disconcerted by movement in one who had been for so long still as death, the flies, maddened, roared up once more.

12

'They say you've been wonderful rich, Soldier, and could be so again... They say you've already drunk away the price of six sloops, to the playing of violins...'

'They do? I wonder who the Devil says that,' commented Read, and turned to gaze absently into the dry bright eye of the Guinea parrot that clung to his coat sleeve. 'To the playing of violins – is that what they say? Well, it could be said there's something not far off poetry in that!' And looking at the young man sitting across the table from him in Sally Turner's, he made an effort to smile. But a picture slid into his mind of a night with fireflies like living stars, and Scipio sobbing outside the shack in Port au Prince where Read had just handed him over to Apolline and Syriaque. Scipio had been told to call Syriaque Uncle Quack-Quack...

'There, little lad, for thou art the only son I shall ever have.' And Read kissed him and gave Apolline money until he should come again. Then he told Scipio to be a good brave lad and keep up his letters and his catechism until Read returned in a ship of their own, in which they'd sail home to England and buy a farm. And with that he split a guinea and made Scipio wear one half, keeping the other to hang about his own neck. But so far he still hadn't gotten the ship...

'That about the violins was told me by your old shipmate, Jack Rackham, so it's not poetry,' persisted the young man. 'He says, sir, that when you and he was on the privateering account together shortly after the Governor's Amnesty in 'eighteen, you took some fine prizes...' But Read had already lapsed into reverie. 'One of 'em had a lading of cacao and rolls of tobacco,' the young man gently persevered, 'that is, if you remember, sir. The other of sugar and pieces-of-eight...'

'Aye, aye...'

'... which ye sold, sir, did ye not, to the factors at the back of Tortuga?'

Tortuga. Was it from Tortuga then that they'd set out for the African coast? What had they shouted? 'A gold chain or a wooden leg, we'll stand by you!' And Read murmured this aloud unthinkingly, but was unable, possibly owing to the excessive smoking of *banghe*, to remember how he'd come into such company, only that before they'd weighed anchor the day had broken up in thunder, with towering black and copper cloud forming and reforming as the boobies flew low over the restless water, grim portent of what was to come.

In the latitude of 22N they fell in with a French ship from Martinique, and being fitter for their purpose than their own, moved their men into her.

'That was the *Royal Fortune!*' he commented aloud to the young man, adding vaguely, 'Exchange is no robbery, or so they say!' He remembered even at that early stage having misgivings about the captain's seamanship, misgivings too well founded, as events were to prove. The captain, a great fellow with a terrible pair of whiskers and a wooden leg and stuck around with pistols like a porcupine with quills, intended turning in at Brava in the southernmost Cape Verdes to careen, but in fact got them so far to leeward of their port that it became impossible either to regain it, or indeed any of the windward parts of the African coast. In the end they were forced to take the Trade Winds back to where they'd come from.

'One hogshead of water,' said Read 'for one hundred and twenty-four of us, which in less time than it takes to tell was down to one half-bottle of water *per diem*...'

The young man saw Read's eyes glaze, and noticed that his companion's finger was tracing nervous arcs across and across the wooden table top as though some inner energy, rigorously suppressed, were forcing its way out . . .

. . . With his inward eye Read saw the man cup his hands, then piss into them, raising them to his lips. But before he had a chance to drink, Read had hurled himself against him, knocking his hands apart. At which the man, his breeches still unlaced, began to cry.

They were by then 400 leagues from Surinam. Down to four mouthfuls of water and six of bread in every twenty-four hours, the rations being doled out by the boatswain at the beginning of every afternoon watch. Some of the men tried to supplement what they got with fish, or even with seabirds they managed to shoot or club down. But the weather, consistently foul, hindered such operations, and in any case their stomachs had grown too weak to digest the food, and the consuming of it only bred the flux.

'Belly timber!' sighed Read, 'which was what that ship called victuals. I saw a man attempting to eat a cut of chewed strap, and his stomach threw it back like a gull disgorging. That was one day by the tally from when the look-out gives a great cry saying a fine sloop is bearing down on us, and that no more than a couple of miles off . . .'

By this time the foul weather had given way to a gentle breeze and clear skies. What astonished those of the men who could still make it to the ship's side, was that the oncoming sloop had no other sails set than her main, besides a foresail and a flying-jib. Nevertheless she came on, slowly and more or less steadily, by which time it could be seen from the state of her upper works that she too had experienced the same rough weather as the *Royal Fortune*.

Seeing her caused some of the men, weak as they

were, to rise in an attempt to caper round the deck, crying out as they did so that there would soon be a square meal for each and drink besides. Others laid down their heads and sobbed like small children, or swore, or prayed incoherently with relief. Read found himself staring woodenly ahead at the oncoming ship, but so penetrated with joy he was unable to articulate a syllable.

The sloop was by now less than quarter of a mile away. Through the glass three men could be seen quite plainly lying at their ease by the forecastle, and as she came on they observed that whoever was at the sloop's helm plainly intended to run under the counter of the *Royal Fortune* in order for the men to board her without the necessity of putting out a boat. When they realised this, the men gathered along the *Fortune*'s sides and gave a feeble cheer, and several waved.

At this juncture, the sloop, now a mere twenty yards away, yawed suddenly and passed clean under the *Fortune*'s stern. Astounded, Read staggered aft. He now had a full enough view of the sloop's decks to see that the helm was in fact unmanned, the tiller swinging lazily this way and that with the motion of the ship. Then, the sloop coming yet further round, he could see that perched on one of the three sleeping men was a huge gull. Its head was buried deep in the man's belly, the skin of which was of the startling saffron colour seen in the victims of yellow-jack. As the sloop passed slowly to leeward, Read saw that the bird was with difficulty withdrawing its head from its feast. It gazed fearlessly at Read for a moment, a fragment of entrail swinging from its beak, then plunged its head once more into the man's carcass. Then Read understood. The other two men, far from sleeping, were also cadavers and, like their mate on whom the gull was feasting, eyeless and saffron-coloured.

How many days after, Read couldn't tell, but he

was himself now lying in the shadow cast by the *Fortune*'s forecastle. The men who were still alive were by this time so weak that he no longer had to cover the boatswain with his pistols as he crawled from one to another moistening their lips with a wetted rag. Above him the main-top was describing concentric arcs across and across the profound blue of the sky. Read attempted to fix his mind on this repetitive yet somehow extraordinarily beautiful motion, sought to draw significance from it, but could not. A gap was widening, it seemed, between his thought processes and what was so mystifyingly taking place. It was as though the essential connection between him and the world outside had been severed or had rotted away.

Then he saw that gulls were congregating on the upper spars, their bodies adjusting smoothly to each movement of the ship, their eyes fixed on him. After a minute one of them slipped off its spar and, gliding downwards, cut across his eyes, screaming and muting as it went. When he wiped the stinking matter from the side of his mouth, he could see that it was liver-coloured and streaked with blood.

For some time he had barely been able to swallow, with his tongue being so swollen. He now turned his head from the sky and the gulls and the sun that had slowly crept round and was burning his face, and began rubbing his cheek back and forth on the planking of the deck to distract his mind from the discomfort he felt. As he did this the gull shrieked again, and as it dived at him he heard the bony creak of its pinions, and suddenly felt its claws fasten in the flesh of his thigh. He covered his eyes with his left hand and, raising his other arm, aimed a feeble blow at it. The claws disengaged, and he felt the rush of air from its beating wings as it rose. Exhausted, he let his head roll to one side. As he did so his cheek knocked against the toecap of a black leather boot.

He felt fingers prise open his jaws, then the air freezing on his lips, which the fingers appeared to have anointed with some fiery substance. His head was raised . . .

He sat now beneath a canopy of stitched banana leaves, his back to the sea which for the time had become hateful to him, the water sussurating gently between the stones and curling round the legs of the bench on which he sat, a wooden trestle before him. He picked up his pen, frowned and at last began to write.

> *The History of Captain Misson.* So I decided that while in this place, which is the island of Johanna on the west side of Madagascar, and off the Bay de Diego, and while still recovering from the fever which has never properly left me, I would write down the life and times of he who saved us – the new-fashioned pirate, the man they call Misson . . .

Misson! Misson! Misson!

> *History, continued.* He had but one eye, the other being lost by the arrow of a savage. The eye was a lively hazel eye like the eye of a viper. His bearing was neat and vigorous, his hair silvered early. He was the younger son of a great French house, of which he ever refused to give the name. His father intended him for the Musketeers, but he being of a roving temper chose the sea as a life which abounded with more variety, and would afford him an opportunity to gratify his curiosity by the change of countries. His father sent him volunteer on board the *Victoire*, commanded by his relation, Monsieur Forbin.
>
> Was from the beginning resolved to be a complete sailor, which made him always one of the first on a yard-arm either to hand or reef, and very inquisitive in the different methods of working a ship. Would

get the boatswain and carpenter to teach him in their cabins the constituent parts of a ship's hull and how to rig her, which he generously paid 'em for. (This from his own lips.)

His ship putting in at Naples, he fell in with one who changed the whole course of his life. This was Caraccioli, a man entirely without colour, that people call albino. He was a Dominican, who became his confessor, and after his companion. This Caraccioli, complaining to him of the corruption of the Church, and that his parents should have given him a sword rather than a pair of beads with which to earn his livelihood, throws off his habit at Misson's suggestion and volunteers for the *Victoire* in company with his friend.

Served together in many actions both in the English Channel and off Brest as well as in Martinique and Guadaloupe, the ex-Dominican meanwhile converting his friend to his own especial form of Deism. Convinced him that all religion was no other than man-made, he running through all the ceremonies of the Jewish, Christian and Mahometan religions to show that, far from being institutions of men inspired, they were no more than what was convenient and necessary. *Sic* the circumcision, said to be the sign of the covenant made between God and his people, known also to the African negroes who never heard of God. Both peoples knowing full well that in hot countries the prepuce consolidates perspired matter which is of fatal consequence and etc.

From here he went on to fall upon Government, showing his friend that every man was born free, and had as much right to what would support him as the air he respired. Such thinking carried well with Misson, who was himself of a generous and bold disposition . . .

It came about that the *Victoire* meeting with the

Winchelsea, an English man-of-war of forty guns, and there following an engagement in which the captain, second captain and the three lieutenants on board the *Victoire* were all slain, Misson takes up his sword, ordering Caraccioli to act as lieutenant . . .

. . . Caraccioli persuaded his friend that with the ship he now commanded (the *Winchelsea* from some unknown cause being blown out of the water and only the *Victoire* left), he might bid defiance to the power of Europe, reign Sovereign of the Southern Seas, and lawfully make war on all the world – since the world would otherwise certainly deprive him of that liberty to which he had a right by the laws of nature. In a word he said so much that Misson resolved to follow his advice.

He called all hands and told them if any were averse to the following his fortune, which he promised should be the same to all, he would set them ashore, whence they might return home and no harm done.

'As we do not proceed upon the same ground with pirates, who are men of dissolute lives and no principles,' says the Frenchman, 'let us scorn to take their colours!' And he orders a white ensign for his emblem with a Liberty painted in the fly, and the motto *A Deo a Libertate* – for God and Liberty – to express their resolution and uprightness. 'And I do now,' said he, 'declare war against all as refuse us entry to their ports, and against all who shall not immediately surrender and give up what our necessities require. But in a more particular manner do I declare war against all European ships and vessels. At the same time,' says he, 'I recommend to you, my comrades, a humane and generous behaviour towards your prisoners, which will appear by so much more the effects of a noble soul, as I am satisfied we shall not meet the same treatment should our ill fortune, or more properly disunion or want of courage, give us up to their mercy . . .'

The proof of this novel philosophy was soon put to the test when, having shaped his course for the Spanish West Indies, he took an English sloop becalmed with her boats off St. Christopher's. Misson took out of her a couple of puncheons of rum and half-a-dozen hogshead of sugar (she was a New England sloop bound for Boston), and without offering the least violence to the men, or stripping them, he let her go. The master of the sloop was Thomas Butler, who owned he never met with so candid an enemy as Captain Misson.

There followed after this a number of engagements of a like kind of which I have no need to be very particular here, save that he took the *St. Joseph*, a galleon of 70 guns with 800,000 pieces-of-eight in silver and bar gold, and the next day a merchant ship bound for London from Jamaica, deep laden with sugars and about 4,000 pieces-of-eight . . .

Misson now called for all hands on deck to consult on the next course they should steer. In this debate the council divided, the Captain and Caraccioli were for stretching over to the African coast, the others for New England, alleging that the ship had a foul bottom and was not fit for so long a voyage. In the event the majority of votes favoured the Captain's side, and they accordingly shaped their course for the coast of Guinea. It was now by the greatness and goodness of Almighty Providence, that they fell in with us of the *Fortune* and saved the lives of those of us that were still alive . . .

This was the manner of my casting in my lot with this man, and my continuing in the *Fortune* as master under his command, for the coast of Angola. Here we met first with a Dutch ship (putting me in mind of Captain Blaise and the old *Virgin*) which was carrying a cargo of cloth, lace, wine, brandy and hardware. Eleven of the Dutch crew came into us, two of whom were sail-makers, one an armourer and one a carpenter. The rest we let go, who were not a little surprised at the regularity, tranquillity and humanity which they found among us new-fashioned pirates . . .

We had now run the length of Saldanhas Bay, about ten leagues to the northward of Table Bay, when we spied a tall ship, which instantly got under sail and hove out English colours. We made a clear ship and hove out our white ensign, and a smart engagement began. Misson gave orders for boarding, and the great number of fresh men he constantly poured in obliged the English to fly the decks and leave us masters of their ship though in this action the albino, Caraccioli, lost a leg. Misson promised, and gave, good quarter to the enemy and stripped not a man. We found on board some bales of English broadcloth, and about 60,000 in English crown-pieces and Spanish pieces-of-eight. The English, knowing whose hands they had fallen into, and charmed with Misson's humanity, thirty of them in three days' space desired to take on with him. He accepted 'em, but at the same time gave 'em to understand that in taking on with him they were not to expect they should be indulged in a dissolute and criminal life.

The English captain was killed in this engagement. Captain Misson was sorry for the death of the commander, whom he buried on the shore, and for whom he made a triple discharge of fifty small-arms and fired minute-guns . . . In addition, one of his men being a stone cutter, he raised a stone over his grave with these words – *Ici gist un brave anglais* – Here lies a brave Englishman . . .

We now doubled the Cape, and made the south end of Madagascar. Our coming to the island of Johanna, on the west side of this greater island, was the beginning of Misson's Grand Design. This was no less than for an 'asylum' as he called it, where he could raise and fortify a small town and make docks for shipping. This would give his men a place to call their own, said he, and a place where, when age or wounds had rendered them incapable of hardship, they might enjoy the fruits of their labour, and go to their graves in peace. The town they were to build was to be named Libertalia, and Misson announced that he would give us the name of Liberi, desiring that in the name should be drowned for ever the separate names of French, English, Dutch, African. He proposed also that our different languages should be incorporated in one common language that was made out of the many . . .

'And the Lord knows how that will carry,' muttered Read to himself. His pen had begun spluttering, and he laid it aside. The tide had receded while he'd been writing, and the sand was growing dry and firm beneath the soles of his feet, the sun beating through the thick-veined banana leaves in hot green light.

The island Misson had chosen for his settlement sloped southward from below the crystalline peaks of the interior, descending in successive bands of tropical forest, dense with filmy ferns, epiphytes and festoons of waxy tree-orchids, to the marshes and crocodile-haunted lagoons of the heat-bound coast where his ships swung at anchor.

On first landing, the impression had been melancholy, a wilderness of broken rice terraces and despoiled cocoa walks, the only sign of a population being the dung of their cattle, its dryness suggesting they'd left at least fourteen days back.

Hunting parties were sent out, however, both to explore the country and in the hope of making contact with the people. With the fever still on him, Read remained with the ships for the time being, but it was not long before men were reporting back, telling of butterflies, many of them bigger than a man's hand, moon-coloured, emerald and velvet black, and of fish, banded and spotted in the same wild hues. When a silver piece was laid under their tongues, it was noted that it remained untarnished, indicating they were good to eat. On the skirts of the marsh, lilies had been seen twice the height of a man, with spathes a foot long, while scouts exploring the north-western extremity of the island had come on a course of slaty rock in the falls of which they'd found stone ferns and what looked like the petrified outline of a huge wingless bird. It was in this same region that they'd glimpsed men with vast ears in which bright metal plates had been inserted, glittering like comets, which suggested that somewhere on the island there was silver to be got.

Nearly three weeks went by, however, before the population were encountered again. This time they found a village enclosed in a wood of thorn so thickly planted, they said, that not even a small dog could have got through it. The villagers were shy and disinclined to venture out, but using sign language, they at last persuaded several of the braves to accompany them back to the ships.

They looked a fine people, Read thought, with smooth dark skin and neat features. Two of them had blue eyes, he noticed. He took in the way Misson made much of them, sending them back to their village afterwards laden with baize, iron kettles and rum, and with a cutlass and a handful of scarlet beads for their headman. So that word soon getting round of such largesse, it wasn't long before Misson achieved his first objective, which was an audience with Johanna's Queen.

It was Caraccioli who told Read of the meeting.

'Salamonger! Captain! Your servant, sir! It is the Gods that sent the White Man!' the Queen had said, impressive in her toga-like *lamber* of striped purple silk. She caused a heifer to be killed, and in company with Misson sat down to eat.

'I swear by the Great God above,' she cried out in the middle of this feast, 'and by the Four Gods of the Four Quarters of the World, that I shall never kill Captain Misson's men so long as they kill not us, or may this liver which I now eat, be turned to poison in my belly and kill me instantly . . .'

All this while it seemed she'd been unable to keep her eyes off Caraccioli. Later, fascinated, she had asked if she might touch him.

'Thinking me a God,' said he, complacently, 'owing to my extreme whiteness.'

As he spoke, his eyes shone like smoky rubies in the dead pallor of his face. He was still wasted by the loss of his limb in the action of Table Bay, but had already mastered his crutches to the extent of being almost as nimble as a man with his full complement of limbs, negotiating every unevenness of the ground, steps even, as neatly as a hopping bird. For it was a bird he put Read in mind of, both in respect of his quick mind as well as his neat physical movements – though a curiously sinister bird.

'All the better for us,' Caraccioli was saying, 'as I told the Captain when the Queen made it known that it was her enemy, the King of Mohilla (an island two hours' sailing distance from here) who had destroyed the rice terraces and driven her people into the woods, "Here is an opportunity," says I, "to hold the balance between these two little kingdoms, and to our own advantage!"' And wedging his crutches tight beneath his armpits, Caraccioli rubbed his hands so briskly together that Read half expected sparks to fly out from between his palms.

'So the Captain now intends to carry the war into the King's country!' said Caraccioli, smiling.

When they returned from their foray Read saw the Mohillan prisoners. The men's thumbs were bound tightly to their ankles with plaited bark strips, and their heads were bowed in shame and exhaustion.

'Captain Misson marries now the Queen's sister,' Caraccioli was saying, as though he were describing the moves in a game of chess, 'and your humble servant likewise the niece of the Queen!'

'Then will this island soon be a-flutter with magpies black and white,' laughed Read, 'that is, if thou carry out thy duties fervently!' Though privately the thought of the albino's concupiscence appalled him.

Yet the prodigious energy of the man was undeniable. It was not so much a case of his word being made flesh, as of his word passing through the medium of his friend, Misson, to be instantly translated into the movement of peoples, the construction of harbours, moles, fortifications, the clearing and tilling of land, the building of houses, and so of the town which was eventually to become their El Dorado.

In spite of his ambivalent feelings Read could not remain untouched by him, could not resist the enticing possibility of progress that had begun taking root within his consciousness, heralding the first stages of an inward transformation away from the hand-to-mouth existence he had led for so long, and towards a new order and purpose.

History, continued. Some little time after this the Captain announced he intended going on a cruise. He hoped, he said, to meet with some East India ships and bring in some volunteers, for the number of subjects being the riches of a nation, he thought our little colony more in need of men than of anything else. Nor would any Libertarian be permitted, as pirates had been, to keep slaves out of the native population, since he personally abhorred even the name of slavery, and indeed he was well known to knock off the chains of any slaves he met with, making them free men besides, and complete sharers in his fortune.

Meanwhile he heartily recommended to those of us who felt the inclination, to choose, like him, a wife from among the black women of the island, but this not as pirates previously, who had each as great a seraglio as the Grand Turk at Constantinople, but rather as wives at home.

Before leaving to cruise the coast of Zanzibar, Captain Misson determined to frame first our island Constitution. This necessity had been put off until a suitable home for the Parliament had been built, but the men falling to very cheerfully, this was finished in about a fortnight . . .

Caraccioli opened the Session. Caraccioli, like a white flame caught in the sunlight slatting through the half-drawn shutters of the Council Chamber that smelt pleasantly of recently sawn wood. Gone was the pirate, and in his place the statesman. His speech, which in other circumstances would have made Read smile, enlarged on the abiding need for order in the new constitution. Were there no coercive laws, he gravely pointed out, the weak would always suffer, and everything tend to confusion . . .

'Supreme power,' he went on, glancing rapidly round the Council Chamber, 'must of necessity be lodged in the hands of one who will use it to punish vicious, and reward brave and virtuous actions!' At which he fervently banged the heel of his crutch on the floor. There was a brief, bemused silence, then the assembled men raggedly growled assent.

Such power, Caraccioli insisted, should be neither for life, nor should it be hereditary, but should terminate at the end of three years, when a new choice should be made by the State, or the choice confirmed for three years longer.

'By this means the ablest will always be at the head of affairs,' he promised, 'though their power being of short duration, no one will dare abuse it! I now propose,' cried he, raising his voice, 'that this chief among us should be our Captain, and that he have the title of Lord Conservator, and that there should attend him all the ensigns of Royalty!'

At this there was again a puzzled silence, followed almost immediately by a roar of approbation, as with one voice the pirates cried out: '*Vive le Capitaine Misson et son Lieutenant, le Scavant Caraccioli!*'

> *History, continued.* All that Caraccioli had laid before us was approved *nemine contradicente*, and Captain Misson chosen Conservator with power to create the great officers of State, and with the title of Supreme Excellence, Caraccioli to take his place during his absence. A Council, in which, as master of the old *Fortune*, I had the honour to be included, was now chosen without distinction of nation or colour. Under its auspices an equal division of our treasure was made, and also of the hump-backed island cattle for which we had bartered with the blacks of Johanna.
>
> Our men now began to enclose land for themselves, sowing it with Indian and European corn and other seeds which they had found on board their prizes. They also commenced the building of the fort . . .

From where he sat, making out a table of his new

possessions (for the moment he had laid the *History* aside), Read could smell the aromatic smoke from the burning brash of the trees they'd felled. He found it invigorating. In the last ten days since the Conservator's return, the volunteers he'd brought back with him had assisted in the felling of no less than one hundred and fifty trees. They were for the most past Travellers' trees – *Urania Speciosa* – their tall trunks affording, when tapped, a supply of cool pure water, and their wood excellent for all kinds of building. Cutting the timber at the water's edge, there was no necessity to haul it, so they could begin the building of the fort on the spot where the trees lay.

'1,354 pieces-of-eight,' wrote Read in a neat hand, 'being one-eighth of the total from the Dutch ship and the English, shared between myself and the eleven other lieutenants . . .

'Six stone jars of rum . . .'

Behind him the morning mists were unveiling the outline of Mount Ambolita with its ridges of crystalline rock in which the eye of the imagination could see gothic spires, cathedrals, the crenellations of crusader castles, or perhaps, seeing into the future, the city of Libertalia.

'3 bales of English broadcloth,

'6 kettles . . .'

Since Misson carried the warfare into Mohillan territory, the people of Johanna had ventured out from the protection of their villages fortified by prickly pear and thorny mimosa, and were cultivating the cocoa walks once more, restoring the neglected rice terraces. These rilled the island's lower slopes, the sun striking a chain of bright fire from the irrigation canals at which the people were so expert.

Two days before, three Mohillan ambassadors had arrived on the island to propose a peace.

'Oh ye Johannians,' they had cried, flourishing the

scarlet umbrellas of their office, having first kissed, then licked the Queen's legs for five or six minutes, 'do not conclude from your late success that fortune will always be favourable to you. She will not always give you the help of the Europeans...'

Seated below the fragrant leaves of the spice tree, they reminded their listeners how the sun rose, came to its meridian height and stayed not there, but declined in a moment. Their speech was soft and musical to the ear, their metaphors pleasing, as they invited their audience to reflect on the constant revolution of all sublunary affairs. How Nature being in continual movement, there was no stability in the world.

'Every tree and shrub,' said they, 'even our own bodies teach us that nothing is durable or can be counted upon...'

They withdrew, and the Queen, taking counsel with Misson, agreed to make peace on condition that the Mohillan King sent two of his children and ten of his nobility as hostages. This to be before the next moon...

They were now five days past the date and still no reply from the King.

'Then we'll sail to them for our answer!' Misson had said...

'3 dozen knives,
'10 widths of scarlet baize,
'6 hatchets...'

Absorbed, Read was a trader once more, able to dream of a landed estate gained in an afternoon, the locust years at last behind him, and returned to that point in his life when, high on hope, he had set out for the Slave Coast with the *Virgin*. Already, for an exchange of a few knives, he had acquired several head of the beautiful island cattle – some streaked like a tiger, some white with black spots, or black with white – together with a number of enormous blonde turtle-shells. The specie he had concealed in a small oak keg at the back of one of the many caves that honeycombed the ridges to the north of the island. He had taken meticulous bearings of the place, which, together with careful descriptive notes, he had reduced to a neat cryptogram for double security. In a little time there would be sufficient to purchase a farm – at home.

As the word came into his mind, his pen hesitated, and he saw quite clearly the big kitchen at Laverstock. An autumn morning, and the music of Sir Harry's pack drawing the Bridewell Soke several fields away was echoing back in a kingdom of sound from the plangent copper deeps of six great boiling-pans hung on the wall. And somewhere Dutchess . . . for a moment his eyes stung. But it was for such as this, after all, that he now laboured.

'2 dozen of felt hats,' his pen wrote slowly.

'3 dozen plain breeches (one pair buyeth an 800lb black ox!),'

He looked up . . . One of the black boys was coming towards him . . .

History, continued . . . this was that as a member of the Council I was to accompany the Conservator to Mohilla three hours' sailing time from here, for the obtaining an answer from the King of that island as to whether or no he agreed to our peace terms. So I closed my accounts with a sigh, having no longer the stomach as once I had for such adventures. And this same black mood pursued me to the quay where the Conservator was waiting. He questioning me what I had been at, says, 'Why, thou art becoming a shopkeeper at last, Soldier!' and laughs, at which, somewhat miffed, I replied that shopkeepers and farmers made the sturdiest soldiers.

I noticed, however, that when we got out on the water, the walls of our little fort had quite a fine air, and said so, the Conservator seeming quite pleased, and saying they would be something more formidable yet when he had taken to pieces the prize he'd taken off Arabia Felix. She being but a heavy sailor, he was preserving her cordage and knee-timber with all the bolts, eyes and other iron work etc., and planting her guns on two points of the harbour where he intended raising batteries.

In due course we anchored off the south-west end of the King's island. Through the glass, I could see men gathering at the sand-bar and a flash of scarlet which indicated the presence of the Mohillan court.

'Then shall we fire off a round both by way of a salute and as a warning,' says the Conservator. Shortly after which, a canoe puts out with one of their Princes as well as a number of fowls, bananas, yams and etc. by way of a sweetener. The Prince assured us earnestly that the King, for all that it was late in the day, did indeed comply with the terms Misson had proposed. He would send the hostages as promised, and desired a cessation of all hostility. At the same time he invited the Conservator on shore.

Our Johanna men on board dissuaded our accepting, saying we would do better to fire on the island and land to exact revenge. But Misson, fearing nothing, accepted the invitation, he being averse to everything that bore the face of cruelty, and thinking a bloody revenge – if necessity did not enforce it –spoke a grovelling and timid soul.

Thus we went, but armed our boat's crew. We were received by the King with a horn of honey in one hand, and a piece of beef in the other as a demonstration of friendship, and dined with him under a tamarind tree . . .

The Conservator at last giving the signal that they

should leave, the King rose, assigning four of his men to conduct them back through the mangrove swamp that lay between their metropolis and the sand-bar where the longboat awaited them.

It was coming towards the start of the rainy season, and the still day was hot and overcast, the vegetable stink of the swamp heavy in the air. Sweating, they walked in single file along the narrow raised path which, when the rains came, would disappear for six months beneath a sheet of brown water. Two of the King's guides walked ahead with lances, Misson behind them armed with cutlass and pistol. The eight armed men of the boat crew followed, while Read, with the remaining two guides, brought up the rear.

He had just paused in his path (his eye being caught momentarily by a violent flash of blue beyond the imprisoning hoops of the mangroves) when he heard a strange, low ullulation. He stepped back. There was a sudden swish, and a whack! and Read saw that there was an arrow quivering in the wood of the tree to his right.

The next moment, the black in front turned and lunged at him. Read heard a pistol discharge, and the man fell against him, his head shot away. A pandemonium of firing now broke out, below which could be heard the insidious whip of arrows. Read turned. Ten yards to his left the crown of a tree was moving. He swung round and fired, and a body plummetted out of the leaves and splashed into the swamp. In the uproar of cursing and shouting which ensued, he became aware that someone to the front and right of him was trying with terrible ineffectuality to scream. Then he saw that one of the crewmen was standing over Misson, and that the Conservator had been hit by an arrow in the throat. He was attempting to wrench at the haft, and with every movement the blood jetted, geranium-coloured, into the air.

History, continued . . . all our bravery would have stood us in little stead, had not the report of our pistols alarmed not only those waiting for us with the longboats, but those of our friends on the *Victoire*. They, hearing this fire, sent immediately the yawls and longboats well manned, and being guided by the noise, put our assailants to flight. We lost by this treachery of the King's seven slain outright, and eight wounded, including our Captain. He, poor gentleman, continuing in his agony to try and pluck out the arrow lodged in his throat, we were forced to tie his hands. But he died soon after with the loss of blood.

So passed away Misson! He being a successful trader, who had been in a good way to establishing himself with a little commonwealth of his own . . .

He was carried to the ship and thence to the island of Johanna. The news of his death travelling before us, his young wife came to us with her little child, asking that we would go with her to perform the last ceremonies to her husband's dead body. This we did, she leading us into the plantation walk, where we found a great many Johanna men and women sitting under the shade of the plantains round the corpse, which had been laid on the ground and covered with flowers.

She first embraced them round, and then the Europeans one by one, and after these ceremonies she poured out a number of bitter imprecations against the Mohilla men whose treachery had darkened her husband's eyes and made him insensible of her caresses. He who was her first love, to whom with her virginity she had also given her heart – for there is among the blacks love, tenderness and generosity which might shame us, and moral sense too . . .

She then proceeded in his praises, calling him the

joy of infants, the love of virgins, the delight of the old, and the wonder of the young, adding that he was strong and beautiful as the cedar, brave as the bull, tender as the kid and loving as the ground-turtle. Then, giving her child to one of the women, she knelt down by the side of her husband's body, and brushing aside the flowers that covered him, put her arms about him and kissed him, then stretched herself along his side as though they had been in a bed together . . .

The movement was so trustfully beautiful that Read caught his breath. In the same instant he became aware of a terrible emptiness in his own breast, a longing for love so overwhelming that it brought the tears into his eyes.

At that moment the woman stirred, then raised herself, and for a second Read thought he saw something glittering like a sprat between her fingers. Then she suddenly gave an ungainly lurch, at the same time furiously driving the knife down under her left breast.

History, continued. Prayers were read over him, and colours flown as would have been done for a captain on a Queen's ship. His sword and pistols lay on the coffin draped in a ship's flag, and as many minute-guns shot over it as the Conservator had years —which was twenty-four.

They dug their graves in a garden of water-melons, fencing them in with a pallisade to prevent their bodies being rooted up by the wild hogs, of which there were plenty in those parts.

'Three days after,' said Read, addressing the young man across the table, 'the blacks came down in two great bodies, at dead of night, each man carrying a piece of meat to throw at the dogs to keep them from barking, and for no known cause they fired the fort.

Caraccioli they hacked to death, as they did forty men and women with their children. We escaped only with our lives.' At which Read's throat closed suddenly and he choked.

A considerable silence fell.

'Jack Rackham says you was the toast of the taverns in Port au Prince . . .' began the young man at last.

'Was I?' said Read, grimacing. Then he roused himself.

'You mean the *Sourire de Venise?*' he ventured softly, and as he said it his mind swerved capriciously, and with great clarity he saw himself sitting alone in an upper room with an unlatched shutter banging again and again and again in the hot wind, and on the table before him a knife, razor-sharp, that he intended using on himself – but couldn't.

'Aye that,' he resumed, 'and the *Oeil Qui Voit Tout* was another . . .' And this time it was a song.

> 'Here's to de cock, who make lub to de hen,
> Crow till he hoarse, and make lub again
> Here's to de hen what neber refuses,
> Let cock pay compliment whenebber he chooses . . .'

The song had a sad fall to it, and must have accompanied some forgotten incident or other, for it turned his heart like a love song, which in a way it was. Then he remembered a man's face being associated with the song. A face of which he had once more become aware during the unreckonable stretches of time after the deaths of Bellamy and the quartermaster, and later of Misson when, once more sick with fever, and overcome with disappointment and despair, he had restlessly haunted the waterside rum shops. A face he had seen before, but in so different a context and so long ago that he was no longer able to place it. A face which, at the time, seemed strangely omnipresent, even in dreams, though that might have been the effect of the calenture or fever, for he imagined through the fever that he'd glimpsed it not only in Port au Prince, but in other harbours he'd called in at during the whole ill-remembered period.

Tall and spare, rather older than Read, the man was only singular in that no one appeared to know much about him, and in that he was not flamboyant in the style of those other gentlemen of fortune who had gold rings in their ears studded with gems ripped from half-a-hundred cathedrals, and who played ducks and drakes with heavy gold coins whose value no one even dared estimate. This man favoured clothes of the plainest, rubbed blue, rusty black, and there was an aloofness about him, a dryness, a solitariness, that momentarily caught Read's attention. This in dives that he perpetually frequented where dagger thrusts were so common that anyone stabbed was left to lie on the floor till the dancing stopped. The man for his part had given no sign of recognition, and Read in consequence had been forced to ask himself whether he must have been mistaken after all.

'He says you once broke a man's back with your bare hands . . .' suggested the young man respectfully from across the table.

'No, my dear young sir, not that . . .' said Read without rancour, and stroked the parrot's head, 'your friend's lying.'

'Very likely, if it's Rackham that says so,' returned the young man agreeably. 'He's a very notable whimsey of a commander, is Rackham!'

'I mind Rackham in the *Kingston*,' volunteered Read suddenly, 'with two Queen's sloops bearing down on him, and he, on the sudden quitting his ship, found himself in the woods at the back of Prince's without either small-arms or ammunition to defend himself. Nothing but bales of silk stockings and laced hats he'd taken off some ship or other . . .' And again Read raised a smile.

'That's Rackham!' cried the young man, encouraged, 'the red-haired son of a whore ever loved such trumpery! Though it was not of that but of Haman's sloop that I wished to speak, sir . . .'

Read looked at the boy. His pleasant sun-burned face had gone momentarily doubtful, as though he were hoping for recognition of some kind.

'If you are thinking to ask me whether or not I remember hearing of your part in the taking of it, Mr. Bonny, yes indeed I recollect it!' said Read dryly. 'As I remember, you was observed going several times on board the ship when it was in the harbour at Providence, pretending to some business with Jack Haman, whose constant employment, as we all know, was plundering the Spaniards about Cuba and Hispaniola. I'm told, though, you went always when Jack was on the shore, did ye not? The better ye might discover how many hands he had working for him and whether they kept watch, and where they lay at night?' The boy had begun to look confident. 'Then one dirty night, or so I'm told, you and Jack Rackham and eight others, all being well armed, takes a boat round one in the morning and rows it out to the sloop which is lying in near shore . . .'

'. . . and goes straight to the cabin, Soldier,' continued the young man animatedly, 'where we sees two fellows lying who belongs to the sloop . . . They waking . . .'

'. . . ye tells 'em you might be obliged to blow their brains out unless . . .'

'. . . so we takes over, slip cable and drive down to the harbour . . .'

'. . . where I'm told the Fort hailed you and asked where you was going at that time of night . . .'

'. . . and we returns them answer our cable's parted,

and that we've nothing but a grappling-iron on board which won't hold us, after which Jack puts out a small sail to give us steerage way . . .'

The younger man looked keenly into Read's eyes, as though trying to assess the weight of his responses, but Read had turned away and was gently scratching the parrot's poll.

'When we gets to the harbour's mouth and knows we can't be seen by any of the other ships owing to the darkness of the night, we hoists all the sail we have and stand out to sea . . .'

Unwillingly thrilled, Read raised his head. The young man's beautiful grey eyes looked gratified. 'Then we calls up the two men from below and asks, will they be of our party? But they not being inclined, we order 'em give our service to Mr. Haman, and tell him, we'll send him his sloop when we've done with it!'

Again Read smiled.

'Well, Soldier?'

'Well?'

'Will you make one of us? Rackham's in want of artists. The sloop's forty ton, and one of the swiftest sailors ever built. "There goes Jack Haman!" they used to say when it was he that had her. "Catch him if you can!"'

'I'm no artist, Mr. Bonny . . .'

'Soldier, before we crack another bottle you ought to know something. Jack Rackham's wanting you for his quartermaster . . .' There was a silence, then the young man held out his hand. 'Shake on it, Soldier?'

Read stared at the proffered hand, noticing its neat shape, and that the nail on the right forefinger had been thickened and bruised violet by a blow. As he did so a curious repetition came into his mind. He heard again the high, hungry sound of fiddles playing, saw the soldiers easing their calloused yellow feet out of their cracked boots to go gravely dancing on the spring grass. Then the woman swept past, holding out her arms in a gesture not to be refused. So now. 'And the Charioteer falls yet again!' he thought to himself, and took the young man's hand in his. It felt pleasantly familiar, thin and hard, and the grip was firm.

13

Two years after, habitués of Sally Turner's were still perplexed that the Soldier should so suddenly have gone back on the account. There were some who said he'd been tricked into thinking they were going to sea as privateers, others that it was a matter of settling an old debt, yet more that it concerned a woman which, in a sense, it had. At the time Read himself would have found it hard to explain such impetuosity unless as the result of despair, but it was only when he got aboard Haman's sloop that he felt an unfamiliar lightening of heart, a shifting of the heavy burden of disappointment and barely endurable loss, a sensation that youth might after all be returning. And as though to mark this he gave up smoking *banghe*.

It turned out that Rackham's was a young crew. Hardly a man over thirty, and many of them, like Read, pardoned under the Amnesty of two years before, but by now weary of working on shore and itching to be back at their old trade. Meanwhile Haman's sloop was all the young man, Bonny, had predicted. Her size and speed rendered her especially fit for working the creeks and bays of the northern coastline, where she could also water and careen in safety. Rackham himself, still nominally armed with a commission from the Governor to privateer upon the Spaniards, not only had an eye on the windward passage from Jamaica (which all good sailors not staying for convoy took as the short-cut to England), but on the lucrative smaller fry, like turtlers and merchant sloops frequenting the inner shipping lanes. Read had not long joined the ship when Rackham, in accordance with the wishes of the ship's council, stretched over to Berry Island to search for prizes.

So it was that, unthinkingly almost, Read resumed a familiar way of life, though like his mates he tended to consider it as an occupation more to do with trading than piracy. Nevertheless, it crossed his mind from time to time, as it did some of theirs, that like some unfortunate spit-dog he might have put himself on a wheel that could prove difficult to get off, so that the ultimate goal of riches and respectability, after which most of them hankered, might elude him after all. For the time being, however, he was content to let the matter rest.

> *December 25th* . . . during this time young Bonny much about me asking details of my former life, etc. which I not totally prepared to give, though his address was polite enough, he still being only a young lad and full of spirit . . . On the third day of searching the shipping lanes we sighted a Frenchman. We struck our Jack and hoisted our Black with the intention of going after him, at which to our great surprise the pretended Frenchman did likewise, accompanying this action with a brave Christmas salute of bolts and nails and any other old iron in true buccaneer fashion, the two captains entertaining one another after with toddy and lemon. After which a chapter from the Bible was read out, followed by the combined crews drinking Christmas Day to one another with the greatest show of politeness . . .

'Soldier!'

Read was smoking, his eyes absently searching the shore where the plumed outline of the palms met the streaked moonlit water. He turned, resenting the interruption (drink had made him melancholy, and his mind had been running on Madagascar), and saw the lad, Bonny. The young man's handsome face looked strained in the soft moonlight, and Read could smell rum on his breath.

'Soldier?'

'Aye?'

'Who is it, Soldier?'

'What fool's game is this? All cats may be grey in the dark, but I know thee for what thou art, Jack Bonny, which is a plaguey bitch's baby!'

'Is that all though knowest of me then, Soldier?'

There was a challenging note in the young man's voice. Read, disconcerted, removed the pipe from his mouth and began industriously scraping out the dottle.

'Give us your hand, Soldier!' said the young man suddenly, and his hand closed over Read's in a dry masterful grip.

'Did ye ever notice I hadn't a beard, Soldier?'

'Damn my blood, Mr. Bonny! I've no concern with your beard nor anyone else's come to that!' At which Bonny gave a quiet laugh, and in one shocking movement carried Read's hand to his cheek. When, having rubbed it roughly back and forth against the jaw-line, he conveyed it deftly into the bosom of his shirt.

The world tilted. Read dropped his pipe. Stupefied, he found his hand being pressed against the breast of a woman.

'O Jesus save us!' groaned Read with all the mortification of a woman.

'Did you never once suspect? Did ye never guess how all this long time I was so greatly fancying you, Soldier?'

The sinewy pressure continued. Feeling that at any moment she might faint, Read managed to trap Bonny's remaining hand against her side.

'Give us a kiss, Soldier!' And before Read could strain away, Bonny's mouth was covering hers like some great sugared flower. Then slowly, beneath

Read's firmly closed lips, the flower opened. But into a night of such darkness, that Read stepped back trembling.

'What is it, sweetheart?' Bonny's slim hand now working free from Read's.

'Sure Mr. Bonny!' Neatly trapping it once more.

'Ann to you, my darling!' Freeing it.

'Ann!' repeated Read foolishly, staring into the girl's upturned face. How drunk was she? How far (if at all) might she be trusted with Read's own secret?

Bonny's face looked oddly remote. It was very pale and the expression was reckless.

'Mistress Ann!' said Read, fighting for time, then (resolving to tell her after all) – 'Ann!'

The relief was so great that she began to laugh.

'Come, Ann!' firmly conveying Bonny's hand (limp and submissive now) to her groin.

Bonny fetched a deep sigh and leaned so heavily against Read that she all but lost her balance. A brief silence fell.

'Sure, Soldier, thou art not wounded?'

'No, not wounded . . .'

'Since a child, then?'

'Since a child!'

'Dry up my bones! Devil take you, Soldier! You've capsized me! You scurvy whore!'

There was a cracked sob, then Bonny began to laugh.

'Two of us, by all that's Holy! Yard-arm to yard-arm! And I dipping my colours as though you'd been a Queen's ship!'

Drunkenness had mysteriously returned. They suddenly threw their arms round each other. Outrageously kissed. Again and again and again, swaying timelessly in one another's arms under the quiet moon.

In the days following they sought out unknown paths, hidden backwaters.

'Dear Christ! I'd be ever happy to roll into the very

scuppers for a sweet moment of repose with thee, Soldier!'

'Sailors, they get all the money,' (sang Read softly)
'Soldiers they get none but brass,
I do love a jolly sailor,
Soldiers they may kiss my arse.
Oh my little rolling sailor,
Oh, my little rolling she;
I do love a jolly sailor,
Soldiers may be damned for me...'

And again they kiss.

How white! they exclaim at such moments, how round, deep, soft, cool, quick, funny, witty, tender! How sweet the breaths of women! How gentle their ways! Tho' powerful strong too! And as for one another's eyes! (into which they gaze enraptured) How fine! Finer than the finest of Brazilian sparklers! Read's especially, though Bonny's... Then fleetingly Read remembers other eyes, grey as Bonny's, but belonging to a tall spare man haunting the rum shops round Port au Prince, as well as sometimes her drugged dreams. Then Read forgets them, for there are their hands to consider...

'Nebba see de day
Dat Soldier run away,
Nebba see um night
Dat Soldier cannot fight...'

sings Bonny, tenderly stroking the ribbed scar that runs over Read's knuckles and up into her armpit; then she locks their fingers together. All the knotting and splicing and scraping and sharpening and priming of pistols these wondrous woman's hands have done! And come to that, how have they conspired all this time to so fool the first sex? How drink so manly? Sing so? Not to say dress, crap and piss so, and that last in the bogs of a Queen's own ship! And now to come alongside one another and tie up so snug at last! At which Read turned and suddenly asked, 'Rackham, what of him?'

'What of him?' Bonny laughed shortly. Her Soldier must know what a passionate whimsical creature her own dearest Bonny is. Quick to throw a man over her shoulder if of a mind to, and dislocate his neck if need be. And that Jack Rackham's neither the first nor likely to be the last she'll splice with, since there was one before him and yet another before that, who was poor James Bonny, that was her husband before she tired of him, weighed anchor and warped into another hammock. Reported for it too, what's more, by one Richard Turney (who she'd see hanged one day), so that the Governor threatened her with a whipping unless she repaired her ways.

She wouldn't deny, nonetheless, that in his softer moments Rackham could be wonderful open-handed, though like all men when the fit was on him, he could also be raging and mean as an Eastern potentate with a seraglio of porcupines . . . Yes, she'd been untrue, and she'd very likely be untrue again, that being her way. Though one day, before it was too late, she intended going on the respectable account, though not yet . . . And very likely not reeved into the matrimonial block with Jack Rackham either, since he was hardly enough of a gentleman . . .

This during an expedition in the longboat to get water. They filled the barrels at an outfall, and leaving them, set off in search of wild hog, following the course of the small fast river by way of the natural escalations in the limestone over which it cascaded. Its passage left a soft mist that collected about the curtains of creeper through which they pressed, eddying beneath the still canopy of silk-cotton and ceiba trees in which the monkeys chattered.

They climbed a number of such natural steps, twisting past tree trunks and stepping over fallen logs sunk deep in moss and fern, then paused, soaked with sweat, to find they had halted before a fair-sized cleft in the rock wall. This was only partially concealed by trailing plants, and, with no other object than that of serving their curiosity, they pushed through. They felt their way tentatively along the dripping rock face for some yards until, glimpsing greenish daylight ahead, they emerged beside a small feed of the river which ran out from a deep spring pushing up through the white sand of the bottom.

January 2nd . . . this was like some green Paradiso. Having nothing to fear we laid aside our weapons and, stripping off our clothes, bathed there. I feeling oddly in my unaccustomed nakedness, such as one might feel who is born anew by baptism. And I was minded of Mother Ross and her discourse on the power of clothes, and how they could make a person, viz. how the wearing of breeches could make a man of a brave woman, and how she could accomplish things dressed thus, that she would not be able to accomplish in her own woman's clothes. And this had struck so deep into my understanding that I began to speculate on this *shedding* of clothes, which is like the putting off of the outer man, which, unlike the innocent Arawaks here who go naked everywhere, is of such importance to us Europeans, we being able to judge instantly of a man whether he be rich or no from his clothes, and of what profession. And it seemed to me I had been forced all my life to use clothes as a protection and as a disguise, and that this had governed my life until now. But that now, being known as I was known by my new friend, I was, not for the first time, obliged to simulate, and could be at peace, like a spring unwound. She lying beside me, the shadows of the leaves spotting her as though she had been a beautiful hind lying deep in a brake, so that my heart was quite conquered by her loveliness. And neither of us at the time feeling any press, even to search for meat in the shape of hogs as we was sent to do, but being free rather to look around, which all my life being subject to necessity, I had not been able to do . . .

January 7th . . . returning again to our Paradiso, I much amused my companion, who is of a more energetic and mercantile cast of mind than I (being ever concerned with the *cost* and *use* of things) by bringing with me a quill and a little ink made from water and charcoal finely ground, and setting myself to try and reproduce in my journal something of what I saw, viz. plants, especially the tremulous mimosa that I had also seen at Wydah, wonderful in that it withdraws when handled, as if ashamed – also a curious fern growing in a tree in a circular nest that has water in it, and into which the leaves of the tree fall when they die, which the fern then consumes . . . as well as a little bird we saw, like a hovering atom of emerald and amethyst and ruby o'erspread with a delicate netting of gold, sipping like a moth from the flowers, which my friend would have caught if she could and brought back for the others to see. But I, preventing her, said we should seek to keep our Paradiso as it was, though truth to tell in the old days I would have shot any such strange creature the closer to examine it. Though now I let 'em alone, and my friend also. For I must confess there is between us now a most gentle sympathy and kindness, she having laid aside her rough boy's manner, and speaking things to me that have both a strangeness and a sweetness in them not encountered by me with anyone, and which after led us to actions that I once, unknowingly, might have been ashamed even to think of, but which by now – no such thing . . .

January 10th . . . It is by this route that my body has at last become my friend. For there was a time, and that not long ago, when I was accustomed to think of my woman's body as a wound (this both at the time of my marriage with Gerhardi and afterwards at the death of the quartermaster). A wound deep and hidden. Men's bodies in this respect being neat and well found. Crested, as I remember being told the old Tudor Queen said sadly before some battle. She spoke then of having a man's heart in a woman's body, she, poor brave Prince, being cloven and liking it not. But my body, in ever appearing to please my friend so, is something for which I am truly grateful, and ever will be so long as I remain upon this earth. Today it came once more in to my head what Mother Ross said which was, 'Ah, that you can never say!' when I told her such affections were foreign to me and not to my taste . . .

. . . So we continue very merry together and mighty content in one another. So that sometimes, looking in the water and seeing our two faces mirrored, it seems another world trembles there, heaven-like, which we inhabit just so long as the days last . . .

January 13th . . . Today I asked her, 'Wherein was thy beginning?' I being curious to know, for she had so white a skin, this being a sign, so it is said, of some greatness inherited in the blood . . .

'Sure, sweetheart, you would have it that I was found in a pretty silk-lined basket hanging from the knocker of a Lord's door!' says she, laughing. 'The truth is, my dear, I was born in gaol, to which my poor mother's mistress committed her, she having missed three silver teaspoons... though I am of some gentility,' continues she, 'for my father was a Cork attorney. This attorney's wife removing to the country for a change of air, my mother, who was their maidservant, warps into his hammock for to keep him company. The mistress returning, and having her suspicions, and reckoning that one good turn deserves another, hides three silver spoons in my mother's trunk and sends for the constable. They breaking the trunk open and finding the spoons, carries her before the Justice. But it wasn't long before my father's wife's conscience smote her and my mother was reprieved. But the attorney never forgave his wife, and he and my mother left Cork together for ever and came to Carolina, where he has a plantation to this day...'

While she lived with her father she had been looked upon as one that would be a good fortune, wherefore it was thought her father expected a good match for her...

'But I spoiled it all, my honey,' says she, 'for without his consent I married a young fellow which was Bonny, who belonged to the sea, and was not worth a groat, which provoked my father to such a degree that he turned me out of doors... So that, my dear, is that,' says she.

'Ah then, my dear,' says I, 'thou art a bastard like myself and none the worse, and I love thee for it. And if I could, I would write it down in poetry such as I used to read with Lady Laverstock, my old mistress. But love,' says I, taking her hand, 'greatly prefers the deed to the writing of it...'

The next time they returned to the Paradiso they had not been long there when they were alarmed by the sound of rapid fire and shouting, and a terrified peccary blundered past them a minute or two later, bleeding heavily from a wound in the shoulder . . .

January 24th . . . Rackham called me late into the master-cabin on some pretext or other, and catching me suddenly by the shoulder, offered to cut out my weasand, saying how dare I make it with young Bonny, he having watched us being so close and going off alone together in the longboat and etc. —he being, he'd have me know, all the time a woman in men's clothes and his common-law wife.

I, standing as steady as I could, asked him how he came to go against his own Articles in thus taking a woman on board, knowing full well how if it was discovered it would enflame the men and endanger us all. At which he flung aside the knife but yet stood glowering, and I found myself thinking, 'There'll be no more green times with thee, my bonny lass, for he'll be ever watching and suspecting of us now!' And I was getting right down in the mouth at the thought (for we have had sweet hours together), when she comes in on a sudden, and coolly taking him by the arm, tells him straight out of my secret, counselling him at the same time to keep the thing close from the rest of the company. This, after considering a moment, he readily promised, both in his own as well as in our interest, laughing greatly at what she told him, and discovering thereafter no further trace of jealousy, though addressing me in private with a familiarity that makes me fear he would as lief now take on two wives.

So by her cleverness are we enabled to continue in our own quiet way some little while longer, though she being of so sprightly and impatient a nature, will likely cast off soon enough, though no harm done . . .

So on into the spring rains, and on into the tropical

summer with moons so brilliant it was possible to read by their light...

June 30th... Venus so bright she cast a little shade in her own right, light enough for me to see my friend's dear face by it... We three are now become what you might call a triplicity together. They wilder than I, and though merry enough, not prudent, so that I from time to time begin to experience the old unease at my continuing in such a life, wishing rather that I might have my own ship and trade for myself as I have all along intended. Though she and I continue very agreeable together, and no doubt always will, her great kindness towards me having changed me in so wonderful a manner from what I was. For it is now as the forecastleman with the bottle-glass legs foretold long ago, that I would come by way of the Hanged Man to know myself, and to rest quiet, being sure at last what manner of creature I was. Though she took up the cards not long ago and 'Soldier! Soldier!' cries she, turning up first the Fool and after the Moon, and then pushing them aside with a grave face, forbearing to read 'em...

July 14th... a ship was sighted beating up on the windward quarter, and through the glass it could be seen she was flying an English flag. When we struck our Jack and hauled up our black silk pennant, the ship responded by striking hers, and without firing a shot, hove to. She and I stood by as Rackham questioned the crew off her, and there came in a man I was very sure I knew, having recognised him for the very Man (or so I thought) I had often seen in the taverns of Port au Prince and other places too long ago to recollect. 'Have we not met before, sir,' says I, going up to take him by the hand. 'Many people say that,' says he with a smile, though with an uncomprehending look, yet taking my hand none the less. His name, he told us, was Joseph, declining to give any other, and that he was a surgeon. He would make one of the company, he said, provided he was not asked to sign Articles, he being a Quaker, and further, that if need be, he could put it out as an excuse that he had been pressed into the pirates' service against his will. 'But I shall make myself as useful to thee as I can,' says he to Rackham, 'though thou knowest it is not my business to meddle when we stand out to fight.' 'No, no,' says Rackham, 'but you may meddle a little when we share the money!' 'Those things are useful to furnish a surgeon's chest,' says Joseph and winks at him, 'but I shall be moderate!'

August 10th . . . we came straight out yesterday on a merchant sloop bound for Hispaniola, and engaged her, thinking to see her strike her flag, but her captain being a sturdy rogue fired on us, and we were hard put to get in with her. But we clapping our helm hard a-weather, and letting go the lee braces of the main-topsail, we laid it aback, and so our ship fell athwart the merchant ship, at which we immediately poured in a broadside of star- and chain-shot . . . Their crew being in the utmost confusion, and their ship having fresh way, run their bowsprit into the forepart of our main-shrouds, so that they could not easily get clear of us, and thus we lay locked. At which Joseph, for fear they might get away from us, and us lose a prize, goes forward with three men to lash the ship's bowsprit to our mainmast. The marvellous thing was this man's negligence of danger, seeming, as some said, to turn back the bullets as he worked, and only having recourse now and then to a little flask of spirits he had with him in his pocket . . .

August 14th . . . sure he is a very extraordinary fellow, this Joseph, his address being so quiet, and his performance in action so very different. He ties well with Rackham who, though a good seaman, has too much of the wild and ungovernable in his temper. Generous on occasion to extravagancy, then quite otherwise, and very much of the coxcomb as to his dress, affecting always to array himself in calico – hence their calling him 'Calico Jack' . . . When this Joseph is with him, however, he shows another side, as though Joseph was able to bring out the rational man in him, and as though with perseverance he might, like another Misson, be brought to become a good trader, and a man capable and worthy of making a Commonwealth. Certainly this Joseph has engaged Rackham's respect, and, I believe, the respect of us all. Strange circumstance that I find him so like that other Man, in which I thought I can only be mistaken . . .

14

Journal, September 4th . . . We have now come into the back end of the year, the weather in these parts hanging sullen, with frequent calms and only faint breezes, which seem like to halt our enterprise for the time being, since all we have to show for these last weeks are seven fishing boats. These we took two leagues off Harbour Island on the Florida coast, along with their nets and other useful tackle, the whole amounting to ten pounds, no great booty, though some of their men joined with us. There is talk now among the ship's company of doubling the Cape and going out to make our fortune in the Gulf of Mocha or the Red Sea, but Joseph discouraged us with this, saying it was a great way, and dangerous by reason of the contrary winds at this time of the year, and that we had best stay as we were for the time being. He showed us another side of his skill yesterday in the treating of one of our men, a negro, injured in the getting one of the fishing boats. This was that a pistol went off accidentally, hitting the man in the foot, so that the ball ploughed up the length of his leg, breaking out at the groin and occasioning him much pain. It was the opinion of all, since the wound began rapidly to mortify, that the fellow's leg must be cut off, and that his life could not be saved without it, since mortification had touched the marrow of the bone and the tendons were also mortified. Joseph gave out that his opinion was otherwise, and that the wound must be probed, in the which he asked me to assist, having learned that I had some skill in that way. We accordingly searched every part of the leg where he suspected the mortification had touched it, and in a word he cut off a great deal of mortified flesh, in which the poor fellow felt no pain. So, under Joseph's guidance, we proceeded till he brought the vessels which he had cut to bleed, and the man to cry out; then with commendable skill he reduced the splinters of the bone and set it, and tenderly laid the man to rest, who found himself much easier than before . . .

September 14th . . . at the first opening of the bandage on Samson's leg there appeared a long red streak running from the wound upwards to the middle of the man's thigh. When I saw it, I asked Joseph how long the poor fellow could live, and he turned and looking gravely up at me answered, 'As long as thou canst!' So that for a moment I was greatly struck, supposing he meant the life of this man and my own were in some manner unknown to me tied together. Joseph now went to work again, opening the leg in two places above the wound, and again cutting out a great deal of mortified flesh, occasioned, it seems, by the too great pressing of the bandage . . .

September 15th . . . we being arrived at Hispaniola and Rackham being minded to take on water and go searching for wild hogs, Joseph and I intend going ashore in the longboat, I with the object of paying a visit to my son, Scipio, and Joseph engaged in some privy business of his own in Port au Prince . . .

Scipio seemed only half to remember. He kept hiding behind Apolline and giggling whenever Read tried to address him. He was speaking only French now, the sweet slow French of the Creole, and Apolline his foster-mother had re-christened him Toussaint. She made him stand on a box with his hands clasped. '*Venez mon dieu*,' she encouraged him to intone for Read. '*Venez, mon doux Sauveur, venez regner en moi au centre de mon coeur.*'

September 16th . . . I left Scipio, having paid Aunt Pol a greater sum than usual, for in my heart I cannot but accept I have seen Scipio for the last time, though he continuing very happy with his foster-mother. I being yet not able to offer him the settled life he should have, this seems the best course. Yet it is a grief, we once planning to sail to England in a ship of our own and buy us a farm together, for I liked to think that I could in some way atone for the sad circumstances of his childhood . . . I returned to the ship to find the captain had taken and killed a number of cattle further up the coast, also some of the wild hogs that abide in the forest there, besides finding three Frenchmen by the waterside that had themselves been hunting hogs. These, whether freely or by compulsion I am unable to learn, came on board, and there was much drinking of punch. In the course of which, while I was about the fo'c'sle, I heard something I misliked out of the mouth of one Zachary Jewell, who said unkind things of Joseph going to Port au Prince, and asking for what purpose did he go and etc. – though he being far gone in liquor at the time, not much was made of it, Rackham and the rest carrying on much as usual, very wild and merry.

I went afterward with Joseph again to see the man that had the wounded leg, and found on examination that the red streak had gone off, and the flesh begun to heal, and matter to run, which was a service also to me who had asked Joseph how long this poor fellow would live, and Joseph replying 'As long as thou canst,' which made me think that in some way my own days were numbered.

During these times that I was aiding Joseph with his business, my mind turned often to the old times on board the *Ruby*, and I told him how I had determined then to go for a surgeon's apprentice when I got home, but in a foolish moment had gone for a soldier instead. Joseph assured me there was yet time for me to do this, I being still young, and he questioned me closely as to whether I indeed liked the life of a pirate. To this I replied that I was coming to hate such a life, it always ending in profligacy such as drinking away our prize-money and etc. rather than turning honest, at which he looked kindly on me and asked whether I might one day give up such a life and turn honest. And I thought (seeing his gentle look), 'Yes, for you! Did you but know it!' But I held my tongue, and bent my eyes on the ground so that he should not see what was in them. For truth is, that for all my reserve, I believe love to have again found me out in this disguise, in consequence of which I grow daily more detesting it, wishing to live my true nature . . .

It was two days after that Read, going to check the lowering tackle of the longboat, heard raised voices and recognised those of Joseph and Zachary Jewell.

'. . . and thou art a right blab!' Joseph was saying, and made to turn on his heel, at which Jewell, a huge man but light on his feet, landed him a back-hander on the mouth. Joseph reeled back, and from where she stood Read could see the colour draining from his face and a trickle of blood go worming down his nostril to his chin.

'Challenge me if it's a lie, then!' shouted Jewell, 'and we'll be resolving this business with swords like gentlemen as to who is blabbing or no . . .'

September 18th . . . this altercation, though I was ignorant of the cause, put me mightily on the hum, knowing Jewell for a hasty and dangerous rogue, and that Joseph's religion forbids him absolutely to kill even in self-defence, to the extent that when in

> action he is obliged to fire at the mast or into the air etc. He nevertheless agreed to meet Jewell at an appointed place on shore, no doubt in the hope of persuading him at the last moment (though in this he won't succeed), or of frightening him by firing through his sleeve or some such thing. Fearing for so good a life, I stept forward, offering to act as second rather than the boatswain as is customary, but privily resolving to insult Jewell and face him myself at a time earlier than that arranged between the two of them . . .

On land it was only just light, and sultry. The morning wind they call the Doctor not yet blowing in from the sea. Mist clinging to the still arches of the palms.

'What care I for his Quakerishness,' Jewell was shouting, 'or which one I takes on, for I'll have his throat out at the end of the day, for your friend's a spy!' And he turned suddenly and discharged his pistol. Read, closing on that instant with him, felt the charge scorch her cheek, her ear go painfully heavy with the noise of it. She was at once possessed by a kind of reasoned fury and her sword, coming suddenly alive in her hand, swooped and snickered, pinking Jewell in rapid sequence in the neck, the knee, the ribs, while Jewell, a heavy and powerful swordsman, thrashed his steel in faster, wider, harder arcs to smash and intercept her.

They fought on in the still heat, the only moving creatures in the landscape. By this time they were pouring with sweat, their breathing beginning to labour, when Jewell, much the stronger of the two, suddenly lifted his arm and, farting with the effort, brought his blade hissing down upon Read's. But a second before, Read had extended her arm like a released spring, to drive the steel under Jewell's arm and between his ribs, feeling it first jar, then run sweetly up to the hilt – at which Jewell gave a great sigh and sagged for a moment, spitted by Read's sword. Then he dropped to the sand, pulling the sword with him, out of Read's throbbing fingers.

Read stood up. The wind had changed. Was now coming off the sea, and it was fully light. Then suddenly, out of the blue sky, rain began falling. Fixing her eyes on a broad striped leaf Read saw, mesmerised, that rain was dropping on to it from the flanges of a yet higher leaf, faster and faster, the warm rain coming down now in a streaming curtain that made a sodden shroud of her clothes. Then, as she stooped to draw out her weapon, she looked up. Standing three yards away watching her was Joseph.

'I've killed him,' said Read simply, and threw her sword into the sand. Joseph walked over and without a word they lugged Jewell's enormous carcass, bumping over the sand and up into the green shade below the cotton trees, the rain drumming on the leaves as on a wooden roof. Then, still without speaking, they set to work, heaving back the streaming rocks to make a stone coffin for Jewell. They rolled him into this face down, covering him first with wet greenery, then with smaller then greater stones, finally scattering these over with beach wrack, by the end of which the rain had stopped as suddenly as it had begun.

'He said you was a spy,' said Read. There was a momentary hesitation as though Read were awaiting either a denial or confirmation of this. 'So I killed him.' Then, trembling with exhaustion, she sank to her knees on the sand.

'Thou shouldst avoid such killing, Soldier,' said Joseph. Then, kneeling beside Read, said softly, 'Greater love hath no man than this, that a man lay down his life for his friend.' And he began gently chafing Read's shaking hands.

'But I myself am not what people think,' groaned

Read through her dry mouth, 'for I am a woman in men's clothes . . .'

'Even so, he might have killed thee, friend,' said Joseph, and put his arm round Read's shoulders.

September 31st . . . our company voted by a majority to return and continue business among the inlets of the north coast of this island (Hispaniola), a decision not much liked among some of the crew, who thinking we were over-trying our luck, were for showing a clean pair of heels in this part of the world and going further northward to the Straits of Florida, or else out to the Gulf of Campechy. Their disagreeing caused a further division in our ship, made already apprehensive by Jewell's disappearance, some saying he was a spy, and others that he'd jumped ship and taken himself to Port au Prince to try his luck in a better company than ours, – Rackham and Bonny being quite careless at the time to seek out the true cause of his absence.

October 2nd . . . in the event the majority decision turned out a fortunate one for us, at least to begin with, for in spite of the weather (it remaining sultry and windless) we plundered two sloops three leagues from Hispaniola, sinking one and keeping the other . . .

October 6th . . . on the fifth day of the month we anchored off Ocho Rios Bay on the island of Jamaica to clean the ship and take on water. Although just coming into the rainy season, the day was lowering but dry. The captain took two boats ashore, I in command of the one, and Rackham with Joseph, his new favourite, in the other. Rackham's boat was ahead and as they rounded a little promontory (for he had taken the precaution of anchoring out of sight of anyone who might be in the bay), we caught sight of a canoe pulled up on the shore with a fisherman beside it sorting out his nets. The moment he saw our boats approach, he dropped his nets and ran into the thick woods that ran close down to the waterside. At this Rackham called for his men to pull harder in order to catch him. When they were just off shore, I could see Joseph clamber over the boat's side and, wading, run into the woods in pursuit of the man, to emerge with him not long after.

With Joseph acting go-between, the man confessed to being only a poor fisherman with a wife and family to keep, and not intending harm to anyone. Since Joseph was disposed to believe the man, Rackham and his officers, with the exception of Bonny, expressed themselves also satisfied, though Bonny was inclined to question the fellow further. But the others dissenting, it ended in their letting him go . . .

October 10th . . . these days following have been exceeding grateful to me by reason of the kindness of my new friend Joseph, and his telling me of the foundations of his beliefs. It seems he comes of a people who, long eschewing visible churches and societies, wandered up and down the country as sheep without a shepherd or as doves without their mates, seeking their Beloved, but not being able to find Him whom their souls loved above their chiefest joy. At last, after much wandering, they came some of them together, not formally to pray or preach at appointed times or places, as in times past they were accustomed to do, but to wait together in silence. And as anything arose in any one of their minds that they thought savoured of a divine spring, so they sometimes spoke – 'Though not always,' says Joseph, smiling, 'to the point . . .'

October 11th . . . a little emboldened, I told him of my system which I had thought on long ago when my old mistress and Mr. Vane and I was at Bruges. Which was that the light and power of God coming whole from Heaven, was as if made to shine through a shutter pierced with holes, so that on one side the shutter was the whole light, and on the other, little shafts of light, the shutter being the portal between earth and Heaven, and the little shafts of light being ourselves, each different, but yet made of the same glorious matter. And I told him I thought that in our deaths we return, our shutter being broke back to that first light, so forsaking our little particular light. And Joseph nodded and said it was very likely so . . .

October 15th . . . when I told him of my own affections on this earth, and in particular that I had not long had with Ann Bonny (for us now growing close, much as a Christian and his confessor, I wanted him to have only the truth and to know me as I was), he smiled and gently teased me, saying it were an association that had been most useful, resulting as it had in the unloosing of the coagulatory solids, and most efficacious in restoring ton and elasticity to the system. Knowing he was making sport of me, for he is sometimes a man much divided between his heart and reason, I smiled and said nothing, knowing that it had not been so with Ann Bonny (to whom I am ever grateful) nor ever would be. Then I laughed and said how he was a very notable joker of a man, and the only man bar one to make me laugh aloud, who am not quick to make laugh. But my heart at this became on a sudden heavy, for I thought of my husband – poor Gerhardi.

'. . . and thou,' says he, 'art plaguey serious!' – as, with the thunder rolling mightily by now among the silk-cotton trees, he sets a-teasing me again. Saying it is by Reason alone that I had been able for so long to play the man and accomplish things no ordinary woman would have been able to do. 'Though thy woman's part,' says he, laying his cheek against my hand, 'is that of a *strong* woman, yet wondrously reinforced by the skills and temper of a *man* . . .'

'And what of this Man, my own Joseph?' I asks him, smiling down at him, for he lay now with his head in my lap. 'Why, my dear,' says he, taking my other hand and studying it closely, 'it is a true observation that in some rational men, perhaps in the *most* rational men, there is yet included, in the wisdom of our Maker, a womanish side to their natures, which is ever desirous of expression. So that in the company of someone of the likes of thyself I feel a peculiar comfort, as though we two together make up a perfect O . . .' And he raises himself up on one elbow, and with a stick describes such an O in the cooling ash of our sweethearts' fire, and I see this O encloses two complementary plume-like shapes, one smooth and gold in the firelight that he says is himself (which is the rational male principle), and the other, being scuffed by his stick, dark, which he tells me is I, Mary Read, the female principle.

'It is a Chinese conceit!' says he . . .

'And thou art a most Chinese blab!' cries I, kissing shut his grey eyes, and shutting with my kisses his nonsense-speaking mouth – a mouth long and thin as my own, and smiling always, even in sleep, as though at some inward joke . . .

October 20th . . . five leagues eastwards from Port Maria Bay we had the good fortune to take a sloop, Captain Spenlow, Master, with a loading of 50 rolls tobacco and 9 bags pimentos. The weather begins to blow dirty now, the rain falling sometimes in cataracts. But as though Providence is yet determined we should take our fill before the final onset of the bad weather, another sloop was sighted the following day in Dry Harbour Bay, at which Rackham stood in and fired on her. The sloop's crew all ran ashore, and we took the sloop and her loading, but when those ashore realised we were pirates, they hailed us and let the Captain know they was willing to come aboard and join him to a man. So that not counting his own sloop, Rackham has by now increased his little armada to four. It was after this that Joseph most earnestly counselled the Captain (and not for the first time) that taking so fine a booty we should all be content and leave off the life we was leading, and return home to become honest men. But Rackham laughed at this and told him, 'Not yet . . .'

October 24th . . . Today I asked Joseph, Was it indeed he I had seen during that wandering fevered time when I was ever about the rum shops of Port au Prince and elsewhere? But he only smiles and puts me off, saying lovers now and ever will see one another everywhere . . .

'But art thou now, owing to the power of love, become at last a true being?' asks he, ever teasing.

'Aye, as true a being as I could be,' says I, choosing to take it gravely. 'But thou, Joseph, what sort of being art thou?'

'Why, Soldier, my dear, I am nought but thy Destiny!' replies he with complacency as our fire, catching a dry leaf, flares and lights up his dear face . . .

'. . . and sure we two will turn honest and buy a ship of our own, and return to England, my dear?'

says I, 'though first returning to the island of Madagascar to retrieve such treasure as is due to me...'

'Aye, surely...'

'...and buy us a small farm, my husband?' For so far as I can understand it, we are married, cohabiting as we do, though we have received no proper comfort of that sort from a regular parson. 'For we have surely not had each other at so cheap a price that we should now throw it all away!' says I. And in the dying flame he turns in my arms and, kissing me, tells me he has changed his mind, and will first tell me something that will please me, and afterwards read me something that will please me more. Then he tells me that, aye, it was he I had seen those many times about Port au Prince and etc. and more.

'For I am the same man,' says he, 'that thou gavest thy hand to long ago when I was run into the Amstell for a reason I will tell you later, and unable to swim or make shift to save myself. And insomuch as thou gavest me back my life then, shall I in turn give thee another life!' And he searches for a little book he always keeps by him and, opening it, begins to read out, 'I, Joseph, take thee, Mary, to my wedded wife, to have and to hold from this day forward, for better for worse and etc.' Then makes me say likewise, and taking a little wire ring from his pocket, slips it over my finger.

'In the Name of the Father,' says he, 'and of the Son, and of the Holy Ghost. Amen.' But conjuring me for the time being to keep it secret...

At about this same hour the Governor of the Island's aide, wig-less and in his nightshirt, was examining closely a much-folded paper brought him by the poor fisherman from Ochos Rios Bay. It was in cipher, and he considered it for several minutes, holding it close to the light of the candle. Then he straightened, and clapping the astonished fisherman on the shoulder so hard as almost to fell him, cries out, 'At last we have them!' and ran limping off to wake his master.

On November 2nd Rackham's sloop, cruising along the northern shore of the island, rounded its westernmost extent at Point Negril, where a pettiauger, or large canoe, was sighted. On seeing Rackham, the pettiauger ran ashore and landed her men, but one of them hailing the sloop to ask who they were, Rackham made answer that *they were trueborn Englishmen.* He then desired the crew of the pettiauger to do him the honour of stepping aboard and drinking a bowl of punch. This, after some debate, they decided to do, nine men in all coming aboard the pirate armed with muskets and cutlasses. This, however, in an evil hour, for no sooner had they laid down their arms and taken up their pipes and glasses, than the lookout reported a sloop to windward, flying the Red Ensign. Rackham, seeing that she stood directly towards them, was instantly alarmed, and at once weighed anchor and stood off. At which moment Bonny, who was standing in the waist of the ship, turned suddenly to Joseph, who was watching the King's ship through his glass.

'How come, doctor, that they could be sensible of our presence here?' He brought down the glass and looked gravely at her. 'Great God, then thou art a spy!' And raising her hand she made to strike him, but he caught and held her by the wrist. 'So kind a doctor, so apparently good a man! By Christ's blood, Rackham will have thy joints torn out for this!' And turning to go, found Read facing her.

'The devil's a spy, and has sent you and all of us to our deaths!' And breaking free, Bonny ran towards the quarter-deck.

'This is, after all, the truth?' asked Read, frowning, 'for we have very little time.' And Joseph nodded.

November 5th . . . 'Why?' I asks. 'Why so, Joseph!' And he looks me steadily in the eyes saying how I should later understand the way of it, and that it was his work to show his love to us by making us honest. And that at all costs. Then, handing me a paper which he said I was to give to the Governor should I be taken, he looks over his shoulder, for the sound of running feet drew ever closer, and he knew they were Rackham's men.

'I love thee, my dear,' says he, 'and always shall, for thou art indeed my own dear wife. But pray, my life being once again in thy hands, deliver me, as only thou knowest best.' And as Rackham and two of his officers leapt down to take him –

'Look up, my Prince!' cries I, and having my pistol, shot him between the eyes . . . And knew very little after, what I did . . .

Epilogue

'Is it you at last, dear Mr. Wafer sir?' For being so wonderfully and beautifully striped, one could easily be misled into thinking he was not there, when all the time there he was, sitting quietly smoking in the shadows of the prison lazarette.

'The child aborted?' queried the chaplain.

'*Oui, monsieur.*'

'Whose was it, I wonder? Some say it was a spy . . .'

The chaplain bent over Read. She seemed to be hardly breathing, her face already set in death, or so he judged, the sweat caused by her fever standing out like rime on her forehead.

'*Elle est devenue douce, trés douce et assez religeuse*,' said Bathsheba. She had heard the Soldier praying aloud sometimes in the small hours.

'Ah yes, they become mighty doose and assey religious at their hanging,' said the chaplain shortly. Then imitating, with some asperity and in a high voice, to no one in particular, ' "I am now with sorrow reaping the fruits of my disobedience to my parents, who used their endeavours to have me instructed in my Bible and my Catechism, and of blaspheming the name of God my maker etc . . ." They all say that. I'm told this one defended herself mighty cleverly at her trial, not but that it was a foregone conclusion. It was her misfortune that some Dutch sea captain or other remembered her face from a former life. Talking of which,' went on the chaplain, 'bring us a touch of captain's rumbo, Bathsheba, this looks as though it may take a little time after all.' And he settled himself comfortably on the chair at the side of Read's mattress.

'They say Jack Rackham was all tricked out in red

ribbons when he stepped up to die on the tree of glory,' he continued, sipping his rum, 'and that before he performed what I believe the pirates call his "dance to no music", he kicked off his shoes in order to confound all his friends who'd said he'd die in 'em. He added moreover, people tell me, that if he could have been an even greater plague to these islands, he would have been, and earnestly wished he had been so . . .'

'*Il avait seulement vingt-six ans!*'

'Vent-sees, did he? They're all young,' said the chaplain, 'and incorrigible . . .'

'*Il recevait des visites de sa femme, Madame Bonny,*' ventured Bathsheba. '*Savez-vous, Altesse, ce qu'elle disait à ce Monsieur?*'

'Aye, everyone here knows,' replied the chaplain. 'That she was sorry to see him in such a case, but if he'd fought like a man, he need not have been hanged like a dog! They tell me that only the two women, Read and Bonny, kept the deck at the last. Rackham and his officers took themselves below to set fire to the magazine and drink to their deaths, I believe. "Strike immediately to the King of England's colours!" Captain Barnet bid them, upon which a woman's voice answering that they'd damn well strike no strikes, she fires on them with the swivel gun.'

There was a note of grudging admiration in the chaplain's voice.

'One of Barnet's officers saw 'em. Knew 'em by their big breasts. Towards the end, he said, which wasn't long, the weather much favouring the King's ship and Barnet's broadside having taken away their boom, this woman Read turns lunatic of a sudden, and runs out and tears open the main hatch, calling on those below to come out and fight like men. On getting no answer from that rabble, she twice discharges her pistol into the hold amongst them, killing one and wounding several others . . .'

251

The chaplain paused and tapped his empty glass. 'Is there more of that, Bathsheba, it's uncommonly restorative in its action! What became of Madame Bonny, then?'

'*Elle a des amis!*' replied Bathsheba, and fell silent, her dark eyes filling with tears. The poor dying Soldier had no friends.

'Amis, has she?' repeated the chaplain. 'I hear the father has a sugar estate somewhere. So that's how she got off.'

'Poor Jack,' Bathsheba heard the Soldier say in a low voice.

'Cast off, my honey, there's nothing to the point to be said on that score!' That was tall Madame Bonny, her face burnt red as a brick and her hair white with the sun. She scared Bathsheba with her loud voice and manly ways. The Soldier's hair was also white. But not with the sun.

Outside the barred window of the lazarette, the dry flanges of the palm trees rasped together in the hot wind, and somewhere a tethered donkey brayed. A sound mourning the ponderous wickedness of the world.

'Has the bleeding stopped, my honey?' And the tall woman, Bonny, who could also be very gentle, drew back the blanket and ran her hand between the Soldier's raised knees, and Bathsheba saw that when she withdrew the old shirt she had pressed between them it was again soaked in blood.

At this the tall red woman rose to her feet, and Bathsheba saw her pace up and down the tiny cell. Six steps by six steps, several times, trying to whistle a tune as though it didn't matter. Then she came back to the Soldier's mattress, and going down on her knees, stretched herself along the Soldier's side and pressed her cheek against hers.

'What time is it?' Bathsheba heard the Soldier ask in a whisper.

'Halfway through the afternoon watch...'

'Not long now...' said the Soldier. 'You have the chart?'

'Hush! We'll take that voyage together when you're out of here!'

'You understand the cypher?' persisted the Soldier. 'The tree it speaks of is a Tangena tree, they use it in the poison ordeal. With that gold you could buy an estate in an afternoon!' And the Soldier smiled.

The red woman, Bonny, with her white hair, turned her head at this, and Bathsheba could see there were tears running down her cheeks.

Silence fell, and it seemed to Bathsheba that at last the Soldier had gone to sleep.

'I had something to say...'

'What is it, my honey...?'

'Is there someone standing by the window? It grew suddenly dark a moment ago.'

'There's no one...'

The Soldier shifted restlessly. 'You have the chart?'

'I have the chart...'

There was a short silence, then the Soldier groaned.

'Take me with you!' And Bathsheba saw tears streaming from the corners of the Soldier's eyes.

'Hush, my heart. When they get me out I'll petition the Governor, and I'll come about and take you off. I will! I will! I swear to you... I'll come back!'

The turnkey came half an hour later. Before she went, the red woman Bonny borrowed a silver dollar from someone and gave it to Bathsheba to buy sweetmeats. But the poor thin Soldier was too sick to eat them, and Bathsheba took them home to the children.

'*Madame Bonny a été pardonée,*' said Bathsheba.

'*Putaine!*' commented the chaplain robustly. 'If that's

the right word. I hear they're trying to get up a petition to pardon this one. Her friend Madame Bonny, perhaps. There was talk of a mitigating letter to the Governor. Some spy in the King's service, I believe, or so they say. It looks a little too late for that now.'

'*Hélas!*'

'Oh, I don't know, it couldn't have been much of a life, ending up as a spy's whore and aborting his child!'

There was a slight movement from the mattress.

'It's getting dark!'

The approaching darkness was familiar, however. It was from just such a void that under the hand of the Demiurge the great and unchanging mangrove swamp had come into being, also the rain forest the old Foin hunter had shown her. And it had been the matrix, too, of some storm either before or after these times, though the Soldier was too tired to frame the particular occasion.

'"Up wind, up sea!" as we used to say, sir, and I mind you telling me of the little black monkeys picking out periwinkles from the roots of the mangroves...'

'Babbling,' commented the chaplain. 'We may be nearer the end than I thought.'

'You're still there, Mr. Wafer sir?' Read's voice was anxious, scarcely above a whisper.

'*Venez mon Dieu, venez, venez mon doux Sauveur...*' began Bathsheba softly.

'... and water so clear you can see turtles browsing six fathom down on banks of sea-grass like our sheep at home...'

'... had your delight been in the law of the Lord, had you meditated thereon day and night (Psalm One, verse two) you would then have found that God's word was a lamp to your feet...' began the chaplain.

'... can you still hear me dear Mr. Wafer, sir? For

I have come back to you. You who from the beginning knew who I was and what it was God intended for me . . .'

'. . . *venez regner en moi au centre de mon coeur, venez mon Dieu, venez . . .*'

'. . . you would then have esteemed the Scriptures as the Great Charter of Heaven, which delivered to us not only the most perfect laws and rules of life . . .'

But the Soldier, curiously, was back at St. Michael Church, Bristol, and thinking of Dutchess. 'If a dog,' she tried to say, 'why not me?' But choked.

In the advancing dark she was just aware of a voice. A voice she had heard before, in bells, or in the sound of a cataract, but until now not understood.

It was now becoming apparent that the darkness was beginning to give way to a small light. This also she had seen before, in the catacombs perhaps, or even long before in some angelic infancy to which it seemed she might be returning . . .

'This darkness, sir,' she tried to say '. . . no darkness with Thee.' But to the two listening this intimation rendered down to a rattling sigh.

'*Hélas! Hélas! Hélas! Vierge Altagrace, Vierge Caridad, Vierge de Mont Carmel . . . touts les Saints et Saintes qui sont dans le ciel . . .*'

'. . . so that if you will now sincerely turn to Him, though late, even at the eleventh hour (Matthew chapter twenty, verses six to nine) he will receive you . . .'

'*Tout rondi-orum dans le ciel. Zo lissandole zo, co lissabagui zo, lissabagui wangan cinque . . . lissandole zo . . .*'

'And do not mistake the nature of repentance as being a bare sorrow for your sins, arising from the consideration of the evil and punishment they have now brought upon you; but your sorrow must arise from the consideration of your having offended a gracious and merciful God . . .'

'*Oh! Oh! Oh!... Pingolo, Pingolo, Pingolo roi montre nous la prie qui, minnin africain... Wanguinan... Wannime...*'

'And the God of Infinite Mercy be merciful to your Soul...'

'*Hélas! Hélas! Hélas!...*'